The Portal Series

BLUE CITY

Charlay Neff

Charlay Marie Books

Charlay Marie/CHARLAY MARIE BOOKS
www.charlaymariebooks@gmail.com
www.charlaymarie.com

Publisher's Note: This is a work of fiction. Names, characters, places, and incidents are a product of the author's imagination. Locales and public names are sometimes used for atmospheric purposes. Any resemblance to actual people, living or dead, or to businesses, companies, events, institutions, or locales is completely coincidental.

Book Layout © 2015 BookDesignTemplates.com
Graphic Design: Andre Hawkins
The Portal Series: Blue city/ Charlay Marie. -- 1st ed.
ISBN 978-1-48357-283-3

Acknowledgements

Where do I even begin when so many people have helped me on this wonderful and fun journey creating The Portal Series. I'm sure I should begin with the one person who has even allowed each individual to be a blessing to me. God. My God has made all things possible, and to Him to give all the glory and thanks. Before I am a writer, I am a Christian, and I believe and will always spread the Gospel of Jesus Christ. Thank you God, for qualifying me! I will use my gifts wisely. To my lovely parents, I thank you for believing in me and doing any and everything to make sure I brought Blue City to life. I'd also like to thank my best friend, Star, for allowing me to pour out every thought, plot, and angle of Blue City onto you. You have always been my biggest cheerleader and best friend, and I love you girl! I obviously can't leave out my wonderful siblings, Nikki and Tisha, who bestowed the gift of literature. I will always be your baby sister, and I'll always look up to you both. I write because of you. Thanks for proof-reading and offering amazing help! Next, I'd like to thank Sonia, Avie, Kirstin, and Richard for being the first four to read Blue City. Because of you, I now have faith in my new series. I also thank Andre Hawkins and Cindy Sherwood, my amazing graphic designer and editor. You have saved my life!!! I will never stray from the two of you! To anyone else who has helped me along the way, you are very appreciated! And finally to my readers...thank you so much for your support! You will never know how much it means to me. I hope you enjoy the read!

CONTENTS

CHAPTER ONE

The Dream

"Read me more, Daddy," Jen bellowed, squirming excitedly under her thick, pink covers. Her father, George Kallis, sat at the edge of her bed, and in his lap sat a black book engraved with silver writing that read The Book of Fairy Tales. He had been on the verge of closing it, having promised Jen a chapter before bed when, as usual, she tried to convince him to read more. "Please?"

George laughed, sitting back comfortably on the bed, mentally preparing for another half an hour of reading. Jen's excitement for the book was exactly what he had hoped for. This was no ordinary book, and it held a very special place in his heart. He had hoped the book would one day mean the world to her as well.

"All right, all right. One more chapter and then it's bedtime for you, kiddo."

"Thanks, Daddy." Jen smiled, pulling her covers up to her shoulders and getting comfortable.

Her bedroom was fit for a princess, with pink and white striped walls that had little pink satin bows trailing down each pink stripe. The matching shelves of the dresser were painted white with pink bows in the place of knobs. The top of the shelves were decorated with a variety of one-of-a-kind, hand-crafted stuffed animals. The pink canopy bed that she slept in had cost her parents a fortune and came complete with sheer white curtains embedded with rhinestones that sparkled like a millions stars at night. A beautiful pearly white vanity sat directly across from the bed, its drawers filled with fake makeup and small toys. It was apparent that George Kallis spoiled his only child, wanting only the best for his little princess.

George turned the page to read the last chapter for the night. He opened his mouth to begin but quickly shut it as an alarming noise filled the room. His eyes darted to Jen's closet. He noticed a white light beaming from the bottom of the door as it began to shake. He felt Jen rise from her pillow to see what was causing the commotion, and once she saw, she jumped into his arms, grasping onto his shirt, frantically. George tried to calm her by running a gentle hand through her hair while shushing her. His eyes never left the door.

"Lie here," he said, placing Jen on the bed as he slowly stood. Jen crawled back underneath her covers, watching in fear as her father neared the closet door and placed a hand on the door-knob. A bright, white light burst through the closet into the room, making Jen shield her eyes with her covers. She heard her father curse lightly under his breath, which was followed by a frightened gasp.

"Daddy," she called to him, not daring to steal a glance from under the covers. "Daddy, what is it?"

Jen strained her ears and heard a weird noise, as if something was being devoured or sucked into a vacuum cleaner. The blaring noise grew louder until it was almost unbearable, and then it quickly ceased, leaving nothing but the sound of Jen's rapid breathing. She wanted to peek over the covers but waited instead for her father to say something.

Silence lingered like the quiet before a storm.

"Daddy?" Jen pushed the covers away from her, sitting up on the bed, staring at the closed closet door. Her father was nowhere in sight.

Jen wondered if he had gone into the closet, so she quickly stood and rushed over to the door. She placed her hand on the warm knob, hesitant to open it at first. With a deep breath, she pushed the door open.

Jen jumped awake from her recurring dream, the one where her father had mysteriously disappeared into her closet. She lay in her bed, eyes momentarily closed as she allowed her mind to finish what her dream couldn't, the rest of what really had happened. She remembered opening her closet door and finding nothing out of the ordinary. Every dress was still hung neatly, and the shoes lined up on a rack attached to her closet door were in perfect order. Panicked, she had thrown every item out of the closet, as she searched for her father. There hadn't been a single trace of him.

Jen had then run out of her room, thinking that her father must have fled while she was still under the covers. She'd run straight to her parents' room where she'd found her mother, Juanita, fast asleep. Jen jumped onto her mother's bed, furiously shaking her awake while reciting in quick waves the horror she'd experienced, pausing between sentences to gasp for air. Her mom had softly assured Jen that everything was okay, and that she must have had a nightmare. But when Juanita searched the house for her husband, she came up empty-handed.

Jen had tried to explain the strange events that had taken place, but her mother hadn't believed her. In fact, no one had believed Jen. Not the police officers who had filed the report and opened a missing person's investigation after Juanita reported her husband missing. Not her closest relatives, who were disheartened that George had left behind his wife and child. Not even Jen's best friends from school.

For many years, Jen lay awake at night, waiting for her father to come back home through her closet door. She'd hear her mother in the next room as she cried for her missing husband. As much as Jen prayed to God to bring her father back, as much as she yearned for it, he never came. Eventually, the police department closed the missing person's case, telling Jen's mother that her husband had left them and didn't want to be found.

It was easier for Juanita to accept that her husband had willingly left than to believe he'd been killed, or to buy into her daughter's bizarre story about his disappearance inside her closet. Jen, however, never let up about the story, causing her mom to put her into therapy. The therapist had stated that Jen created the story so she wouldn't have to face the hard fact that her father left her and her mother behind. Jen learned not to speak about what had really happened the night her father disappeared.

Deep down, though, Jen still knew the truth, and when she

was old enough, she began searching frantically for the answers online. Unfortunately, the search engine results mentioned possibilities like alien abductions and black holes. In the end, the results were nothing but farfetched garbage that didn't help her at all. Eventually, she gave up on finding the answers and allowed herself to believe, finally, that her father had willingly left. It was easy to do, since her real memory seemed like a distant dream. Maybe she had imagined it all.

As she struggled to wake up and shake off her dream, Jen pushed the memory of her father out of her mind and pulled the covers away from her body, revealing a pink tank top and white pajama shorts. After stretching, she stood and went to her closet and placed a hand on the doorknob. Images of her father's disappearance instantly resurfaced, sending a chill down her spine. As hard as she tried to keep the pain at bay, it never stayed away for long. At times, she could almost see the white light blazing from the door.

Large hands wrapped around her waist, causing her to shriek. Jen turned so that her back faced the closet door, and her eyes landed on a pair of blue tennis shoes. A familiar body softly pressed up against her.

"What did I tell you about wearing clothes to sleep?" Eric growled, nuzzling at her neck. He pushed himself away long enough to take in the sight of her bare legs.

Eric was everything a girl could want. He was tall, blond, very attractive, and athletic. He played varsity football, and being a talented quarterback gave him a promising future of going pro. He had good manners—aside from his lustful side. He was also the committed type. Once his eyes had set on Jen, they hadn't traveled elsewhere. Sure, plenty of cheerleaders and other girls had thrown themselves at him during the occasional party, but he had stayed committed. "On second thought, I kind of like the whole 'half dressed' thing."

Jen instinctively lifted a hand to the cross dangling from her neck while pushing Eric away with the other hand. She was a devout Christian and tried not to encourage Eric's lusting behavior. Once he was a few feet away, she turned back to her closet.

This time, she opened it, grabbing two items off the hangers without checking to see if they matched. She only wore pastel colors, so everything seemed to match anyway. She shut the closet door and walked over to her bed, laying her clothes down while trying hard not to pay attention to her boyfriend's amorous stare.

"If my mom ever finds out that you sneak into my room before school, she'll kill us both," Jen warned, staring down at her choice of attire. It was a soft blue tube top with a pair of tan shorts, and even though her outfit was plain, she knew she'd look amazing in it.

She was glad she had inherited her mother's curves and thin waist. Her mother was a beautiful black woman, and her father was from Germany. From him, she inherited bright hazel eyes and fair skin. Her hair was what she hated most, as it was a big mess of unruly brown curls that was often hard to manage. Despite her struggles, everyone loved her hair, and she got compliments wherever she went.

Eric couldn't stay away from her, though his parents firmly warned him about interracial dating. They weren't necessarily racist, but they didn't believe in mixing races (even if she was half white), saying it polluted blood lines. Eric didn't dare tell Jen that, of course, and so she never understood why she wasn't invited to his family gatherings or hadn't been introduced to his parents.

"Good thing your mom will never find out," Eric said, walking slowly toward her while continuing to take in the sight of her. He placed himself directly behind her and wrapped his arms around her waist, kissing a spot on her neck just above her necklace. "We have a half an hour before the bus comes."

Jen pulled away and turned toward him, staring at him firmly. "Perfect. That gives me just enough time to get dressed."

He pulled her close again.

"How about we just lie in your bed and get creative."

Jen rolled her eyes at his comment. Even though she liked Eric, she still didn't think their relationship would last through the school year. Sure, he was almost perfect, but Jen was changing. She didn't feel the same pull toward him or any of her friends. She spent most of her days feeling as if life had more to offer. A lot of times, she caught herself drifting off, wondering about her father and his whereabouts. It had been ten years since she had last seen his smiling face. Being seventeen didn't mean she was too old to need her father.

Deep down, Jen knew something weird and supernatural had happened that night. She'd even begun entertaining the once ridiculous thought of an alien abduction, having spent weeks researching white lights that came from closets to no avail. Overall, she wished she'd never stuck her head underneath her covers that night. If she hadn't, she'd know exactly what had happened to her father.

Footsteps sounded in the hallway and seemed to be quickly approaching, causing both Jen and Eric to freeze in place. She lifted a finger to his mouth, signaling him to remain quiet just as Jen's mother knocked on the door.

"Jen," her mom said on the other side of the door. The handle started to move.

Crap, Jen thought. I'm so busted.

"Don't come in, Mom! I'm naked!" she yelled, signaling for Eric to hide in her closet. Eric quietly darted across the room, closing the closet door just as the bedroom door opened. Her mother peered into the room with a smile in her eyes. She glanced over to the closet door and then to Jen, her happy eyes now shadowed with doubt.

"I thought you were naked," her mom said, moving farther into Jen's room with sass only she could manage. She was a beautiful, dark-skinned woman with a full figure and a keen fashion sense. She wore a white and pink tribal print halter top with faded blue jeans, nude heels, and a necklace and bracelet set she'd gotten from Tiffany's.

"I thought it would keep you out of my room, but I guess that didn't work," Jen said sarcastically. She wasn't the type of girl to be rude with her mother, but she was willing to do anything to keep her mother from knowing a boy was hiding in her closet.

Her mom shook her head but kept her tone light. "I made you breakfast. French toast, scrambled eggs, and bacon. Come eat before it gets cold."

Jen nodded as she watched her mother leave her room and close the door behind her.

Eric burst out of the closet as soon as the bedroom door shut again. He held a stuffed animal in his hands with a coy smile.

"I just made out with this teddy bear in your closet. She's a better kisser than you. Please don't dump me," he begged. Jen rolled her eyes, sitting down on the edge of her bed, momentarily relieved she hadn't been caught. "I was deprived of this morning's make-out session and I needed a quick fix. Teddy happened to be there."

"For the record," Jen said, staring at her favorite stuffed animal in her boyfriend's hands, "Teddy is a boy."

Eric laughed, quickly tossed the teddy bear to the floor, and walked over to the window, preparing to leave. Jen stood and met him as he hung halfway out of the window and planted a soft kiss on his cheek. She tried to pull away, but he pulled her back in for a real kiss.

"See you at school, Mutt." And with that, Eric jumped from her first story window.

Twenty minutes later, a clean Jen sat at the kitchen table, entertained by her mother as she washed the dishes and danced to Michael Jackson's Thriller. When Jen was little, she and her mother would dance around the house, knowing every single move to the song, as her father sat back on the couch and watched with a content expression.

Jen admired the amount of love her parents had for each other, despite the hateful stares they received whenever out in public for being an interracial couple. Her parents taught her it wasn't the color of the skin, but the depth of heart that mattered. Jen remembered how they used to slow dance at night and how her father would gaze deeply into her mother's eyes and whisper sweet nothings in her ear. It didn't make sense that he would just leave them both without a moment's notice.

Jen grew used to the sound of her mother crying at night, truly believing her husband had left her. Her mom became depressed, and she stopped working and doing things for Jen that a mother normally would like cooking dinner for a seven-year-old and remembering school events. Her mother's depression had been very hard for Jen, and she tried hard to forget it whenever the memories resurfaced. Who wants to remember that kind of pain? Who wants to remember a mother who forgot her own child in the midst of her own sorrow?

Jen had even lost her friends. They'd all laughed at her and called her crazy for thinking her father was taken by a mysterious white light. She became the weirdo, the loner, a zombie. A group of kids even came up with a game that they'd play at recess where whoever touched Jen would become a zombie. That kid would have to chase the other children until another one of them was caught. The child who had been caught would also turn into a zombie and start chasing the other children. The game would continue until all of the kids were like Jen: zombies.

Jen felt she'd deserved to be called a zombie. She'd walked around with her head low and shoulders slumped, with lifeless eyes and a mouth that didn't open much to speak. The kids around her hadn't understood what had made her seem that way. They'd had their fathers and loving mothers. They'd had secure homes and good holidays. Jen had spent her holidays alone, watching TV reruns and classic movies while her mother slept her holidays away.

Jen's mom eventually started coming around again when Jen was twelve. Her mom had been lying in bed as she always did, when it occurred to her that her husband had been dead for five years and that Jen was almost a teenager.

Juanita's eyes had drifted around her room as she relived the past five years. When was the last time she cooked Jen dinner? Did her hair? Made sure she bathed? Sure, Juanita had been there at times, but not as much as she should have been. While she had been overly concerned about the husband she'd lost, she hadn't considered the daughter she still had by her side.

On that day, Juanita promised herself she would spend the rest of her life giving Jen what she needed most—a mother.

At first, it was difficult for Jen to adjust to a caring mother, one who made her breakfast in the morning while singing to old school music as she had done before her dad had disappeared.

She had to get used to a mother who smiled again and looked at her with affectionate eyes. Jen had been afraid that her mother's newfound drive for life would be temporary, so she kept herself at a distance. Eventually, her mother's love won her over, and Jen had forgiven her for the past five years she'd spent alone.

However, those years had hardened her and made her wary of other people. She didn't trust a soul anymore. She knew too much for her age, things her peers didn't even think about.

Jen had been able to cook a full course meal since she was eight. She'd been writing checks in her mother's name to pay bills since the age of ten. Once, when she was eleven, she'd even had to drive her mother's car to the grocery store because the rain had been too bad to walk and the cabinets had been bare once again. This happened often during times when her mother entered into phases of deep depression and couldn't get out of bed. The phases would last a few weeks, and then her mother would snap out of it, partially, long enough to handle whatever Jen had been forced to deal with while her mom had been locked up in her room.

"Eat quickly, baby," her mother said while they sat at the table eating breakfast that morning, snapping Jen back into the moment.

"I know," Jen said, stuffing her mouth with a piece of French toast drizzled in syrup.

"And you better tell that little boyfriend of yours that if he comes back to my house, staring at my baby girl, who barely had any clothes on by the way, he's gonna meet the end of his days." Jen dropped her fork. "Mmm-hmm, didn't think I knew, did you? I could hear yall's conversation from clear down the hallway. Let it happen again? Not in my house you won't."

With that, her mom walked out of the kitchen, leaving Jen surprised. She absentmindedly dangled her fork in the air, which still had a piece of French toast stuck on the end, long forgotten.

Eric was waiting for Jen by her locker and smiled his deadly, sexy smile as soon as she emerged through a crowd of students. Jen sighed, barely glancing at him as she opened her locker. Eric frowned, confused by her change of mood. Jen hadn't even sat with him on the bus, choosing instead to sit next to a girl she barely knew and pretending to be deep in a conversation.

"What's wrong?" he asked, rubbing her back.

Jen grabbed a few books from her locker and shut it, finally meeting Eric's curious stare. "My mom knew you were in my room this morning. Thanks."

Jen began walking to her next class as Eric followed closely behind, feeling amused. "So what did she say?"

"Pretty much that she's going to kill you if you ever step foot in my bedroom again," Jen said, rounding a corner. She cut through a couple who were holding hands while whispering to each other and quickly entered her classroom before Eric could say anything else. He laughed it off and headed to his own classroom.

The first half of the school day passed by quickly as Jen worked hard to stay under the radar. At lunch, she took a seat next to her best friend, Daniela, a cute Hispanic girl with dyed gray hair cut into a bob. Danni, which was what her friends called her, wore a red nose ring and had a pierced bottom lip that made her look rough around the edges. She had a firecracker personality with a bad attitude to match and didn't care who disliked her.

When she was thirteen, Jen started at a different school after her mom learned about the bullying. Jen's first friend at her new school had been Daniela, and they'd managed to continue their friendship into high school. Danni was also disliked and had lost her dad. That gave them something in common, and so when they met during gym, they became instant friends.

"I hate this school, I hate the teachers, and I definitely hate the guys," Danni began, with a thick Hispanic accent, watching as Jen settled in at the lunch table. "Guess who got dumped today? My little sister. Guess who dumped her? A senior. Jen, she's a sophomore. I didn't even know she was dating a senior! When I see him, I'm going to cut his eyes out for looking at my sister!"

"That's harsh," Jen said, taking a bite of her pizza. Danni momentarily forgot her anger as she stared at Jen's choice for lunch.

"Milk with pizza? That's disgusting. But not as disgusting as the image in my head of me feeding my sister's ex his own ey—"

"I'm eating," Jen interrupted, setting her piece of pizza back down on her plate with a frown.

"Okay, I'll stop talking about it," Danni replied with a sigh. "Guess what else happened? Mr. Johnson says I cheated on my math test."

"Well, did you?"

"Si, I cheat on every test. If you lived in my crazy house with five younger siblings and no personal time, you'd find it hard to study too. I explained that to Mr. Johnson and you know what he said? 'If you can find time to get two piercings and I don't know how many tattoos, then you can find time to study. I don't need your excuses, Miss Rodriguez. Go see the principal.' God, I hate his stupid English accent. So then I go see the principal and he gives me two days of detention. And then after I leave the principal's office, my sister is in the hallway crying. You can imagine what happened after that. Like I said, I hate this school, these teachers, and these stupid boys. And since I can't take my anger out on the school, I'll take it out on my sister's ex."

"Wow," was all Jen said. Every day, there was some sort of drama with Danni.

Danni pulled her cell phone out of her purse and showed Jen a picture of a Hispanic boy with a mischievous grin. "This is my sister's ex. I had her text me a picture of him so I could know what he looks like."

"You're really serious about hurting him?"

"Well, I'm not gonna cut his eyes out, but I'll shove my fist down his throat," Danni said, looking around the lunchroom for him. "She said he's wearing a red t-shirt and dark jeans."

"You're going to get suspended," Jen warned.

"Who cares? My mom needs help around the house anyway. The young ones are driving her loco."

"What am I gonna do for a week if you're gone?" Jen asked her, feeling the sadness already swelling in her chest.

"You have a boyfriend," Danni said, still intently scanning the room. "Bug him."

"Ugh." Jen put her face in her hands, remembering this

morning's events. "My mom found out that Eric was in my room earlier. I don't know why she just didn't bust him out then and there; she waited until after I got dressed to say something. She said she's gonna kill him if she finds him in my room again. And when I told him, he laughed. He thinks everything is funny. He can never take anything seriously, which is so frustrating." Jen lifted her head, wondering why Danni hadn't said anything in response. She usually would have interrupted her with a smart remark, but Danni hadn't been paying attention. She was already halfway across the cafeteria.

Jen stood, watching Danni as she approached a short Hispanic guy with a red shirt who was facing away from her as he chatted with a group of boys. He had no idea what was coming his way, but Jen did.

Danni tapped him on the shoulder, and he turned to face her. She mouthed a few words Jen couldn't hear from her distance. The boy laughed and turned back to his friends. Danni grabbed his shoulder and yanked him toward her. At this point, most of the kids in the cafeteria had turned to watch the confrontation.

The boy almost fell, but he quickly found his balance. As soon as he steadied, Danni's fist connected with his jaw. He fell to the ground, holding his face, and Danni jumped on top of him, swinging wildly. Within seconds, his friends pulled her off of him as she, kicked, screamed, and cursed at the top of her lungs. Teachers from every direction rushed to the cafeteria, breaking through the crowd of observers to get to Danni. Once the teachers had her, they escorted her out of the lunchroom, but she kept her head held high with pride. Right before Danni disappeared in one of the hallways, she turned toward Jen, finding her eyes.

"Sorry," she mouthed.

And then she was gone.

CHAPTER TWO

White Light

That night, Jen lay in her bed, studying for her midterms, which were two weeks away. Unlike Danni, Jen had all of the time in the world to study. She didn't have any younger brothers or sisters to bother her, and her mother worked late into the evening, which meant she had the house mostly to herself.

When Jen got home from school, she called Danni, but her mother answered, saying Danni was grounded and not allowed to talk. Jen knew Danni would sneak in a phone call later that day to explain the horror she'd had to face once she got home.

Jen took notice when the clock turned seven. Right after football practice, Eric always climbed through her window, smelling like a fresh locker room shower. They were both seniors and planned to attend the same college on full scholarships, his thanks to football and hers thanks to good grades. He seemed the most excited about it, taking it as a sign they were meant to be together. Jen looked at it as a bad omen. She didn't want to go into college with a relationship, so she planned to break up with him soon. She anticipated that his hurt would follow them through college and would bring drama. But in the end, Jen knew the breakup would be for the best. She just didn't love him.

Sure, he was a good guy at heart and loved a good laugh, but he was also very childish and extremely hormonal. Anytime they were alone together, Eric tried to talk her into having sex with him. Because of her strong Christian beliefs, Jen wanted to wait until marriage. Eric had said he'd respect her wishes, but his hormones always outweighed his words, and he'd end up trying to have his way with her time and time again.

A sound from the window broke Jen out of her trance. She didn't have to turn around to know that Eric was climbing through her window and would soon be jumping onto her bed, rolling her over on top of him. She sighed and closed her laptop, counting down the seconds before her bed indented and wishing she hadn't worn revealing pajamas.

"Hey, babe," Eric said, flopping down on her bed. He wrapped his arms around her and rolled her over on top of him until she was facing him, just as she'd predicted. He looked into her eyes and smiled. Jen pulled away as his head rose a few inches from the bed, so that he could meet her lips with a kiss.

"What did I tell you about sneaking into my room?" Jen asked, having to strain against his grip to sit up.

"Your mom never said anything about me sneaking into your room at night," he explained, proud of himself for finding a loophole. Eric quickly pulled her back to his chest. "Now, where's my kiss?" Jen tried to pull away again, but he held on tight.

"I'm studying."

"I didn't ask if you were studying," he said, hands roaming down to her bottom and squeezing. She pushed harder on his chest, causing him to loosen his grip, and rolled over so that she was lying on her back right beside him. He climbed back on top of her, smiling down, and she finally gave in, allowing him to kiss her.

"Good girl," he said, earning himself another firm shove against his chest. He landed on her side, laughing softly. "Let's me have my way with you."

"What?" Jen laughed. "No, Eric. I'm serious, I'm studying. And you should be, too. We have midterms in two weeks."

"It's always the same excuse," Eric huffed.

"It's a valid excuse. Some of us didn't get into college because of sports. We earned our full ride by studying and getting good grades."

Eric sighed. "So you want me to leave?"

"Please!"

"Fine," he said, getting up from her bed. He started to walk toward her window but stopped. After a few seconds of silence, he turned toward her. "My best friend heard your best friend telling someone that you were planning on dumping me. I didn't believe it. But should I? I mean, here you go, pushing me away, denying me my rights as your boyfriend. No matter what I do, you find something to be irritated about. You come up with excuses for why you can't be around me. Then when I'm forced to sneak into your bedroom window just to get some alone time with you, I'm the bad guy."

Jen watched the pain on his face as he shared his revelation with her. She felt terrible inside, knowing the truth of what he was asking. He wanted to know if she still wanted to be with him, and she hated her answer. Eric was charismatic and fun—he was everything a girl could ever want—but Jen couldn't open up her heart to him the way he needed. She had too many unresolved issues to deal with, and she couldn't afford to let another person love her, only to walk away. She had "daddy issues" and wouldn't allow herself to give her heart to anyone.

"So tell me," Eric continued, "are you planning on breaking up with me?"

Jen sat up, tearing her eyes away from his. She took a deep breath, hating what she was about to say. She remembered when she'd first met Eric, how he and his friends had stared at her, thinking she was different. He'd never been attracted to a black girl before. At the time, he hadn't known that she had white in her, but it wouldn't have mattered. She wasn't fully white, and so his parents wouldn't approve. Still, it didn't stop him from continuing to stare at her that day.

After a few weeks, he had finally mustered up enough courage to ask her out. At that point, he didn't care anymore what his friends or family would think. She was a goddess, a beautiful caramel creature with curls he wanted to play with. He hadn't been able to resist touching her hair on their first date, loving how the curls had bounced back in place after being stretched. He loved how round and full her butt was, and how her hips curved, reminding him of an hourglass.

Jen finally met his eyes and nodded.

"I haven't been feeling this relationship lately and—"

"It's a yes or no question," he cut her off.

"Yes." Jen sighed. "Yes, I've been planning on it."

Eric gave her a curt nod and headed to the window. He put one leg out and paused.

"I should've gone with my first instinct and avoided dating a black girl. My parents would've hated you anyway."

And with that, he left.

Jen was hurt by his words and spent the rest of the evening staring around her room in deep thought. Truth was, she knew his parents, being wealthy and conservative, wouldn't have wanted her to date their son. In a way, she was doing Eric a favor; it made her feel slightly better about her decision to break up with him.

Eventually, Jen's thoughts wandered to her father, picturing the night he'd sat on her bed, reading her a bedtime story.

Jen hadn't really changed her room around since she was little. Her walls were still pink, as were her covers, and she had a new vanity dresser similar to the one she'd had as a child. She still had her stuffed animals, although they were now packed into boxes in her closet. Her white bedframe was no longer a canopy.

Jen reached over and opened her nightstand, pulling out the old black book her father had been reading to her the night he disappeared, The Book of Fairy Tales. The book was a compilation of love stories, but the story her dad had been reading that night had been a love story that took place in the future, where a prince and princess fell in love while trying to save their kingdom. Her favorite part had been when the prince, who had been stubborn and closed off to love, finally admitted his feelings for the princess just as they were on the verge of dying. Jen had always wanted to be the princess in that book, and grew up imagining the man of her dreams would be as handsome and dreamy as the prince she envisioned. She found herself wondering if Eric was her prince, but laughed at the thought. He was an athlete, not a prince, and she'd just dumped him. Jen placed the book neatly back in her dresser and lay down on her bed, imagining her Prince Charming taking her completely by storm.

Jen hadn't realized she'd dozed off until a noise from her closet frightened her awake. She rubbed her eyes, turning toward the sound, and waited a few seconds to see if she'd hear anything else. After a minute passed, she chalked it up to something falling from one of the shelves in her closet. She closed her eyes and dozed off again.

ZAP!

The closet door burst open as a rush of air and white light exploded into the room. She screamed, sitting up in her bed while shielding her eyes from the light until they adjusted to its brightness. Jen felt a thousand emotions at once—fear, wonder, suspicion, dread—and finally, the pain caused from remembering her father. She found herself getting up and walking toward the light in a dazed state while simultaneously recalling the first time she'd seen such brilliance. She wouldn't make the same mistake twice; she wouldn't hide from the light this time. Instead, as she neared the closet door, she invited the warmth that spread across her skin from the bright light.

Jen stood inches from her closet, listening to the distant sounds that seemed to be coming from within the light. Now, being as close as she was, she realized it wasn't just a white light, but some sort of entryway, judging by the large frame that seemed to keep the light contained within its borders. Strange, she thought, as she took a step closer.

The light slowly began to swirl into a circle, resembling a hurricane contained within the frame. Its middle opened up, revealing something that made Jen take a few steps back in fear. Peering into the hole as it grew, Jen saw an alley and nearby buildings.

She slowly raised a hand to the center of the circle, wanting to see what would happen if she touched it. Jen's thoughts ran back to her father, wondering if that was what he had done, wondering if she was making a mistake. She blocked out her fears and drew her hand even closer to the light. Without another moment's hesitation, her hand melted through the surface, almost as if she'd stuck her hand in water. Although heat radiated from the light, the liquid feeling was cool and calming. Jen continued sinking her hand into the frame until it reached her elbow, and then she pulled her hand back out, examining it. Nothing bad had happened to it.

The hole began to shrink until it was just big enough for her enter. Jen realized she was staring at some sort of portal, and wondered if she'd find her father if she stepped through it. God knew she'd dreamed of finding out what really happened to him. As the hole continued to shrink, Jen knew she had a quick decision to make, one that could cost her own life.

Nothing mattered more than finding her father, and she'd risk her life to know the truth. It was possible he was in trouble and needed her help, and if she found him, she could bring him home. Jen had made her choice. Without another moment of hesitation, she stepped through the shrinking hurricane, disappearing from her room.

CHAPTER THREE

Blue City

Asher stepped outside of his favorite pub and took in a deep breath, not minding the stench of sewage and metal in the city air. Blue City, his glorious home, was founded in 2189, right after the invention of the hover bug, the world's first flying car. It took over a hundred years, trillions of dollars, and millions of robots to build it into the city it had become: a blue paradise that everyone wanted to visit. There was no other city in the world quite like Blue City. Other cities didn't have skyscrapers that soared past the clouds so high that the naked eye couldn't make out the top of the building when standing on the Bottom Ground, the lowest street level. Other cities didn't have human-like robots working in restaurants and stores, doing all of the manual labor, while the rich men fattened themselves up on expensive lobster and caviar. Nor did they have a sea of tourists crowding the Bottom Ground, bringing even more money to the city by visiting the many attractions.

Blue City was a vacation city, similar to the old Las Vegas, with large casinos, hotels, amusement parks, and theaters filled with show girls and magic shows. All of the attractions that lay within the skyscrapers were advertised on the glass windows, creating their own light shows at night.

Asher thought the best part of the city was the night sky view, when hover cars zoomed past in the sky on transparent, neon blue streets, which glowed brightly against the dark backdrop. There were multiple layers of streets that started from the Bottom Ground and continued into the sky, all heading different directions, all extremely complex to those who had never driven on them. From the ground looking up, it seemed as if the neon streets intertwined. The intricate, overlapping streets suggested the possibility of a hover bug accident waiting to happen; however, the streets actually kept people from crashing into each other and falling out of the sky to a certain death.

The neon lights were merely an illusion, an image coming from strong projectors built into the surrounding skyscrapers. At one point, the government thought about building high roads, but found it to be too costly. Instead, they perfected the projectors, making the blue streets seem real and quite lovely at night. The light show in the night sky was something that Asher never got tired of as he stared up at its beauty from the Bottom Ground.

Asher followed in the footsteps of his father, Commander Thomas Moore, and worked for the government as third commander in the army. At the age of nineteen, he was the youngest commander and took pride in his position. However, getting to such a high ranking had come with a big price.

Asher was raised by a man who never showed any affection and constantly taught him that emotions were a weakness. He was disciplined with beatings and harsh punishments, once having to stand for twelve hours on thick, sharp pegs because he'd talked back to his father. Asher had been able to carefully position himself in a way that didn't cause the pegs to rupture his skin.

He didn't understand why his father punished him so harshly knowing that, had Asher fallen, the pegs would have caused him to bleed to death. There had been a few times when Asher had almost fallen, his twelve years of life flashing by in his mind, but luckily he'd found his footing. And although he had hated his father's disciplinary methods, he could attest to it being the sole reason that he was fierce and strong.

Asher had fought and outsmarted his way into his high position, beating out a bunch of overly qualified recruits, reporting directly to his father, Commander Moore. Usually, Asher's job was located overseas, supervising military units and boot camps, but lately he had been assigned a simple job that consisted of patrolling the streets of Blue City. Recent riots and a decrease in the police force due to funding cutbacks had taken their toll on the city, causing a large amount of unrest. Asher's job was to make sure the locals were acting level-headed.

Asher never understood why someone as highly ranked as he was had been given a job that police officers should have been doing. Even though he still held his title, it made him feel as if he had been demoted. Every now and then, Asher would get what he considered a fun assignment, where he'd go on high speed chases to catch criminals flying through the sky in hover bugs. He'd get to bust major drug operations and rescue illegal slaves from slave houses. However, lately, he'd been bored with just patrolling the streets and couldn't wait for his next big mission.

Outside the pub, Asher looked up at the evening's display on the billboards. His eyes dropped to a hover bug entering an opening in one of the skyscrapers, called a Sky Garage. He then looked down at the cement sidewalk with all of its cracks and imperfections, a reminder of the old generations that had once walked past.

Blue City had been built just north of New York and was twice the city New York used to be due to its greatness. Asher had heard stories of the once glorious city, but what stood out more than any other was the city's demise. The city had been attacked during World War Three, and all of the once-beautiful buildings had come crashing down. The war continued for ten years, and afterward, Old America had begun to rebuild. However, settlers never dared to rebuild directly over New York and instead moved to the land just north of it.

A few men came out of the pub and clumsily brushed past Asher, muttering apologies once they saw his harsh gaze and military uniform. He watched as the men stumbled away and continued walking down the street. A yellow taxi hover drifted inches from the Bottom Ground and waited until each of the men got inside before gliding swiftly onto the neon roads in the sky.

Asher reached into his pocket, pulled out a piece of gum, and brought it toward his mouth. A bright light suddenly exploded from an alleyway, causing him to jump back in surprise and drop his gum on the Bottom Ground. He looked around, wondering if anyone else had seen the blast of light, but nobody was around. Asher couldn't believe his eyes. Time travel had been banned for years. Very rarely did a criminal attempt to time travel, and when caught, death wasn't the worse punishment imaginable.

Look what we have here, he said to himself, quickly turning down the alley and walking toward the portal. Asher stood to the side of the metal barricades, watching the light begin to swirl and form into an opening. He pulled the shooter from his holster and pointed it at the middle of the circle that was opening up. First, he noticed a feminine hand come through its center and then disappear again. Moments later, Jen stepped through, falling to the ground, looking slightly dazed.

The portal disappeared, leaving Jen alone in an alley, or so she thought. Her eyes landed on a pair of black combat boots and traveled up a metallic military uniform to a strange looking gun pointed at her. She glanced from the man's gun to his face and took in the sight of his stern, full lips, straight nose, and deadly, piercing blue eyes. Her breath caught as her eyes darted back down to the gun pointed at her.

"Stand up," Asher commanded with a low and serious growl. Jen obeyed, quickly rising to her feet and brushing off the debris that had gotten on her skin. She didn't have time to be embarrassed that she was in her usual braless tank top and pajama shorts when a gun was pointed at her head.

The exterior of the gun was smooth and polished white, with a thick, blue tip, reminding her of the types of guns used in space movies. Bright green liquid energy seemed alive as it surged through the gun, making it glow. Was it electrical?

Before she could lift her eyes to his face again, he lowered his gun and pushed her backward until her back hit the brick of a building. Her breath caught in her throat as she slammed against the wall and instinctively tried to push him away. She didn't understand what was going on. First she was in her bedroom, and then she was walking through a bright light into the hands of a man who now held her captive. The only thing she knew in that moment was fear.

"Who are you?" Asher asked, his face inches from hers as he practically spat in her face. Even though she was afraid, she couldn't help but notice how dark and intriguing he was. This man was very attractive in a dangerous kind of way that called to her. He stood strong and stiffly, his thick brows and piercing blue eyes shielding something deep and sinister, which made Jen believe she was right to be afraid. His hair was cut extremely short, which was typical for a man in the military, and it made the angular curves of his cheek bones more prominent. Yes, he was both beautiful and deadly, and Jen wasn't sure which was worse.

"J...Jen Kallis," she said, shaking underneath his gaze.

"Ms. Kallis, you do realize you've committed a federal offense?"

"W-what?" Jen blinked rapidly, trying to wrap her head around his words.

"Time travel has been banned for fifteen years, or did you not get the memo growing up?" Asher asked with a hard tone.

"T-time travel?" Jen was horrified; she would have sank into the floor had the man not been pinning her to the wall. "I don't understand. Where am I? Do you know my father?"

Asher was confused as to why Jen was pretending not to know the law, unless...

"Ms. Kallis, what year are you from?"

"T-two-thousand-and-s-sixteen," she answered, looking fragile under his firm grip. He loosened his hands but kept her firmly pressed against the building.

"Do you understand what you just did by using a portal? You committed a federal crime. But of course you wouldn't understand that if you weren't from this time period." Asher sighed and absentmindedly let go of Jen, taking a step back, in deep thought, while keeping her within his line of sight. Jen took the time to really study his profile.

His name badge read "Asher Moore, Third in Command." She could tell he was a few years older than she was and belonged to some type of military unit. His dark brown buzz cut looked perfect against his olive skin. His jaw line was strong and his high cheekbones caused his eyes to slightly slant. Most of all, he really did look like someone from the future.

"Where am I?" Jen asked, regaining Asher's attention.

"Blue City, of course," Asher said with a hint of attitude. "Land of the robots." Jen took in the bit of information with a deep swallow.

"My dad—he came through the portal ten years ago. Can you please let me go so that I can find him and go home?"

Asher laughed.

"Opening that portal would've definitely showed on the radar at the Capitol Building. Government officials are most likely on their way as we speak. No matter where you try to run, you'll get caught."

Dread filled every inch of her. "What will they do to me?"

Asher shrugged, hearing the nearby sirens and lifting his eyes to the sky. Just as he suspected, the officials were only minutes away.

"Probably take you in for questioning and possibly send you back home. That is, if your story adds up. Otherwise, they'll torture you until you come clean. After that, they'll kill you to set an example." Jen gasped.

"Would they have done that to my dad?"

"I don't know what the protocol was ten years ago. It's possible he could've gotten away or been taken in."

Jen heard the sirens approaching and began to panic. She looked up at the sky and noticed the cars flying past on bright roads and large skyscrapers that disappeared in the clouds. She was overwhelmed by the sight and appeal of it all, as it all looked like a scene right out of a sci-fi novel. Jen glanced back at the soldier in front of her and watched the gun dangle aimlessly in his hand.

"Can you just send me back?"

"Nope," Asher responded nonchalantly, not even bothering to meet her eyes. "I don't have a portal, and as I've already stated, the portals are off limits."

"Then let me go! Tell your people that the criminal escaped before you got here."

Asher outright laughed and then quickly sobered. He leaned closer to her face as he continued to trap her against the wall.

"You're serious, aren't you?"

"Please help me," Jen begged while gripping his arm. "You know I'm not a criminal. I'll find my own way out of this place if

I need to."

Asher sighed, looking up at the sky. The officials would be there any minute. Even if he let her go, she wouldn't be able to escape on her own, knowing nothing about Blue City. Her strange clothes would also be a giveaway, preventing her from blending in. Any officer or soldier could stop her for questioning along the way, and he knew she wouldn't have the kind of answers needed to get past them.

Asher entertained the idea of helping her. He had an uncontrollable pull toward a thrill, and this little adventure would definitely satisfy that desire. If anyone could get out of the situation they were currently facing, it would be him. Asher was almost as high as authority went and having a father directly associated with the president would help him get out of trouble if they were caught. Asher groaned deeply, having made a decision.

Without a word, he pulled Jen by the arm and ran to a door on the side of the building. He opened it, surprised it hadn't been locked, and pulled her inside. They found themselves at the base of a stairwell that ventured to the top of the skyscraper.

"Come on," he said, pulling up her the stairs. "Quickly."

Jen followed behind, not understanding what he was doing. Had he decided to help her? If so, what was his plan?

"Where are you taking me?"

"Somewhere far from here. We can rent a hover bug on the twentieth floor. If we don't hurry, they'll find us."

Jen followed him up to the twentieth floor. Halfway up the stairwell, she slowed down and had to push herself to keep up. Her legs burned in a way she'd never felt before, and each step caused her to moan. Asher, who was at least eight steps ahead of her, kept shouting back at her to hurry. He didn't seem the least concerned about her pain.

Insensitive prick, she thought to herself and busied her mind with throwing insults at him to keep herself distracted from the pain. They finally reached the twentieth floor, and Jen noticed that Asher hadn't even broken a sweat. She envied his stamina—twenty flights of stairs was probably child's play to him. Asher reached out, steadying her when she almost collapsed in exhaustion.

"Get it together," he said with blatant indifference. "I don't need you drawing any more attention than you already will. Don't look like a tourist, no matter how interesting things look. Okay, Ancient Meat?"

"Ancient Meat?" Jen asked, surprised that he'd already given her a nickname, and a terrible one at that.

"From the looks of it, you're no older than eighteen, and being eighteen in the year two thousand and sixteen would mean you're around two hundred and six years old. That's pretty ancient."

Jen shook her head and looked ahead of him as he opened the door to the twentieth floor. He quickly pulled her through the door and signaled for her to start following him.

Although Asher warned her against staring, Jen couldn't help but look at the men and women who were walking around what appeared to be a shopping mall. Almost all of them were dressed in different colored liquid bodysuits, and the women wore bright-colored hair pieces twice as big as anything she'd ever seen.

Each person looked a lot tanner than what she'd considered normal and seemed to take as much interest in her as she did them. Jen fully understood how different she must look and wanted to disappear. Asher noticed that she'd slowed and reached out to grab her hand, yanking her forward.

Jen would have fought against his firm grip, but she was again distracted, this time by a few kids hovering above the ground on a floating board. She also noticed strange adults who traveled stoically on similar looking boards that seemed to surge with their own liquid energy like the gun Asher had.

Asher noticed her staring.

"Those are robots," he said, pointing to the people on floating boards. "You can tell them apart from actual humans because they glide around on those boards. They also have limited facial expressions. You'll see a lot more of them, because as I said earlier, this is the Robot City. This building is pretty much like all other commercial buildings on this strip. There are five malls, three casinos, and two hotels all in here. The Bottom Ground has a bar, and I believe there's also a gym somewhere."

They began walking past all types of people. One woman had purple and red curls and wore a pink pixie dress made of a flowing material Jen had never seen. The heels and sides of her stilettos were missing, almost making her shoes look invisible, and she seemed to be walking on the tips of her toes. But despite her strange clothes, she looked comfortable in them, and she smiled as she passed them, bowing her head to Asher in respect.

"The hover rental is just across this bridge." As he said it, Jen noticed a large bridge appear ahead of them that seemed to connect to the opposite side of the building. She stopped in her tracks, causing a couple behind her to stumble. Asher pulled her aside, letting the couple pass, and gave Jen a look deadly enough to make her cower. He grabbed her hands and pulled her forward. "What was that about?"

Jen nodded ahead at the large, unique bridge before them. The floor of the bridge was transparent, and there were no railings, meaning one could easily fall off. The only reason she could tell it was a bridge was the neon green lights that trailed along edges of it. She watched as the couple absentmindedly stepped on the bridge and stood still as it began to glide them across.

"It's easy," Asher snorted as if reading her mind. "There's a sort of force shield on the bridge that prevents you from falling off. Completely safe."

They now stood inches from the bridge, and Jen glanced down over the edge, noticing similar bridges on each level below her transporting people. She then looked above her, seeing more bridges connecting to other parts of the building. Some floors had multiple bridges while other floors seemed to have bridges that were out of order. It was all a very intricate and appealing sight.

Jen wasn't as afraid anymore. She watched as Asher stepped onto the bridge and turned toward her, holding out a hand. She quickly stepped onto it, having realized she was holding up the people behind her. She felt the suction of the bridge seeming to grasp her leg, holding her in place. She met Asher's approving stare and almost laughed. She hadn't known the bridge would do that. Asher smiled for the first time, knowing he'd deliberately left out that detail just to see her reaction. It had been a while since he'd met an adult with a child's joy and view of their world. Even the tourists were used to Blue City and didn't get as excited about its charms.

Jen heard shouting and looked above as a dozen officers piled onto the bridge directly above them. She returned her gaze to Asher, who raised a finger to his mouth to keep her silent. She nodded and lifted her head to the commotion above.

"We need reinforcements on every floor in all nearby buildings on the block. The fugitive couldn't have gotten far," an officer above her shouted, causing her heart's pace to quicken. She lifted a hand to the cross around her neck and silently prayed that those guards wouldn't look down and notice her standing there. They got to the other side of the building, unnoticed, and Jen was thankful when Asher stepped off the bridge. He held a hand out to her and she took it, feeling the pulling sensation lift from her ankles. She stepped off the bridge with a sigh and felt a rush of adrenaline.

"That was awesome!"

Asher frowned, his thick eyebrows making him look menacing.

"Seconds ago, you were scared out of your mind. We don't have time for excitement, Ancient Meat. They're on to us." He pulled her toward the entrance of the hover rental store. Jen was confused by Asher's sudden mood change. Hadn't he laughed with her on the bridge? She sighed and followed him in silence.

A man appeared on an animated sign gleaming above the entrance of the store. He stared directly at Jen, telling her to come inside and take the ride of her life.

"Welcome to Hover Rentals, where you can rent the latest hovers and scooters for however long you need. Come inside and see what journey awaits!"

Asher reached into his pocket, pulled out a gadget, pointed it at the rental store, and pushed a button. "This will shut off all of the cameras. We don't need to leave any evidence." He pulled Jen inside the store, passing the eager robots that had begun greeting them. One was a beautiful blonde with an expressionless smile. She looked at Jen and waved.

"Hope you find a rental that meets your needs." Jen was surprised by the accuracy and human-like quality of her voice. The robots in 2016 sounded like robots, not like humans.

"Why are there so many robots?" Jen asked Asher. He didn't seem interested in answering her, so she redirected the question. "Where are you going to take me?"

Asher ignored her second question, too, giving all of his attention to the robot running the front register. Jen sighed, turning away from where Asher stood, and began looking around. There were models of different hovers sparkling throughout the room. She walked up to an intriguing purple car; it seemed to glow from inside the same way the hover boards had. She opened the door and sat on the driver's side, noticing that the steering wheel was replaced by a stick, and the dashboard was covered in different buttons ranging in color and size. The seats were extremely comfortable and seemed to automatically adjust based on her body size. It was a feeling Jen could get used to.

"What are you doing?" Asher asked, nearly scaring her to death. "Now is not the time to be curious. Come on."

He walked away as she got out of the car and quickly trailed behind him. Asher had a pair of keys in his hand and followed a male robot gliding through a door.

They were now in a garage that opened to the outside. A blue road began right at the opening, making Jen gasp in appreciation. She'd only seen the roads looking upward but now she was actually going to see what it was like to ride on them. The hover car roared to life, making her jump. The robot stood aside, smiling at Asher.

"Enjoy your trip and please use Hover Rentals again."

Asher grabbed Jen's arm, quickly pulling her around to the side of the hover. He opened the door and motioned for her to get in. Jen was hesitant, having never driven in a flying car before, but she forced herself to slowly sink into the hover bug.

Apparently it wasn't quick enough. Behind her, Asher signed, lifted her up, and sat her inside the hover himself. Jen could deal with him practically dragging her through the building, but she didn't appreciate him sweeping her off her feet and putting her into the hover the way he had. Once she was inside, he closed the door and walked around to the other end.

Controlling, Jen thought to herself.

Asher got inside the hover, pressed a big green button, and flicked a few switches. Jen felt the hover lift off the ground and squeezed the sides of her seat for support. It was a strange feeling to be floating in a car, and Jen wasn't too excited about the idea. Asher pressed a few other buttons, and the hover slowly began to move.

The hover bug floated onto the neon street as Jen pressed her forehead against the glass window on the passenger side as her fear began to vanish. She was mesmerized at how effortlessly the car floated in air and dared to look down at the cars below her. She did everything in her power not to shriek in excitement. Asher pushed a few more buttons and the car took off, pressing Jen against her seat.

"Seatbelt," Asher said, looking in his rearview mirror at the cop's hover bug that had just dropped down behind him from a Sky Garage above. "This trip might get a little bumpy."

It didn't take long for the cop's sirens to sound behind them, causing Jen's heart to jump out of her chest. She quickly reached for the seatbelt, clicking it into place. Suddenly, the hover dropped, making Jen's stomach flip as they glided downward. She let out a shriek, holding onto the side of the hover for support.

Asher let up on the stick, causing the hover to stop falling and level out. Jen realized he'd dropped down three streets to get away from the cop, but in a matter of seconds, the hover was trailing them again. Asher gripped the stick in anger and jerked it to the right. The hover shifted, throwing Jen to the side, and just when she thought she'd been thrown around enough, the car shifted to the left, entering another lane. She turned around and saw that the cop was keeping up and another one had joined behind it.

"There are two now, Asher!"

"You might want to sit back for this," he said, and the hover accelerated as he lifted it into the air.

They soared upward at heightened speeds, zooming past other hover bugs, while narrowly missing them. Asher decided to lower the hover into a lane a few levels below so that he could blend in with traffic. Jen kept watching behind them and noticed that the cop still trailed them, clumsily dropping down into their lane.

"Stop or we'll shoot!" the officer called from a loudspeaker. Jen faced forward in her seat and looked at Asher, who cursed under his breath.

"Not if I shoot first."

Asher flipped the hover in the air, causing it to loop backward until it was positioned behind the last cop car. Asher pressed the button on top of the stick repeatedly as green light flashed from the front of the hover, hitting the cop's hover in the back. The cop's hover stalled and began to fall from the sky. The first cop noticed and swerved to the left, narrowly missing another round of shots Asher set off, and disappeared behind a building.

Asher didn't follow the cop, knowing that he and Jen were given a perfect chance to get away without being trailed. He figured the cop would circle around and continue the chase, so he kept his eyes open. He lifted the hover up three more levels, getting onto the expressway and heading east toward his condo. He looked over at Jen, whose face was filled with panic and excitement. He'd almost forgotten how different this experience was for her, since it was her first time being shot at in a hover bug flying in the sky. She would definitely have a story to tell her friends once she made it back home.

Asher was thankful for Jen's silence as it gave him time to figure out what they'd do next. It seemed hard to get her to stop asking questions once she got started soon after the chase ended. Jen asked about the buildings, the hover bugs, the robots, the advertisements lit up on buildings, the economy, and the world in general. She was worse than a tourist seeing Blue City for the first time, and he didn't have the patience to deal with it. He would help her find whoever she needed to find and figure out a way to get her home. Hopefully, they wouldn't get killed in the process. Still, the thought of the challenges ahead intrigued and excited him. He lived for thrills and felt as if he had been playing his favorite video game. He thanked his father's stern discipline and training in helping him become the best. This was all fun and games for him.

Jen closed her eyes, exhausted from the last half an hour of the crazy yet exciting world she had found herself in. A small part of her wondered if she was dreaming. Maybe she had fallen asleep while studying and managed to dream up Blue City. Jen pinched her cheek and felt pain, which let her know that she was, in fact, more than 200 years in the future.

Another thought dawn on her. The night her father disappeared ten years ago had really happened; he hadn't left her and her mother behind. She now had a chance to find out where he was and bring him home. But what if he didn't want to come home? Or worse, what if he had died? Jen could barely fathom the thought. She tried to fight back the tears that threatened.

"You're about to cry," Asher observed. Jen hadn't realized he'd been staring at her while driving. She felt small under his scrutiny and turned her head even farther toward her window.

"It's all so overwhelming: the cars, the roads, the buildings, being chased by cops. I'm just trying to process it all."

Jen waited for Asher's response, but he said nothing. She glanced in his direction and noticed how low his thick eyebrows were on his forehead. He looked to be deep in thought. Jen welcomed his silence and tried to force herself to focus on the bright roads and the odd, angular shaped cars that passed by, oozing orange flames from behind. An hour ago she was breaking up with her boyfriend and now she was a fugitive in the future, running from the cops. She just wanted to close her eyes and pretend that it all really was a dream.

CHAPTER FOUR

Smart Condo

A sher drifted the hover near the side of a building as the stainless glass window opened in front of them, revealing a large three-hover garage. Two expensive looking hovers occupied a parking space, leaving one left for their hover. Asher glided the hover into the garage, turned it off, and stepped out. Jen followed quietly behind, watching as he walked up to a square sensor on the frame of his door. He put his right hand up to a built-in machine that copied a single fingerprint, and after a few seconds, a green light flashed, causing the door to his condominium to open.

Asher cockily strutted into his condo and then stood aside so that Jen could enter. The first thing she noticed when she stepped inside was a large, open room with wooden floors and white walls. A large sliding glass door took up the whole back wall, and Jen could make out the glistening glass from other buildings nearby. She was surprised by how plain and bare Asher's apartment looked compared to everything else she'd seen in Blue City so far.

"Where is everything?" she asked, turning around to Asher. He was greeting a female robot who had seemed to come from nowhere, as there were no other doors around. Her name tag, pinned to her white and black polka dot shirt, read 'Hi, I'm Mary!', and she wore the same emotionless smile that Jen noticed other robots sporting. Asher leaned toward the robot, whispered something quietly, and watched the robot disappear into a door that Jen hadn't noticed before. She blinked and then gave her attention to Asher, who walked past her toward the middle of the open room.

"Anna," he called, looking around the room at nothing in particular.

"Nice to have you home, Mr. Moore," said a voice from

above. Jen lifted her eyes to the cathedral ceiling to see where the noise came from but found nothing. "What may I help you with?"

"Please set the living room."

"Gladly, Mr. Moore."

Suddenly, the walls began to break apart and the floor shifted underneath Jen, causing her to stumble. A large beige couch protruded from the floor, followed by two chairs and two sets of nicely decorated end tables. One of the white walls had completely shifted upward, revealing a TV screen that spanned the wall's length.

"Anna, show the news," Asher said, motioning for Jen to take a seat with him on the couch.

"As you wish, Mr. Moore."

Jen studied Asher as he casually walked over to his couch and flopped down. She slowly followed him, but sat down more cautiously, having noticed how expensive his couch must have been. It was the finest material she'd ever seen. Jen fought back the moan that was on the verge of escaping her mouth as she sank into the soft, heavenly cushions. The large TV screen clicked on and an image popped up of an attractive anchorwoman staring intently at the camera. The image of the woman and her surroundings seemed to stick out from the actual TV, making it appear as if she was standing directly in from of them. Jen fought back another urge to get up and touch the TV screen. It was way cooler than the 3D TVs she had been accustomed to. For those she'd needed 3D glasses to view the special effects.

"For the first time in over ten years a portal was unlocked and opened on the east side of downtown Blue City around noon today," the anchorwoman said. "A getaway rental hover bug was spotted by law enforcement fleeing the scene. However, it got away after shooting down a police bug. Thankfully, the officer survived. The Enforcement is currently investigating the situation and hopes to have a suspect soon. We are asking for anyone who may have a possible lead on the suspect to call our Crimestoppers Hotline immediately. The Enforcement would like to remind people that time travel is a serious felony that can be punishable by death. An example will be made out of anyone who breaks this law."

Jen stopped listening to the anchor and turned her head toward Asher who, once again, looked to be deep in thought.

"Asher," she began, studying his expression. He never seemed to be in the mood to answer questions, but his peaceful face seemed promising. "Why are the portals banned?"

"Why else?" he asked, sarcastically. "People wanted to change history. If history is altered, even slightly, it could cause a ripple effect on the timeline of humanity, completely changing the future. There are men in this world who would do anything to go back to monumental moments in history and change the course of events.

"Something like that happened over fifty years ago. A man named Johnson Howard had a plan to go back to the time when the scheme to blow up the Twin Towers had been hatched. He wanted to completely change the mission so that three other major cities would be bombed, causing a national crisis beyond anything America had ever seen.

"Thankfully, the Enforcement interceded, discovering a secret organization that aimed to change every major moment in history. The Enforcement has been trying very hard since that incident to make sure nothing like that happens again. The portals should've never been invented in the first place."

"So you don't believe in time travel?" Jen asked out of curiosity.

"If God intended for us to play with time, he would've given Adam and Eve a portal."

"If the Enforcement closed down the portals, why did one open up, allowing me to come through?"

Asher looked at her as if she'd finally asked a question worth answering.

"That's what I've been asking myself over and over. Portals don't just open up by themselves. It takes a person with skill to do so. How did you discover the portal?"

Jen nodded and explained the series of events from the day her father disappeared to the moment she decided to step through the portal, based on curiosity and an eagerness to find her father. Asher listened to the story with mild interest. His robot, Mary, eventually reentered the room carrying bags of clothes. She removed an outfit from the bag and handed it to Asher.

"Is there anything else I can do for you?" Mary asked. Jen was stunned by how lifelike she looked, despite her emotionless smile. Mary even had a set of freckles that covered her nose. Asher nodded.

"Take the rest of the clothes to the guest bedroom and put them away." He then turned to Jen, handing her a set of clothes.

"The bathroom is on the right. The door will appear once you're close enough. I need you to change into something more modern. The clothes should fit you perfectly. And just in case you're wondering how Mary was able to shop for your things so quickly, I'll explain. There's a mall a few levels below. Mary was able to measure you within a second's time, scan an online selection of clothing, order the clothes online, and have them ready to be picked up in less than two minutes. Too much to take in, Ancient Meat? I'll let it marinate. I need to make some phone calls and will be in another room. If I'm not back by the time you're dressed, make yourself at home. Anna and Mary will help you with everything." His tone was dismissive.

With that, Asher stood and walked to the wall where a steel door appeared, and he quickly disappeared inside the room. Jen watched as the door molded back into the wall, amazed. Asher's dismissive tone was forgotten instantly.

"I don't think I could ever get used to that," Jen said out loud. She stood and walked to the wall on her left side, as Asher had instructed, and watched as a steel door, identical to Asher's, materialized, revealing a rather empty bathroom.

Once Jen stepped into the bathroom, the door disappeared behind her. She turned to face the mirror, which had been the only object in the room, and studied the droopy, hazel eyes that looked back at her. Her caramel skin looked pale in comparison to how it had looked a day before. A shower was definitely what she needed. She turned to face the rest of the bathroom, wondering how she would wash with no shower.

Jen thought back to what Asher had said about Anna helping her out. She hesitated, hoping that simply calling her name would work. "Anna, where is the toilet?"

Suddenly, a small hole in the floor appeared and grew wider as a toilet rose from its center. Jen laughed, completely taken back by this "smart house."

"Anna, I want to take a shower."

And just like that, water sprung from the wall, falling into a drain that appeared on the floor. Jen changed out of her clothes and stepped into the soothing shower, allowing all of her fears to wash away. The hot, steamy water seemed just the right temperature as it beat down on her skin in a therapeutic way. She almost melted with pleasure.

"I could get used to this," Jen said, and laughed quietly to herself.

Asher stood in his bedroom, which was desolate and void of any sunlight. He preferred it that way. He kept a thick black curtain pulled shut against a wall-length window because he couldn't stand the sun in the mornings. He hadn't realized his bedroom faced the east when he purchased his condo, and he didn't dare move into one of the smaller rooms.

Asher took out his holo-phone, pressing a button and then letting go so the little silver gadget floated in the air in front of him.

"Ring Gunner."

The holo-phone floated a distance away as a yellow light flashed from the top right corner, casting a circular light on the marble floor in front of him. A second light flashed red on the bottom left corner of the holo-phone, picking up his image for transfer. As the phone read his image, it converted another image onto the yellow projection in front of him. A body began to form from the light.

A young man appeared before Asher. A large cut was centered on his right cheek as if someone had sliced his face open years ago. His eyes were black, the color of death and despair, and large veins protruded from his neck as he took in the sight of Asher. Gunner clenched his hands into veiny fists and tilted his head to the side, cracking his neck. Gunner then growled and spat at Asher. Of course the fluid didn't land on Asher since he was only an image, but it didn't matter to Gunner.

Why did you call me?" His voice was deep and held a promise of wrath. Asher's cocky smile was just as ominous.

"You owe me a favor."

"I owe you nothing," Gunner growled.

"I broke you out of jail."

"You're also the one who put me in jail."

Asher recalled the memory. He had been affiliated with Gunner, a twenty-six-year-old drug lord who'd had a high stakes' job, something Asher thought the military would never find out about. There had been a promise of a five hundred thousand dollar payment, if he killed a man named Roster Hills who happened to be another big-time drug lord. It wouldn't have been the first time that Asher had to kill a man, so he'd agreed to do it for the money.

Somehow, the police had been tracking the drug lord and were on the verge of bringing the whole operation down. They were there when Asher killed the drug lord, rushing into the underground compound with guns pointed every way. Gunner had been watching from a hidden place and was arrested while Asher narrowly escaped, glad for the mask that had kept his identity a secret.

Gunner believed that Asher had purposely tipped off the police, having him arrested while Asher got away free with the money Gunner had paid him. After waiting a few years to make sure things were clear, Asher devised a plan to break Gunner out of jail in exchange for a favor, something Asher would decide when and how he wanted it. Once Gunner had been freed from jail, he'd punched Asher in the face, knocking him to the ground, and had taken off. Asher let him go, knowing Gunner would deliver his favor one day. Now, Asher was calling in to collect it.

"Like I said before, Gunner, I did not—"

"You're a military commander who works closely with the police, the same dogs who put me in prison! You're either with them or with us. You're a traitor," Gunner spat, cracking his knuckles in front of his chest. It took everything Asher had to remain cool, but he was boiling with silent rage. If Gunner tried to spit at him again, he would lose it.

"I will be collecting my favor tomorrow."

"You don't know where I am." There was a hint of humor in Gunner's eyes, even though he looked ready to destroy Asher.

"Actually I do," Asher's smile was as cocky as ever. "One of the perks of being third in command is that I have access to all the goods used to keep tabs on a man like you. And you have something I want. A kid named Lark, boy genius. The kid knows everything about anything. I heard through the grapevine that you're using his intelligence."

"Why do you need him?" Asher noticed Gunner hadn't denied his claim.

He may be of use in helping me solve a mystery relating to the portals." Asher took a step toward the holographic image of Gunner, wishing they were face to face. He wanted to see Gunner's look of defeat firsthand. "I'll be there at thirteen hundred hours. Have the boy ready."

Jen was once again standing in the living room, wearing a liquid gray jumpsuit meant to sleep in. The jumpsuit reminded her of a onesie, although it looked more uniform-like and was pointed at the shoulders. Although the outside of the jumpsuit seemed sleek, it was actually one of the softest things she'd ever had the pleasure of wearing. Jen silently walked around the living room, thinking about how cool the future was. She had just begun getting familiar with telling her smart phone what to do and now she was telling a condo what to do. The thought of it was thrilling. However, it wasn't enough to keep her thoughts from the idea of finding her father. The complicated mission ahead made her stomach knot.

Asher had not yet returned from the other room, so Jen took a seat on the couch and noticed a plate of food. The sweet aroma made her stomach growl, and she involuntarily licked her lips. If she had been at home, she would have been in bed. Yet she found herself sitting here in this new world eating a plate of grilled zucchini, tomatoes, caramelized onions, mushrooms, and lobster tail while staring out at the neon blue street lights that decorated the late evening sky. She now understood why it was called Blue City.

Jen stood, walked over to the window, and watched as the street lights continued to brighten in preparation for the ever darkening night. Hover bugs seemed to be everywhere in the sky. Since she didn't understand the roads and rules that kept them from crashing into each other, it all seemed very chaotic.

"I see you found the food Mary brought you."

Jen turned around at the sound of Asher's voice as he casually leaned against the wall with folded arms, studying her from across the room. He had changed into a pair of black slacks and a dark blue t-shirt that had a thick silver stripe going down the right side. Jen couldn't make out the expression he wore because his eyes always seemed to be shielded, but she noticed how tight his face had gotten from the last time she'd seen him. Whatever was said on that phone call couldn't have been good.

"Yes, the food is delicious." She looked out the window, noticing the dark ocean in the backdrop behind the buildings. "You have a beautiful view, Asher."

"This is one of the best buildings on this side of town."

"Do you live with your parents?"

Asher snorted, taking a seat on the couch.

"I'm twenty and old enough to have my own place. Besides, my mother died when I was young."

Jen frowned and looked down at her feet. "I'm sorry to hear that."

Asher shrugged it off, walking over to the couch and taking a seat. He picked up an uneaten mushroom from Jen's plate and popped it in his mouth. "I was three. I barely remember her."

"And your father?" Jen lifted her eyes to meet his.

A shadow crossed over Asher's face as he focused on the table in front of him. "He's...alive."

Jen watched him, waiting for him to finish but realized he didn't plan on doing so. She decided to change the subject, seeing how easy it was for Asher to choose not to answer any more of her questions.

"How can you afford this place?"

"I'm third commander," Asher said with pride. "I'm loaded."

"So, you're in the army? And you're risking your position to help me?"

"Don't worry about me, worry about your father," Asher replied. Jen nodded and decided to change the subject. She made her way to the other couch and sat next to Asher.

"Is every condo like this?"

"The good ones are. Every house in Blue City has advanced technology a lot different from your time period, Ancient Meat. According to your standards, even the poorest house here would be luxurious."

"My standards?"

"You know, ancient standards. You had to manually turn on every single light. You had to run bathwater and cook your own food. You didn't have robots, and your furniture and electronics weren't safely tucked away within your walls in case of a burglary. Your time was closer to the caveman times than ours."

Jen felt offended by his view of her time period but shook it off quickly. It seemed part of his nature to be a jerk. "What year is this, anyway?"

"Twenty-two, twenty-two."

"2222?" Jen asked with wide eyes.

"Such a tongue twister when you say it like that," Asher told her, running a hand through his hair, as if it were long enough. He must have had long hair at some point before he'd joined the military, Jen thought, while picturing him running a hand through long brown locks. The gesture made Jen look away in fear of finding it attractive. Asher was definitely her type of guy, even though he was rude and indifferent. His attractiveness wasn't something she welcomed as it could only be a distraction for her. "Twenty-two, twenty-two works just fine."

"It's amazing how far the human race has come over the last two hundred years," Jen said, looking around.

"That could be a bad thing. Crime is at an all-time high, birth rates are low, food supplies for those less fortunate are hard to come by, and new diseases have surfaced. I'd prefer the simplicity of life in 2016. Sometimes it's unbearable living in twenty-two, twenty-two," Asher told her, momentarily dropping his guard and allowing Jen to see the hurt in his eyes. He looked up at her, noticing the concern in her own eyes and quickly masked his face. He didn't want her to be concerned for him. It was his job to care for other people, not the other way around. "Tonight, you'll need to get a good night's rest. I made a few calls to a man who will loan us a boy that may have some information about the portal opening ten years ago. The problem is, this man and his people are the bad kind of men, the kind who would love to kill me. It's going to be risky."

"What happens if he won't cooperate?" Jen asked.

Asher's eyes darkened as he pulled up his shirt, revealing the white gun he'd pointed at her earlier.

"Then I will make him cooperate."

CHAPTER FIVE

Lark

The rental hovered close to a glass building, nearly 3,000 feet in the air. These buildings were three times the height of any building Jen had ever seen in her small hometown in Ohio. She marveled at how this structure had what appeared to be liquid glass and watched how its surface rippled in waves as the strong winds blew in its direction.

Just then, the liquid glass window directly ahead of them opened up in the same way the garage to Asher's home had. Jen wondered if every window on every skyscraper opened up. She turned to ask Asher, but his expression was dark and serious, as if he was concentrating on something harsh. She turned back in her seat and decided to let it go.

The hover floated into the dark garage where two guards stood against the wall on either side of the garage door. They wore black jumpsuits and thick, black sunglasses that hid their identity. The men began moving toward either side of the hover bug once the engine cut off. Asher quickly turned to Jen, his expression desperate.

"Do you trust me?"

The question took Jen by surprise as the passenger door opened. Before she could respond, a set of hands yanked her out of the hover. She shrieked, nearly falling to the ground, but the man balanced her roughly and then pushed her toward the door. Asher had been given the same treatment and now stood next to her with his hands raised. The man behind him pointed a shooter at his back.

"Don't even think about doing anything stupid. One blast and you can say 'bye bye' to your little girlfriend."

The men guided Asher and Jen through a door into a large, open factory. Complex machines pushed black packages onto large trays, which were carried away by robots. Farther back, another machine poured liquid into the black packages that were then sealed and dropped onto another machine, which stamped and labeled each bag.

Jen had no idea what the liquid being poured into the packages was, but she knew that whatever it was wasn't good. She lifted a hand to the cross dangling around her neck, saying a silent prayer. A thousand things ran through her mind, starting with her wondering how an illegal company managed to operate inside a skyscraper with hundreds of other businesses on different floors. She wondered what other types of illegal activity took place within the building.

The guards brought them to a stop in the middle of the factory and patted both of them down. The man touching Jen seemed a little too friendly when he patted her backside, and she did everything in her power not to reach back and smack him. Once the two guards were satisfied, they began leading Asher and Jen down a path through the factory to a back door that opened up into a narrow hallway.

One of the guards led the way, putting Asher and Jen in the middle as the other guard stayed in the back. They went through another set of doors, which opened up into a nightclub blasting loud music. The style of music was similar to techno, but wasn't like anything Jen had ever heard before. Performers who were nearly naked danced on nearby stages and cages that glowed in different colors. Jen looked away, focusing instead on the back of the guard's head.

The guard stopped in front of a door down a long hallway, where the music from the club was at a more tolerable level, and knocked three times. He then opened the door and stood aside.

"Enter."

Jen's heart rate sped up as she entered the room first. How did Asher expect her to trust him when he willingly threw them into the arms of danger? She shivered as a pair of dark, ominous eyes met her from a maroon couch. In fact, everything in the room was maroon. Jen shifted her gaze to Asher, who stood next to her with a tight smile. His hands clenched and unclenched at his sides as he stared at the man ahead of them. Jen noticed he seemed to be battling a strong urge to do something.

The two guards took a stance behind them, never letting their shooters drop from pointing at Jen and Asher's backs. The man sitting on the couch slowly stood, cracking his knuckles as he smiled at Asher. A low growl sounded in the back of Asher's throat. If Jen had thought Asher looked dangerous, she now knew how mistaken she'd been. The man in front of her, with a sickening scar that ran down the side of his face, was ten times more frightening.

"What good is a man who can't keep his word?" Gunner asked as he walked over to an end table, picking up a glass of wine and swallowing its contents. "That is what my father taught me. It's what he lived by. No matter what he promised, he made sure he followed through."

Gunner signaled to a guard that Jen hadn't noticed standing near a double door to her left. The guard opened the door next to him and stepped inside. Moments later, he returned with a freckle-faced redheaded boy, wearing thick, black glasses, who looked no older than fourteen. The boy lifted his glasses and looked at Gunner with questions in his eyes. He turned his curious gaze to Asher, and then he looked at Jen and gave her a goofy smile. The boy quickly wiped the smile off his face as Gunner began to speak.

"My father would agree that it is best to honor the favor I owe you, regardless of the past." An evil smile played on Gunner's lips. "Unfortunately, my father is not here. I killed him many years ago. And I am not a good, honorable man, Asher. If you want my boy, you will have to take him." His deep, amused laugh echoed throughout the room. Gunner knew he had Asher now. In his head, there was no way that Asher would be able to kill three of his armed guards plus himself. Asher was simply outnumbered, and it was all so comical to Gunner. Gunner had waited for this moment since the first night he'd spent in prison. However, Gunner didn't weigh in the fact that Asher was third in command and had an uncanny ability to get himself out of any situation.

Out of the corner of Jen's eye, she saw Asher spin to the ground, kicking out and knocking the man who was guarding him to the ground. In the same breath, he managed to do a front flip while grabbing the knife from the guard's pocket, using it to stab the second guard in the leg. The man fell to the floor with a yelp, blood gushing from his leg, and Jen knew he'd be dead within minutes. Asher quickly stood, watching the guard closest to the freckle-faced boy spring into action by pulling the trigger on his shooter.

Green light shot through the air, barely missing Asher as he pushed Jen to the ground. The shots hit the wall, exploding into smoke, leaving large holes the size of a human head. A line of fire followed Asher as he ran toward the wall doing a kick flip while flinging the knife at the last guard. It went straight through his head, causing him to fall back against the wall.

The first guard Asher had taken down was now standing. Asher turned around and kicked the guard back into the wall. The man reached for his shooter, pointing it at Asher, and tried to shoot, but he wasn't quick enough. Asher managed to snatch the gun out of the man's hand and turned it on him. Green light shot through the shooter, hitting the guard directly in his chest. Jen looked away as blood splattered onto the wall.

Asher turned around to face Gunner and then cursed under his breath once he realized that both the couch and Gunner were missing. He must have gone under the floor boards and escaped. Asher sighed and went to Jen, helping her to her feet. He could see the fear in her eyes along with the tears that threatened to escape, but he didn't have enough time to reassure her. Gunner was gone and more of his guards were sure to be on their way, ready to kill them.

"Come on," Asher said, quickly moving over to the redhead who was watching Asher as if he was a ghost. The boy hadn't moved an inch during the whole ordeal.

"A-are you going to k-kill me?" the boy asked through chattering teeth. Asher rolled his eyes and grabbed the boy's arm.

"You need to come with us. We need to question you." The boy nodded and followed Asher and Jen out of the room.

A few minutes later, Jen found herself running with Asher and the boy as they traced their way back through the nightclub.

They'd knocked a few drunken men over in the process of leaving, and heard shouted obscenities and saw raised fists as they passed. When Jen also heard shooting behind her, she dared to look back.

Five guards were pushing their way through the crowd toward them. The commotion caused the paying customers to hide under tables in fear of a shootout. The performers began to scream and run off the stage. One girl screamed helplessly from the stage, not being able to take cover in enough time. Asher opened another door and allowed the boy and Jen to go through as he shot back at the guards.

Jen took the lead, running through the factory that would take them back to the garage. She stopped in her tracks, seeing the threat ahead. Not even twenty feet away stood two more guards. She looked behind her, past Asher, noticing that there were now two other guards chasing them.

They were trapped.

Asher was already a step ahead of Jen, taking out the last two guards behind him with the shooter. He pushed his way past Jen, aiming the shooter at the two guards in front who had begun taking their own defensive stances. Asher fired, but nothing happened. He looked down at the shooter, noticing that all of the green energy was gone. He cursed, quickly pushing Jen and the boy against the wall as the first round of shots flew past them.

Asher looked around. He noticed a picture directly above Jen's head. One thing his father had taught him through all of the beatings was that a weapon could be made out of anything. He managed to dodge a few more shots as he grabbed the frame, slamming it on the ground. Thick glass broke on the floor around him. Jen and the boy cowered, screaming as the two guards drew closer. Asher knew he had only seconds to act before one of them got shot.

He picked up two pieces of glass and quickly flung them through the air with skill, managing to hit both guards in the chest. He knew it would only momentarily stun them, but it would give him enough time to kill them. As the guards stumbled backward, holding onto their chests, Asher ran toward them. He grabbed one of the shooters from the closest guard's hand and shot both guards with little effort.

Asher let out a sigh and smiled cockily, and then turned back around and saw Jen and the boy crouched on the ground like children. The sight caused him to wipe the smile from his face in irritation. He turned back to the dead men, grabbed the second shooter, stormed over to where Jen was standing, and shoved the shooter in her hand.

"What good are you if you can't defend yourself?" He turned away from her and began walking away, not waiting for a response.

Jen watched in shock as he walked past the two guards, completely unaffected by the fact that he'd killed over ten of them just to get one boy. As logic and reason began to kick back in, she realized that he had also done all of this to help her. He'd risked his job and his life to help find a man who may or may not even be alive. She didn't understand why, but she wasn't complaining. She'd accept his attitude, even if she didn't like it.

Snapping out of her reverie, she followed behind Asher, looking back to see if the boy was behind her. He met her eyes, as if wanting to trust her, but then looked ahead at Asher and tensed. Jen could tell that he didn't know what to make of Asher, and she realized she really didn't know what to make of him either.

In her eyes, Asher was like a super human. How many people could defend themselves and two others against a group of men with weapons? Asher had speed and agility, but it was his quick thinking and uncanny intuition that truly impressed Jen the most. Even though he didn't express himself well, it was obvious to Jen that he had a heart. He was in the military and chose to go against commands to help her. No selfish man would have risked his own life just to help her, especially one in his position. Maybe that's all Jen really needed to know. Asher was trustworthy—m deadly but trustworthy.

No one said anything as Asher drove the hover back to his condo. He welcomed the silence as he thought about what they had in store next. Eventually, he stole a glance at Jen, who seemed to be drowning in her troubled thoughts. He could tell she would spend the rest of her day trying to get over the last twenty minutes of her life. He shook his head, hating her weakness. She needed to toughen up if she planned on finding her father. Blue City wasn't meant for ancient meat like her.

Having made it safely to the apartment, Jen welcomed the warmth of Asher's shower. She moaned as it rhythmically poured down her back in a massaging manner. Never in her life had she felt so relaxed and, at the same time, so on edge as she did now. She looked down at her trembling hands and thought about how much she missed the comfort of her mother. Jen could only imagine the amount of worry she was putting her mother through, having been gone a whole day without leaving any word of her whereabouts. She hadn't thought about how her mother would have to suffer through another loss and the depression that was sure to follow. If Jen could do it all over, she might have stayed home. At least she'd have been safe.

Mary came into the bathroom and set another pair of weird looking clothes on the long sink before exiting. Jen continued looking at her shaking hands, watching as the water poured onto them, continuing its journey downward and into the drain. If only she could wash away her fear as easily as she washed away the suds on her body.

Jen wondered if her father had ever experienced anything like what she'd just witnessed back at the factory. She sincerely hoped he hadn't. As she continued to clean herself, she imagined a more tranquil Blue City, one where her father sat on the beachside, drinking something fruity and thinking about how good his life was. However, she doubted that he had been that lucky. If anything, her father was in a bad position, which made her even more desperate to find him.

Jen hoped there was a good reason for barely escaping death just to get that boy. How could he know anything about the portals? Even if he did, how could that knowledge help them find her father? Jen wished Asher weren't so closed off, so that he could explain his thoughts thoroughly. For now, she would just have to trust him, and even that was a task in itself.

Jen could tell by the darkness in Asher's eyes that he was haunted by his past, as if a shadow of pain and regret followed him wherever he went. He didn't seem open to friendship or kindness and seemed incapable of any kind of affection or soothing words. He also looked at her as if she were a burden, just one more thing to slow him down. She wanted to prove herself worthy, but there was still a lot she didn't know or understand about Blue City.

Jen wondered what type of guy Asher would have been if he had been born in her era. She imagined him being a popular college student who partied a lot and was proud of all the girls who threw themselves at him. Jen couldn't help noticing how attractive he was. If it weren't for his tough exterior and terrible social skills, she could see herself actually liking him as a person.

After finishing her shower and dressing in a bright purple liquid jumpsuit, Jen returned to the living room. The boy was sitting on the couch, eating as if he hadn't eaten in days. A second plate of food heaped with white rice, sautéed vegetables, and baked chicken sat across from him. Jen looked around for Asher, but he was nowhere in sight. The boy looked up, giving Jen a goofy smile.

"T-that's your food right t-here," he said, pushing the brim of his glasses up his nose. He lowered his head and began to stuff his face again. Jen took a seat beside him and pulled her plate of food toward her from the other side of the table. She hadn't realized how hungry she was until the aroma of the baked chicken hit her nose. It smelled absolutely delicious.

"Where's Asher? Why did he leave you alone?" Jen asked, thinking that if the boy had wanted to, he could have escaped. She didn't take Asher as being careless.

"H-he told Anna not t-to let me out. These s-smart condos are built to k-keep people trapped inside, as well as people from outside coming in. That's common knowledge," the boy said, looking at Jen curiously.

"Do you always stutter?" Jen asked bluntly.

"It's a n-nervous condition."

"Oh. Well, what's your name and how old are you?" she

asked, after swallowing her first bite. The boy lifted his head up from his food long enough to say "Lark and fourteen" and then returned to eating. Jen nodded, taking another bite of food. It was just as good as the first meal she'd eaten. "I'm Jen."

"Y-you seem different," Lark observed, taking another bite. Jen picked up on his thick Blue City street accent; it sounded very similar to a New York accent. It seemed odd coming from a boy who looked like a nerd. "Y-your mannerisms are different. Are y-you from Blue C-city?"

"No," Jen said. "I'm actually from the year 2016."

Lark froze. "You're the c-criminal who opened the p-portal yesterday. I s-saw it on the news."

"I'm not a criminal," Jen protested. "I was just sitting in my room when the portal opened. My father, he came through ten years ago. I just want to find him. Asher believes you may have some information."

The boy froze again, looking off into the distance. Jen noticed sweat begin to drip from his forehead. She set her plate down, anxious for answers.

"If you know something, anything..." Jen reached out and caressed his arm. The nurturing gesture made him pull away.

"N-no." Lark shook his head, blinking back a distance memory. "I d-don't k-know a-anything about the portal opening t-t-ten years ago. I c-can't help you."

"But I just saw that look in your eyes. You know something."

"I just t-told you," Lark said more firmly, setting his plate of food down on the table. "I don't know anything."

Suddenly, a pair of hands grabbed Lark's shirt from behind and pulled him over the back of the couch. Jen gasped as her eyes followed the commotion. Asher straightened Lark into a standing position and turned him toward his frightening eyes.

"Either you help us or I kill you," Asher warned. Lark looked from Asher to Jen and a tremble rolled through his body.

"F-fine," he breathed. "I'll t-tell you everything I know.

CHAPTER SIX

Pink Flamingo

A single chair raised from the floor adjacent the couch. Asher took a seat as Jen and Lark sat next to each other on the couch. Asher played with what looked like an ink pen, flipping it in his hands over and over again. His eyes narrowed as he watched Lark, who was fidgeting nervously with his hands. Lark looked up at the pen in Asher's hand and swallowed hard, seemingly afraid of it. Jen didn't understand why Lark would be afraid of a pen until Asher clicked the button on the top.

A laser pointed directly at Lark's chest, and he began breathing deeply.

"You only have one chance to answer my questions correctly. If I believe you're lying, I'll press the button again."

"What happens if you do that?" Jen asked.

"He'll be shot in the heart by this little laser," Asher answered, without taking his eyes off of Lark.

"That's a little harsh." Jen said. Asher pointed the laser at her, his eyes narrowing into slits. Fear coursed through Jen's body as she shivered in response.

"Do you want to find your dad or not?" Asher asked.

Jen's mouth dropped. Her anger replaced her fear. The mission of finding my father would be pointless if I were dead. How dare he point that laser at me for voicing my opinion? Who does he think he is trying to scare people into obedience?

Jen wanted to scream at him, but she put aside her anger as she thought about the whole purpose of taking Lark. She needed to find out what had happened to her father and then go home, hopefully bringing her father with her. Jen lifted her chin and stared at Asher with a new confidence.

"I do want to find my father, and if you ever point that laser at me again, I will rip your heart out and feed it to you." Jen mentally patted herself on the back, knowing that Danni would have been proud. She watched Asher's lip twitch before pointing the laser back at Lark.

"You hear the girl? She wants to find her father, and you're going to help us."

"Tell me what you know about the portal opening ten years ago," Jen demanded, getting to the point. From the corner of her eye, she saw Asher look over at her, but she kept her eyes planted on Lark.

Lark looked down at the laser pointed at his chest and hiccupped. "I k-know a man. J-john Foster. H-he said he witnessed it happen. T-the man came through a p-portal downtown on the B-bottom Ground. John s-said that there were men on our side w-waiting for him. It l-looked like one of the m-men d-deliberately snatched that man o-out of the portal. J-john saw them place a b-bag over the man's head and c-carry him away.

"J-john ran into the guy on the street a f-few years later. Said he was b-beaten a-and bloody and in v-very poor shape. J-john o-offered him help, b-but the guy shook his head, m-muttering something and then r-running away. John said h-he never saw the guy again. That's all I know. A-a-ask me anything else and I can t-tell you. I know pretty much e-everything. But there isn't a lot of w-word around the streets about this. W-whoever knows the t-truth is doing a good job at k-keeping it a secret."

"You mentioned that her father said something to your friend before running away. What did he say?" Asher asked, putting his hand on the button of the laser. Lark's eyes widened.

"H-he...he didn't say. I swear. T-that's all I know."

"Where can we find John Foster?" Jen asked.

"L-last time I saw him, h-he worked down at the Pink F-flamingo. It's one of those f-fancy casinos you have to have a m-membership to get into."

"Age minimum?" Jen asked.

"T-there isn't no age m-minimum if you're a member. It's one of the p-perks," Lark explained. "John usually w-works at night at the poker table. I can take you to him. M-maybe he can answer the r-rest of your questions."

"Sounds like a plan." Asher sat back, content with the small lead. Jen wasn't so ready to relax. There was something bothering her.

"How are we going to get in if we need a membership?" Jen asked, turning toward Asher. He met her gaze, coolly.

"I'm a member," he said with an arrogant smile. "Mary!" he called. Moments later the robot appeared through the farthest wall and floated over to Asher.

"What can I help you with, sir?" Mary smiled mechanically.

"Please prepare my best suit. I'll also need another suit for the kid. And for the lady." Asher's eyes lowered as they roamed over Jen's body, sizing her up. Jen wanted to squirm under his heavy gaze but tried to remain as still as possible. "A formal dress, cobalt blue, size four."

Jen blinked in shock by his accuracy. "I thought you said she can measure me herself."

"She can," Asher said with a cocky grin. Jen felt insecure under his gaze as he watched her knowingly. She cleared her throat, turning toward Lark.

"Thanks for helping us," she said.

"I don't h-have a choice, do I?" Lark laughed nervously, scratching his head.

There was something sincere about Lark that made Jen trust him. She didn't know exactly what it was, but she did sense that Lark was just a teenage boy who was trying to survive in a tank full of sharks. It turned out that sense was right. Lark had adapted to life by becoming what people needed him to be, so that no one would have a reason to kill him. When he was eleven, he got his first job working for a wealthy Russian thug and learned the ins and outs of the black market. He then worked for an Italian mobster, where he had been asked to spy on another mobster, reporting back everything he heard. He'd gotten caught after three months and was almost killed. Thankfully, he'd been a faster runner than his pursuers.

If Lark had lived in the year 2016 he would have been a freshman in high school, the type of kid who was slightly awkward and had one weird best friend. He was the type that would sit with only three people at his lunch table and talk about fantasy video games or quantum physics.

It was strange how different their times were. Jen thought she'd had it tough having to practically raise herself during her mother's depression, but Lark was a kid who'd had to find his place in a man-eats-man society. He didn't have to tell her anything about his past. It was written all over his face. Jen was sure a lot of teenagers in Blue City grew up too fast. It made her appreciate her life more.

Asher's holo-phone vibrated in his pocket. He stood, excusing himself from the living room, and went into his bedroom. He pulled his holo-phone out, let it float in the air, and watched as an image materialized. Commander Moore appeared, tall and regal in his metallic suit, looking mighty and powerful. Asher might have admired the commander had he not been his father. Asher could never see past the horror of his childhood.

"Good 'noon, Commander Moore," Asher said with a firm salute.

"I didn't hear from you yesterday. I thought I'd make sure you were alive. Now that I see you're well, I'd like to discuss a serious matter with you. Did you hear of the portal opening yesterday? Cops had a lead on the getaway hover bug, but one hover was shot down and the other lost his lead. They ran the license plate and found out it was a rental. A fake name was used to purchase it. Police searched the video footage, but there was none. We have nothing, except for a few witnesses, who said they saw a suspicious male and female enter the rental store.

"I need you to keep your eyes open. You're better than some of the best cops and detectives. If anyone can figure out what happened, it's you. We'll let the police department handle their jobs, but I do want you to keep an eye out and get as much information as you can. I'm fighting for this case to be considered a terrorist threat, so that it falls in my jurisdiction. Report any suspicious activities immediately."

Asher closed his eyes, contemplating telling his father everything he knew. He could come up with a lie about how he found the girl, something Commander Moore would believe. His life would then continue as normal and he wouldn't have to worry about the stupid girl and kid.

It occurred to Asher that at that very moment, he could have been sneaking off to a back alley, hooking up with a random girl from a pub. Girls were constantly throwing themselves at him, and because the government provided him with all of his shots he didn't have to worry about contracting STIs or AIDS.

Asher knew he could take the easy way out by turning the girl in, but his gut feeling told him to stick with the plan. He fought back the urge to tell his father the truth. For now, he would pretend to keep an eye out for the "criminal" who had entered through the portal.

"I'll do my best," Asher promised his commander, staring him straight in the eyes as he spoke the lie. There was no going back now...

"What's the plan?" Jen asked as she walked into the immaculate casino. The blue dress Mary had picked out for her was too far ahead of her time, and she felt as if she were a walking piece of shark bait. The dress puffed out in weird, unnatural angles below her knees, and the sleeves that hung off her shoulders looked like fins, giving the illusion that she was being swallowed by a great white shark. The silver heels she wore were the only normal looking thing on her body.

Asher walked slightly ahead of her, giving off a confident vibe that made the nearby women turn to watch him. His buzz cut shined under the bright lights, and he wore a pair of expensive aviators that reflected the casino. His black tuxedo was tailored to perfection, showing off the firm muscles in his arms as he walked. He was definitely the better dressed of the two.

Jen had thought he was giving her a backhanded compliment by correctly guessing her size and ordering what she should wear. Now she only wondered if he purposely wanted her to look ridiculous. However, judging by the dresses that other woman around her wore, hers wasn't out of place.

Jen focused on the actual casino. The floor was an elaborate glass aquarium; different types of fish swam by in groups. Even some of the walls and ceiling had fish swimming inside. It was as if the casino itself were inside a giant fish tank. Jen also noticed large, lifelike pink flamingos that stood on either side of every entrance. The female waiters serving drinks were also wearing flamboyant pink flamingo costumes.

Slot machines and glass chairs occupied by gamblers hovered a few feet off the ground. Jen watched a chair lower to accommodate an overweight woman as she took a seat. Once she was adjusted, the chair floated upward again so that she sat perfectly at the table. Robots zoomed past on hover boards, holding trays of neon-colored drinks, stopping at nearby tables and offering service. Women dressed in outrageously shaped gowns with expensive pearls chatted with men in suave suits similar to Asher's in a way that signaled they were part of the upper class. Lark pointed in the direction of the poker tables.

"This way," he said, avoiding Jen's questioning eyes as Asher often did.

Both Asher and Jen followed behind Lark as he led them toward the tables. Jen watched a man lose at blackjack, slamming his hand down on the table in anger. He then got into a heated debate with the dealer.

"One more," he shouted. "One more game!"

Another man, a little farther down, kissed a beautiful brunette passionately, and then rolled a pair of dice. Moments later, his hands lifted up in celebration.

"Ten thousand dollars," he proclaimed, kissing the brunette in excitement.

Jen ran right into Asher, who had stopped to wait as Lark's eyes scanned the tables for John Foster. Asher turned around, eyeing Jen.

"S-sorry," Jen muttered awkwardly.

"He's right there," Lark said, pointing at a man in his early thirties. John was freshly shaven and sported a challenging smile as he dealt out cards with ease. He had an attractive face and a smooth demeanor, which made it easy for people to come to his table. He also knew how to rig the game so that players would lose if they began winning too much money.

There were two empty chairs at his table. Asher and Jen walked over and took a seat as Lark stood a distance away. Asher raised a hand to be dealt in. Jen didn't know anything about the game and decided to watch John intently, noticing how he sized Asher up immediately. She also noticed the little smirk John got when he knew someone was going to lose and how he glanced quickly at one of the players right before he won. Asher purposely lost the first few hands just to get a feel for his opponents. After that, he won the next five hands, racking up different colored chips in celebration. After the seventh hand, a robot glided over to the table, telling John to go on his break as the robot took over. John nodded and walked away.

Asher grabbed his chips and excused himself from the table, following closely behind John. Jen and Lark followed in Asher's footsteps. John entered a side door with a sign that read "Employees Only." Asher caught the door just before it closed, allowing Jen and Lark to enter first.

"Excuse me," Jen said, watching as John turned around. He frowned at the sight of them.

"This area is prohibited to casino members," John said with an English accent.

"We know." Asher took a step forward with his hands outstretched to show he wasn't a threat. "We just have a few questions for you."

John looked at Lark with recognition and then nodded at Asher, closing the distance between the two of them. "How can I help you?"

"We know you ran into the man who came through the portal ten years ago," Asher said. "There was something he muttered to you that night after he had been beaten. What did he say?"

John's nervous eyes flickered to Lark as he shifted his weight onto his left leg.

"Yes, I remember that night. The bloody man kept mumbling, 'Burdock, Burdock.' I don't know what he was getting at."

"Was there anything else that he might have said, any other tips?" Jen asked. John met her desperate eyes.

"No, that was all."

"Thank you." Asher tossed the man his bag of chips and began heading back out the door.

"Wait," John called. "There's one more thing. The men who

took George Kallis...they wore military uniforms."

"Thanks," Asher said, and again turned toward the door to leave.

Once they were back in the hover bug, Asher revealed that he knew what Jen's father had meant when he'd said "Burdock." It was the name of an underground house that offered shelter and protection to runaways and innocent people hiding from gangsters and criminals. The location often changed due to the risk of criminals finding the hideout and shooting it up.

Asher knew of the location since the government helped fund the home. They kept track of who came and went and made sure enough security circled the place in case of an attack. It didn't make sense that the military would house someone they brought through the portal there, especially not a criminal. Asher was third in command and very little happened under his nose without him being aware. Something wasn't adding up.

Right now, Burdock was located in Old New York, down in an old subway station off of Chamber Street. The only thing he needed to get inside was his uniform. His fingerprints would tell them the rest once they ran them through the system and pulled up his information. This was a mission he'd need to make alone. As soon as he told Jen this, she began to panic.

"You can't just go by yourself! What if something happens?"

"I can take care of myself," Asher responded, amused by her concern.

"Take me with you. Find a way to get me inside."

"I can't. The place is heavily loaded with security."

"You're a commander in the army! Can't you make them let me in?"

Asher laughed. "Oh, if only life were that easy, Ancient Meat."

"Don't call me Ancient Meat," Jen argued, folding her arms in defiance.

"Why? It suits you, Ancient Meat. Maybe I should call you 'child,' since you like to whine so much."

Jen moaned and shifted in her seat so that she was facing the window. Asher laughed and continued driving. He looked through the rear view mirror at Lark, who was passed out in the back seat. Children, he thought. I'm definitely surrounded by children.

CHAPTER SEVEN

Surprise

Jen sat quietly in Asher's living room, watching as he put his shooter in his holster and checked his other pockets for gadgets he might have to use in case his plan turned sour. She hadn't spoken to him since the car ride back to his condo and wanted to continue her stubborn silence. At the same time, she had so many questions she wanted to ask. Asher looked at her, raising an eyebrow with a small smirk as if he was expecting her to begin talking at any moment. Jen couldn't stand that self-assured, egotistical smirk and envisioned the day where she'd get to smack it off of his face, most likely for calling her "Ancient Meat."

Shaking her head, she dismissed the thought, amazed at how violent her thoughts had become in the last two days. She wondered if she'd be the same person she was before coming here, once she got her father back and went home. She was sure her mother had sunken into a deep depression, now that she knew Jen was now gone too. It was something she didn't want to think about. Jen felt as if she was running out of things to safely think about, things that wouldn't upset her. She shifted her gaze to Lark. He sat in a chair with his head bobbing back and forth as he tried to fight sleep. The sight was enough to make Jen laugh, even though she felt like doing anything but.

Asher had commanded Jen and Lark to stay in his apartment while he handled Burdock. Lark seemed perfectly content to follow the order. It wasn't his battle to fight, after all. He'd said all he knew. Jen, on the other hand, sat restlessly, wanting to do more than stay put and drive herself crazy with her thoughts until Asher returned in one piece. She looked over in his direction.

"All right," Asher began, grabbing a circular gadget off the table. It had shiny purple and silver coating and seemed to hum when Asher touched it. Jen silently wondered what its capabilities were as she eyed it. "I'll be gone for a few hours. Keep the kid within your eyesight."

"Why won't you just take him with you and drop him off somewhere? He's told us everything he knows."

"We may need him again. It's best to keep him with us until we have your father."

"Gee, thanks for filling me in on this," Jen sarcastically stated, earning her a frown from Asher.

"I don't answer to you."

Jen stood from her seat and walked toward Asher, whose eyes widened in amusement. She stood inches from his face, fuming.

"I'm not asking for you to answer to me. I'm asking that you treat me like an equal and let me know your plans as soon as you make them!"

Asher nodded, but his amused expression hadn't changed. He cleared his throat, obviously trying to fight back laughter. Jen knew that it was funny to him, seeing how she tried to stand up to him as if she had a chance. She'd come far within one day. Jen knew that Asher would've expected her to go into a catatonic state after the morning's events but surprisingly, she remained calmed. Asher had to give her credit for keeping up with him. She even wanted to accompany him to Burdock.

"Okay," he agreed. "I'll let you know whatever plan I make as soon as I make it."

"Fine," Jen said, crossing her arms.

"Happy?"

"No, take me with you." Asher laughed outright at her comment.

"What? You can't stand being away from me even for a few hours? Will you miss me that much, Ancient Meat?"

"No," Jen answered, almost too quickly. "I just, I don't want you to get hurt." Asher smirked and took a step toward Jen, closing the gap between them. Her breath caught in her throat as she stared back into his piercing eyes. She wanted to move away, but his inviting, fresh scent held her in place.

"So then you care about the state of my body?" he asked with a low voice.

"I...you..." Jen paused, opening and closing her mouth in search of the right words. She couldn't think with him so close to her. She didn't want him to know that he affected her, so she pulled herself together within a few seconds. "You're no good to me dead. If you're reckless and get yourself killed, I won't be able to find my father or get back home. Now can you move? Your closeness is uncomfortable."

Asher chuckled and moved away from Jen, walking toward the door. He made sure his back stayed turned against her, so Jen couldn't see his expression.

"There's a gun underneath the couch, just in case you find yourself in a position where you need to use it." And with that, he left.

Asher flew the hover bug over the ruins of Old New York. It was a desolate land with miles of rubble from fallen buildings. There wasn't a single building that still stood—not even a bridge. When the sky was as gray and sullen as today, the old city looked like a wasteland.

He'd seen old pictures in history class of the once glorious city. The cars still drove on the Bottom Ground back then, and the streets were always filled with tourists, shopping on Fifth Avenue or in Chinatown buying knockoff designer bags. He couldn't imagine himself living in a time period where everything had to be done manually, and yet he'd do anything to leave Blue City.

Asher thought that Jen must have loved New York; he knew he would have. If he was ever able to time travel, it would be the first place he visited. Maybe he could find a way to go back with Jen, whenever he managed to figure out a way to get her through the portal. He would go back to 2016 and move into a nice condo, much like the one where he currently lived, and find a job that had nothing to do with the military.

As Asher slowly glided over the rubble, he noticed a flag that stuck up from a crumbled building, waving proudly among the gray and black scenery. A nation still stood, despite the world's hatred, despite its own nation's hatred toward those within it. Below that flag lay Burdock, if Asher remembered correctly. He lowered the hover until it was inches from the crumbled heap and waited.

Within seconds, two military men glided toward him on bright gold military hover bikes. He didn't dare take the rental after hearing that the police had the license plate number. All it took was for one cop to run the plates to discover who he was.

The two military hovers resembled a mix between a motor-cycle and a jet ski, and let out blue fire from the exhaust as they soared in the sky. The military had special access to these bikes and would frequently use them instead of hover bugs due to the bikes' speed and mobility. Asher could get his hands on one of the bikes easily and seriously thought about dropping his car off at the military base to pick one up.

The men recognized Asher immediately, saluting in respect. Asher saluted back and watched as the men circled around, sig-naling for him to follow. Up ahead, a piece of a fallen building began lifting up, revealing a disguised entryway. Asher followed the two military men inside and descended down a fluorescent blue tunnel that was once a part of the subway. The old railroad tracks below were seemingly untouched even though the city above was destroyed. Up ahead, Asher could make out a sign that read "Burdock," and behind that, an underground house ap-peared.

The old Victorian-style house had been built fifty years ago and had once been used as a refugee shelter for those who had survived the attacks on Old New York. It had a big front porch that wrapped around the sides with a few benches and chairs that were sprawled about the porch, mostly for decoration. The house seemed small from the outside, but actually ventured three levels into the ground. Without the right security access, it was impossible for a criminal to get below the first level, and many of them would have been unaware that Burdock even ex-isted. Asher parked his hover bug on top of the subway tracks and got out, following the two military men inside.

Back at Asher's condo, Jen sat on the couch, watching Lark as he slept peacefully in the armchair. He seemed younger as he slept, as if nothing bad could meet him in his dreams. He was barely a teenager and still had thin, puny limbs that hadn't yet built their muscle. Even his voice was young, barely deep enough to convince anyone of his manliness. A part of Jen wanted to take him back to 2016 where he could have a good life. She felt strange caring about a boy she'd only just met. Her mom once told her that it was because she had a heart of gold.

A half an hour passed before Lark awakened, first shifting in the chair, and then rubbing his eyes. He noticed Jen staring and gave an awkward smile.

"H-wow long h-have I been asleep?" he asked.

"Since we got back from the car ride, but we've been back here a little over a half an hour," Jen answered.

"W-where's Asher?" Lark yawned, looking around the living room.

"He went to Burdock."

"D-did he tell you w-what he was planning on doing with m-me?"

"Yeah," Jen began. "He wants to keep you around until we have my father. He said you might be able to help us more."

Lark sighed, sitting back.

"I c-can't wait to s-see the day w-when my expertise is n-no longer required. I'm t-tired of being forced to w-work for people." Lark lowered his head, staring at his hands, unable to meet Jen's concerned expression when talking about such a touchy subject. "I n-never knew my pops. My m-mom, she left me w-when I was eleven. I came h-home from school one day and f-found a note s-saying she couldn't do it anymore and h-had only enough m-money to get herself out of B-blue City. She said once s-she had the money, she'd send for me.

"I w-waited around for two months, p-patiently living in that apartment even a-after the electricity and h-hot water went out. I stole f-food from markets, pickpocketed men, and w-whatnot just to get by. I stayed near my old house for a few years, thinking I'd f-find my mom, thinking she'd come back, but she never did."

"I'm so sorry," Jen said, placing a hand on top of his for comfort.

"I bet you felt something similar when your own dad came

through the portal."

"Yeah." Jen nodded. "I kept waiting for him to come back through my closet, but he never did. It didn't help when my own mom was trying to convince me that he left us."

"I'm sorry too," Lark said.

"Hey," Jen said with a laugh. "Your stuttering is gone."

"It means I'm getting comfortable around you now," Lark admitted. He stared at Jen for a while, finally deciding he liked her. She had stood up for him when Asher pointed the laser at him, and she seemed genuinely interested in him. There weren't many people like that in Blue City.

"You know, I actually want to help you find your dad. We're a lot alike since we both have been trying to find something. I gave up on my mom, but I believe in your cause."

Jen's heart warmed as she smiled at Lark. It would be nice having someone else around who actually had a heart, because Asher acted as if he didn't. Plus, Lark could help her understand her surroundings better, things Asher hadn't taken time to explain to her.

"Do you really think we'll find your dad?" Jen was surprised by Lark's question.

"I hadn't really thought about not finding him. I don't even want to think like that. I just..." Jen paused, trying to hold down her emotions. "I want to be as positive as possible. I will find him and we will go home."

"What if he doesn't want to go back?" Lark cleared his throat, immediately regretting his question. The pained look on Jen's face was torturous. "What I mean is, Blue City is t-tempting. Once people are here, they don't want to leave."

"Did you hear what your friend said? My dad was beaten and scared out of his mind. Whoever took him probably put my dad through hell. He must've escaped and ran to Burdock. Why would he want to stay in this place?"

"What doesn't make sense is why he'd run to Burdock to escape the military when the military funds it. They'd know he was there." Lark had a point and Jen knew it. A light bulb clicked on in Jen's head. It didn't make any sense, at all, unless her father wasn't running to Burdock, but from it.

The door to the garage burst open before Jen could answer Lark. Three men dressed in black jumpsuits and masks rushed inside, pointing shooters at Jen and Lark. A cloaked figure walked inside the condo and lowered his hood. The gash that ran along the side of his cheek stretched as he sneered. He took in the sight of the apartment, of Jen and Lark's alarm, and smiled wickedly.

"G-gunner..." Lark said to the intruder, hiccupping nervously.

"Surprise," Gunner replied, with a smile full of mischief.

Asher stood inside what looked like a jail. Thick black bars separated him from a woman at the front desk who had been preoccupied with a file sitting on her desk. She was a chunky, pasty-skinned lady with bright orange curls pinned on her head, shaped like a large beehive, and she wore a crooked nametag that read "Teresa." Little green glasses hung off her thin nose as she looked down at a file. She had small red lips that looked out of place on her round face, and her tight eyes darted back up at Asher as if she needed to keep an eye on him.

"George Kallis, you said?" Teresa asked, placing the file in a desk drawer and standing up. Asher guessed her age to be around sixty and had a bad back, which would explain why getting up and sitting down seemed more difficult. She wobbled toward a dingy-looking filing cabinet, searching through the drawer labeled J-M. "We still file the old way to prevent hackers from getting information. His file should be in here some-where...let's see...ah, here it is." She grabbed a tan folder and walked back to her seat. Once she was back in the chair, Teresa looked up at Asher through her green glasses, watching him with suspicion. "Why do you need this file?"

Asher, who had been casually leaning against the counter, straightened and gave Teresa his most charming smile. "Gov-ernment business. Private matter." The redhead blushed slightly and nodded, keeping her face tight as she opened the file and began to read.

"George Kallis, age fifty-three, height six-foot-two, admitted at Burdock on January 12, 2215, departed on March 16 of the same year." Teresa flipped to the next page, scanning it intently before skipping to the next page. Frowning, she looked at the last two pages in the file. "That's strange. A page is missing. It doesn't state why he was admitted."

Asher sighed, wanting to punch the wall. He'd been so close to finding some information that would explain the night John Foster had mentioned. There had to be something else—some type of clue that would lead him to Jen's father. He watched as she read something with interest.

"Says here that George Kallis escaped Burdock. I don't know why anyone would feel the need to escape this place. We provide a great life for our runaways." She read another paragraph. "It also says he shared a room with a Mr. Clint Burns."

"Pull his file," Asher said. He watched as Teresa returned to the filing cabinet and grabbed another file. She took to her seat and began flipping through seemingly unimportant information. Her index finger stopped on a spot halfway down the page, and she pushed her glasses farther up her nose and read aloud.

"Mr. Clint Burns was released two days prior to Mr. Kallis' breakout. He was admitted because he had witnessed an assassination and a hit was put out on him. His personal information is listed...where he used to live...where he worked...where he is now staying..."

"Give me his current address," Asher demanded, barely containing his excitement. He was getting closer to figuring everything out. Teresa wrote the address on a piece of paper and handed it to Asher through the bars.

"Good luck."

Asher nodded and quickly left Burdock.

Lark slowly rose to his feet, joining Jen by the couch, hoping to protect her in any way possible. "H-how did you find us?" he asked Gunner.

"Asher isn't the only one with resources," Gunner laughed, walking farther into the room, observing his surroundings with faint interest. "Where is he?"

"Gone," Jen said, faintly above a whisper. It didn't take a

rocket scientist to see that Gunner was a cruel man, one who probably killed just for the fun of it. Without Asher's protection, Jen felt helpless. She didn't have his keen sense of survival or the ability to get herself out of any situation. Thankfully, Jen remembered the gun Asher said was under the couch and contemplated grabbing it. But she wouldn't know how to use it if she tried, and that act of false courage could wind up getting herself killed.

"Too bad. I wanted him to watch as I destroyed his home the way he destroyed my club!" In a fit, Gunner grabbed the corner table and threw it across the room, making Jen jump. He pulled a black and red gun from under his shirt and pointed it at the chair Lark had been sitting in. He shot a hole through the center of the chair, leaving a trail of dark smoke. He then turned and shot a hole in Asher's wall.

Mary glided into the room, completely oblivious to the danger as she smiled at Gunner. "Hello, sir."

Gunner pointed the gun at Mary and blew her to pieces. An uncontrollable shiver ran through Jen's body as she watched what was left of Mary collapse to the ground. She had to remind herself that Mary was just a robot, not a real person. Gunner turned toward her with a deadly sneer, pointing the gun. Lark quickly stepped in front of her.

"P-please, don't kill her," Lark pleaded.

"She helped him take you from me!" Gunner screamed, punching his hand through the wall closest to him. He then backed away, trying to calm himself, but to Jen, it didn't work. He was manic.

"W-we could...we could u-use her as bait," Lark suggested, trying to come up with a way to stall Jen's death. "We c-can lure Asher to us. O-once he finds out t-that you have, her h-he'll come running r-right into whatever t-trap you'll have."

Gunner looked at Lark as if he wanted to kill the boy, but then his sneer turned into a smile.

"Smart boy. That's why I like having you around." Gunner looked at his three men. "Put the girl to sleep and bring her with us."

"No." Jen backed away as one of the guards approached her.

She looked at Lark, who wouldn't meet her eyes. She wanted to punch him for siding with Gunner. He was a liar, a cheater. He made her believe he was on her side, but the moment an opportunity arose, he ran back to the man he should have seen as an enemy. Lark was only trying to save her, not harm her. He was only trying to buy her some time.

Jen tried to fight off the man who approached her, but he was too strong. He held her struggling body against him, lifted a finger to the pressure point in her neck, and pressed hard. A few seconds later, Jen's body collapsed against him.

CHAPTER EIGHT

The Great Escape

A sher was about to get into his hover bug when his holo-phone buzzed inside his pocket. He pulled it out, letting it do its magic. Seconds later, Gunner appeared before him with a content smile. Asher's hands clenched into fists; he didn't have time to worry about Gunner. He was seconds away from hang-ing up his phone, but decided to play along with whatever game Gunner would throw at him.

"Out from hiding so soon?" Asher asked, earning himself a grunt from Gunner.

"You'd be surprised. Tell me, Asher. Where's the boy?"

"Safe and far away from you."

"Is he?" Gunner chuckled. "And what about the girl? Is she safe, too?"

Asher didn't have time to play mind games. He was ready to move on to his next mission. "Why did you call?"

Gunner laughed, showing off his decaying teeth.

"I paid a visit to your condo. Nice bachelor pad. It could use some fixing up at this point, but you probably won't live long enough to do that."

Bull, Asher thought. Gunner was bluffing. There was no way he had been able to find out, in that short amount of time, where Asher lived. Not only that, it would have been impossible for Gunner to breach Asher's security system and get inside. Satis-fied with that thought, Asher decided to disconnect the call and go back home. That was, until he saw Jen's limp body tied to a chair in the background.

"Where is she?" Asher asked, trying his hardest to remain cool. He couldn't let Gunner know how affected he was; it would give Gunner the upper hand.

"The girl?" Gunner smiled, looking behind him at where Jen lay unconscious. "Why, she's in my possession, along with the boy."

"Where are you?"

"Come and find me." Gunner's image flickered and then disappeared. Asher kicked a loose rock and screamed loudly.

Shut up, a familiar voice said in his head. He recognized it as his father's stern, unaffectionate voice. There were times when Asher felt so low that he could almost hear his father talking to him. He could even see his father standing in front of him, looking down at him in disgust. Shut up, you idiot! Just look at you, screaming like you want to cry. I didn't raise a cry baby! You have five seconds to pull yourself together before I send you to the pegs. Asher could almost feel the pain in his feet from the long hours spent on the pegs, reminding him it was time to straighten up. Now, complete your mission...and that is an order.

Asher nodded at the image that began to disappear in front of him. Even if his father had been an illusion, he was right. Asher had a mission to complete, and he was more than willing. The mission was no longer about a bored commander wanting an adrenaline rush and an interesting story to tell, but about him prevailing. He would rescue Jen and reconnect her with her father, even if it killed him...

Jen jumped awake as if from a bad dream. The last thing she remembered was trying to fight a guard as Lark watched and did nothing. That traitor, she thought. He went right back into that man's arms after practically professing his loyalty to her. Jen should have known she couldn't trust him. After all, he was a boy just trying to survive.

She heard movement behind her and stretched her neck to see who it was. Lark sat in the corner, watching her silently. He slowly stood and began walking along the cement wall until he stood directly across from her. Jen instinctively tried to stand, her intent to choke Lark, but she quickly realized her arms were chained to a chair by white handcuffs. She strained against the chains, feeling helpless.

Once Jen calmed her breathing and nerves, she began to observe her surroundings. They were in a dimly lit basement that smelled of mildew and sewage. Water dripped from the leaky pipes that covered the ceiling and seeped into the walls. A dull light dangled above her head and flickered as it swung side by side. There was also a door to her right, and Jen wondered if it led to freedom. On the side of the door was a scanner much like the one Asher used to get into his house. Only those with access could get in and out of the room. Jen wondered if she'd ever make it out of the room and silently prayed that she would.

Jen returned her gaze to Lark, who stayed a distance away as if afraid to come too close. His weary eyes kept glancing at the door as if someone was going to walk in any moment. He dared to look at Jen and opened his mouth to speak. He quickly closed it, deciding not to risk making noise and drawing Gunner's guards.

"I hate you," Jen screamed.

"Shhh!" Lark put a finger to his lips with wide, fearful eyes. "Be quiet. Y-you don't want them to hear us."

"I hate you, Lark," Jen bellowed. She tried to lift her hands, forgetting again that she was chained to the chair. "You said you'd help me. You lied."

"I am h-helping you," Lark said, his voice barely above a whisper. "If I h-hadn't told Gunner to s-save you as bait, h-he would've killed you. I bought you t-time. Asher will save us."

It took a minute for Jen to allow his words to sink in, and even though she understood Lark's reasoning, it didn't help much. She was still handcuffed to a cold chair. Lark's life wasn't in danger; hers was. If Asher failed to kill Gunner, she'd die and Lark would live.

Asher, please don't fail, Jen thought. I need you alive. Jen didn't realize how much she'd actually relied on Asher until that moment. Her life was in his hands, and the choices he'd soon be making would fall back on her. One wrong move and they both were dead. Jen started shaking, knowing that the odds were against them once again.

"Do you think Asher can get us out?"

"I d-don't know," Lark answered honestly.

"Then we need to have a backup plan," Jen said, and Lark

nodded as if he was already a step ahead of her.

"We're in a b-basement in an old f-factory Gunner used to u-use before he went to prison. T-there's an exit on the first f-floor, but getting to it will be t-tricky." Lark stopped talking as the door opened and a guard walked in. He looked over to Lark, who stood against the wall, seemingly harmless, and then to Jen, who was staring back at him in fury. Moments later, the guard put his hand on the scanner and waited for the green light to flash. The door opened, and he left the room.

"That guard h-has been coming in h-here every five minutes. H-he has the key to your handcuffs. I c-can try to fight him and t-take his shooter and s-shoot him and then—"

"Lark, do you really think you can take down a trained guard?"

"I can t-try," he said. "It's better than j-just sitting here."

"Okay," Jen said, trying to clear her mind and focus on the task at hand. "Say you manage to take down the guard and we break out of this room. How will we get out of this building?"

"T-that's where things get t-tricky, and you n-need to listen closely."

Five minutes later, the guard came through the door, taking a few steps inside the room. He hadn't noticed Lark, who stood on the side of the door ready to attack. Lark kicked the guard in the back of the leg, watching as he stumbled and fell onto one knee. The guard reached for his shooter at the same time that Lark extended his foot, hitting the guard in the side of the head with brutal force. The guard dropped to the floor and was still.

Lark laughed out loud, impressed with himself. "Well, that was e-easy."

"Grab the keys," Jen demanded, ready to be free from the chair. Lark bent down, searching the guard's pocket, and pulled out a black round gadget. He pointed it at Jen and pressed a button. With a loud click, the handcuffs fell to the ground. Jen stood, rubbing her wrists, ready to do whatever needed to get out alive.

Adrenaline pumped through her veins, as she thought about escaping. Never in her life would she have imagined that she'd be doing something so dangerous and life threatening. She had to praise herself for being able to keep up mentally and not check out. She'd once thought Danni was the strong one. The girl had a mouth piece, a nice right hook, and was tough on the exterior. But Jen? Jen was levelheaded and didn't fight because she feared the consequences. She always tried to think situations through, eventually deciding something was either too risky or just plain stupid to do. She didn't drink, rarely cursed, never inhaled a cigarette, and read her Bible. She was a good girl who was about to find out just how bad she could be.

Lark grabbed the shooter from the guard and examined it.

"W-we should have enough e-energy if we use t-the shooter wisely." Lark looked up at Jen with uneasy eyes. "I-I don't like to s-shoot these things. Will you do it?"

"I don't even know how to use it," Jen confessed. Lark walked over to where Jen stood and showed her the shooter.

"You just p-pull the trigger. It's like a g-gun but more advanced. It z-zaps out energy that kills its v-victim instantly. I guess in that c-case, it's worse than a g-gun since guns don't always kill. That's why I d-don't want to use it. I d-don't want to kill anyone."

"So you'd rather me kill people?" Jen asked, incredulously.

"You're of legal a-age. I'm not. So t-technically, I'm not even allowed to h-hold it."

"I'm only seventeen!"

"Legal age in B-blue City is sixteen. Geez, you r-really are ancient. D-did you even have electricity w-where you came from?"

Jen scoffed, "For a boy genius, you know nothing about the past. Give me the gun."

"It's c-called a shooter," Lark corrected her, handing her it.

"Whatever." Jen sighed. "I've never noticed how annoying you are."

"Well, I've b-been told I'm really a-annoying when my life is on the line," Lark stuttered sarcastically and then hiccupped nervously. Jen rolled her eyes.

"So, what next?"

"We l-leave this room, take d-down whoever is in the w-way, and find the nearest e-exit. We can d-do this, Jen. We aren't going to d-die, so stop shaking."

Jen looked down at her hand that was holding the shooter, noticing for the first time that she was shivering uncontrollably. "Right," she nodded, trying to stop her hand from moving, but it didn't work. "Right," she said again.

"Snap out of it," Lark said, walking to the door. "We g-got some butt to kick."

Lark used the guard's badge to open the door, and they began climbing a set of white stairs. Lark stayed ahead of Jen, since he knew the way to the nearest exit. At the top step he peeked around the corner to make sure the wide hallway was clear. He signaled to Jen, and they quickly entered into the hallway, walking as fast as they could.

They eventually came to a dead end, forcing them to either turn left or right to continue. Lark paused, forgetting which way to go. Jen noticed and sighed.

"Which way?"

"I f-forget. It's been m-months since I've b-been here. I think we s-should go left."

"Lark, we can't afford mistakes, we have to know for s—"

"Hey!" Jen and Lark snapped their heads to the right, seeing a guard fifty feet down the hallway, pointing at them. "What are you two doing?"

"I guess w-we go left," Lark said, grabbing Jen's hand and pulling her down the hallway.

"Get back here!" the guard called from behind, but Jen and Lark wasted no time running as fast as they could down the hallway.

They came to another dead end, but didn't waste any time deciding which way to turn. They made a right and continued running. Jen stole a glance behind her and was glad that she didn't see the guard. Lark pulled her down another hallway, and then another, until Jen couldn't even keep track of how many hallways they had run down.

Finally, Lark came to a stop, breathing hard, while having to lean against a wall.

"We don't have time," Jen said, anxiously looking behind

her.

"W-we're lost."

"What?" Jen wanted to shake Lark but refrained. "I thought you knew your way around!"

"We were being c-chased; I had no time to t-think about where we were going," he said, breathing deeply between every other word. "J-just...just give me a few seconds."

"There you two are!" Jen froze at the sound of the voice behind her. Her back was facing the guard, but she knew Lark could see everything, and she studied his face for a sign. Lark's eyes widened in fear as he quickly snatched the shooter out of Jen's hand. He aimed it at the guard and shot.

Jen screamed and quickly turned around, seeing the guard crumple to the ground. His own shooter lay a few inches away from his twitching hand. Jen turned to Lark, whose eyes had gone blank as he stared down at the guard.

"I k-killed him," Lark began. "I-I killed him. I had to. He...H-he..."

"Lark."

"H-he was going to s-shoot you. If I h-hadn't, you'd be dead."

"Lark," Jen yelled, shaking him out of his stupor. "You did what you had to do. You saved my life." She regretted shaking him when she saw the tears in his eyes, but she needed him to snap out of it. If they hadn't stopped running, the guard would never have caught up, and Lark wouldn't have needed to shoot him. "We have to find an exit. Think. Where do we need to go?" Lark blinked back his tears and nodded.

"T-there's an exit on every side of the b-building." His eyes were still trained on the guard. "We s-shouldn't be f-far from one."

"Give me the gun back," Jen said, taking it out of his hands.

"It's a shooter," Lark said, finally looking at Jen. She smiled, glad he was coherent enough to catch her mistake.

"Let's keep moving."

Jen grabbed Lark's hand and guided him down the hallway. Jen knew he was still in shock from killing the guard, so she took over the escape mission. They ran down three additional hallways in search of an exit but came up short. She was beginning to lose hope and slowed her pace, until an alarm went off in the building. Jen froze in place, staring up at the red flashing lights that blared from the ceiling. The sirens were so loud she had to cover her ears as she winced in pain.

"We're caught," she yelled to Lark, who was struggling against the loud noise as he covered his ears with a pained expression.

"W-what?" he shouted back.

"They know we've escaped. What do we do?"

"W-what?"

Jen shook her head and grabbed Lark's hand, continuing their journey down a long, desolate hallway. Suddenly, a guard appeared in front of them and stopped the moment their eyes connected. The guard reached for his shooter, but Jen was quicker. She aimed the shooter in her hand and fired.

She missed.

The blast from the shooter flew over the guard's head and hit the wall behind him, leaving a large hole. He quickly pointed his shooter at Jen and fired. Fortunately, Lark had pressed them against the wall, and the blast blazed past them. Jen lifted the shooter again, aiming more carefully, and pulled the trigger three times. The last shot hit the guard, knocking him against the wall. He collapsed on the ground and shook wildly as white foam formed at his mouth. Within seconds, he stopped moving.

Jen didn't have time to stop and feel sorry about killing him. Another guard had rounded the corner and began shooting instantly. Lark pulled Jen to the ground as she fired back. A shot hit the guard in his leg, and he collapsed on the ground.

"We n-need to go back the other way," Lark yelled over the sirens. Jen understood and nodded. They quickly turned around and started running in the direction they had come from. As soon as they turned down the hallway, they came to a stop.

Gunner stood ten feet from them, and he was accompanied by three masked guards on either side. Jen raised the shooter and fired, but nothing happened. She looked down at the shooter and noticed there was no more green fluid. She'd wasted their remaining shots on the previous guard. Jen dropped the shooter in defeat and looked up at Gunner.

"You've managed to kill three of my men," Gunner said to Jen. "Not bad." He lowered his eyes as he glared at Lark. "And I see you've helped. I should've known not to trust you around a girl, you hormonal imbecile. What good are you to me now?" Gunner turned his head toward the guard on his right. "No more waiting for Asher. Kill them both."

The guard lifted his shooter and pointed it at Jen. Her breath caught as she waited for him to shoot. From the corner of her eye, she saw the guard to the left spring into action and shoot the guard to his right. Jen's eyes drifted to the rogue guard, who quickly turned his shooter on the last guard and shot again. In less than a second, he shifted and pointed the shooter at the back of Gunner's head.

Gunner smiled and then laughed. "Well, I'll be da—"

The guard shot Gunner in the back of the head, causing his brains to splatter on the ground and nearby walls. Gunner's knees slowly buckled underneath him, and the rest of his body leaned forward until he fell face down.

Jen looked up at the remaining guard, not understanding why he'd killed his own people. She heard Lark laugh next to her, but she didn't understand why. Too much had happened for her to begin piecing it all together. The guard moved toward Jen, causing her to take a retreat in fear. The guard paused, lifted a hand, and removed his mask.

Asher's cocky smile greeted Jen, and she wanted to cry in relief. Tears welled up in her eyes as she took a few steps toward him. Jen didn't understand how Asher had managed to save them, but he had. Her slow pace turned into an outright run until she stood in front of him, wrapping her arms around his neck.

"Asher," she cried. She felt his chest shake against hers as he laughed.

"I should save you more often, Ancient Meat," he said, and gently pulled her away.

"How?" she asked, searching his eyes.

"I'll explain later, but now we have to go."

CHAPTER NINE

Insensitive Jerk

Jen and Lark sat in Asher's destroyed living room, listening intently as he explained how he had managed to break into Gunner's compound. Even though they were safe, Jen's hands still shook uncontrollably and tried to mask it by playing with her fingers. She was thankful that Lark was focused on Asher and that Asher was being extremely self-absorbed. She didn't want them to know she was beginning to crack after having killed two people.

"It wasn't hard finding you two," Asher said. "I had Mary embed a tracking device into your jumpsuits."

Jen froze. "You did what? I feel violated."

"I needed to make sure I knew where you were at all times in case something bad happened, like today," Asher said, rolling his eyes, as if Jen was the unreasonable one.

"Who even thinks to do something like that?" Jen asked.

"Smart people. But you wouldn't know what that is, would you now, Ancient Meat?"

"I have a name. Try using it, stalker," Jen retorted.

"I saved your life," Asher said, lowering his eyes as the conversation grew more heated.

"We were doing just fine, thank you," Jen responded.

"Yeah? You had a shooter with no energy, and you were up against three guards, plus Gunner. Let me explain exactly how I saved your life. Maybe you'll be a little more grateful. As I was saying, I tracked you to Gunner's old factory. I managed to take out the first guard at the gates and put on his uniform so that I could blend in. The other guards didn't even question me as I entered the building.

"I still had to kill them, so that we could make a clean escape. I'd spent over ten minutes walking around the building and checking empty rooms looking for you two. Then the sirens sounded. Shortly after that, I saw Gunner storming down a hallway with two guards. When he saw me, he asked me to join him. I knew then that if I followed he'd lead me to the two of you. Apparently, I was right. If I hadn't been there, you two would've died."

"I'm forever indebted to you," Lark said, having lost his stutter the moment they entered Asher's house. "Next time, I'll make sure I'm the one saving you."

"I'm not a man who needs saving," Asher smirked. He focused on Jen, noticing her trembling hands. "Are you okay, Jen?"

"Yeah," she said, too quickly. "I'm fine. Just wondering how you're going to fix up your condo. Gunner almost destroyed everything."

Asher looked around the room, taking in the large holes in the wall, his broken chair and table, and Mary, his robot, laying in pieces on the floor. He'd paid a fortune for her, and now she was destroyed. But he knew a man who could fix anything, so he planned to drop off Mary to be repaired as soon as things settled down. As far as his walls...

"Anna," Asher called to the built-in computer system.

"I am at your service, sir," Anna responded.

"Repair yourself."

"As you wish, sir," Anna replied.

The holes in the walls began to morph, as the shattered and rugged edges enclosed until the wall was restored. The broken table pieced itself together by an invisible force and stood as if it had never been damaged. The process took less than two minutes, momentarily distracting Jen from her true issues. She met Asher's unreadable gaze and wondered how long he'd been staring at her.

"How is that possible? How can it just repair itself?" Jen asked him.

"Technology," Asher told her. "I'm no scientist, and if I were, I'd probably spend all day explaining exactly how my walls regenerated." He sat back in the chair with a deep sigh. "On to more important things. My trip to Burdock proved itself to be rewarding. Turns out, your father had stayed there, for three months to be exact. He eventually broke out."

"Why would he do that?" Lark asked.

"I asked myself the same question," Asher replied with a bored tone. "My conclusion is that he didn't trust Burdock, and that's most likely because he didn't trust the military. The question is why? Why did Mr. Kallis feel as if he couldn't trust them? There may be someone who knows."

"Who?" Jen asked, sitting up straighter.

"A man named Clint Burns. He shared a room with your father during his stay at Burdock. He may have an idea. I was able to get his address and was planning a trip to his house tomorrow," Asher said.

"Great," Jen said. "I can't wait to question him."

"No." Asher sighed, looking annoyed by her words. "You stay here with Lark."

"What?" Jen couldn't hide her frustration. "Why?"

"You need to rest; you've had a difficult day."

"Then I'll get a good night's sleep and be ready tomorrow morning," she argued.

"No, you need more than one night's sleep. Just look at you." Asher's eyes traveled to Jen's trembling hands. "You're on the verge of going into shock. Another risky mission could put you in a catatonic state."

"I can handle this, Asher. I'm just a bit shaken up. Lark, tell him!" Jen looked next to her, where Lark lay sleeping peacefully. He'd fallen asleep that quickly. Jen wanted to shake him awake and scold him for always falling asleep, but instead she turned back to Asher, ready to plead her own case. "This is my father we're talking about."

"And I've agreed to help you find him. However, I didn't agree to do this on your terms. I'm doing them on mine. What's the point of finding him if you just end up dead in the process? You'll stay here where it's safe."

"The last time you left me alone, I was kidnapped by your enemy. Do you really trust leaving me here?"

"That enemy was eliminated, so you have nothing else to worry about," Asher promised. "You're safer in here than out there."

"You sound like a parent. How old are you anyway?"

Asher snorted. "I'm sure I've already told you how old I am. I'm nineteen."

"You act much older than that. Most nineteen-year-old guys I know work at a pizza shop and have no idea what they want to do with their lives. And here you are, all mature, brooding, and cocky. You're also extremely headstrong and stubborn."

"Headstrong and stubborn mean the same thing," Asher smirked, crossing his arms, completely entertained by her tantrum.

"Well, you're still both!" Jen fired back. "My point is, you can't boss me around." Asher unfolded his arms and slowly leaned forward. He absentmindedly licked his lips as he held Jen's gaze. The motion was extremely sexy and made Jen momentarily forget her anger toward him. Her eyes drifted to his lips and quickly found their way back to his eyes. Asher noticed, but he was too involved in the argument to care.

"I can and I will. I'm done discussing it," he told her and then stood to his feet. "Clean yourself up and get ready for bed. You'll have to pick out your own nightclothes since Mary is broken. Everything is in the bedroom closet. You won't see me for the rest of the night, and I'll most likely be gone by the time you wake up."

Asher turned to leave, waiting for his bedroom door to appear, which seemed to take longer after the repairs Anna made to the wall. Jen quickly stood and silently followed Asher into his room before his door disappeared on her.

Asher was halfway across the room, walking toward his bathroom while he removed his shirt. Even though the room was dark, she could make out a wound on his side. Her soft gasp made him pause just outside of his bathroom door.

"What are you doing in here?" he asked without turning around to face her.

"I wasn't done talking to you. You don't get to decide when the conversation is over." Jen began to walk closer to him, wanting a better view of his wound. She could tell it was fresh, something that must have happened while he was saving her life. She momentarily forgot her anger toward him. "What happened?"

"It's nothing," he said, sounding annoyed, which Jen was realizing was his usual tone.

"It doesn't look like nothing."

"Do you have to be so nagging?" Asher spun around to face her with wild eyes. Jen refused to back down, even though he looked as if he could hurt her. She was starting to learn a couple of things about him—that he was all bark and no bite with her and that she could handle him and his hot temper.

"Allow me to clean it."

"I can do it myself."

"Do you have to be so stubborn?" Jen asked in a mocking tone. "At least let me repay you for saving my life today. It's the least I can do."

"Fine." Asher sighed. "I'll get the first aid kit."

Jen took a seat on Asher's bed as he disappeared into the bathroom. She took the time to study his room, which held nothing pleasing to the eye. His dark walls were bare; there were no pictures in fancy frames of happy memories, no high school football trophies or academic awards. It was nothing but a plain room with a bed and a nightstand. Jen couldn't imagine sleeping in such a depressing bedroom.

Asher returned with the first aid kit and took a seat next to Jen. He leaned forward, giving her access to the wound. Taking a closer look, she could tell it wasn't serious and that some rubbing alcohol and bandages would do the trick. She opened the first aid kit and found the supplies she needed, quickly dabbed some alcohol onto a piece of cloth and held it up to his wound. Asher's back arched as he sucked in air due to the burning sensation. A part of Jen wanted to laugh at his response. She guessed he wasn't such a tough guy after all.

"I can't stand the thought of sitting in this house and driving myself crazy, wondering what's going on with you," Jen confessed as she tended to his wound. "Doing absolutely nothing at all when I'm so close to finding my dad is mentally tiresome. I've spent the last ten years waiting for this moment, and now that it's here, I can't just sit back and do nothing. You have to understand."

"I do understand," Asher told her, his voice softer than she'd ever heard it. She briefly wondered if her speech had worked its magic on him. "But I still can't let you go. If you do, then Lark would have to tag along. I can't watch you both. It's better if you stay."

Jen bought herself some time to think as she wrapped a bandage around his waist. She needed to find a soft spot, something that would make him cave. Unfortunately, she didn't know him well enough to know what that soft spot was. The only other thing she could do was cry. Boys hated to see girls cry, no matter how tough they acted.

The first tear came with ease. Jen hadn't realized how badly she needed to cry, as the tears easily rolled down her cheeks. She'd been so good at holding it together, but now that she let her defenses down, there was no going back. Asher heard her sniffle and turned to face her, sighing when he saw the tears.

"Why are you crying?"

"I—I don't know." She turned her head away in embarrassment. Now that she was crying real tears, she didn't want him to see them. Her plan had backfired. Jen went to stand, but Asher pulled her back down. He raised a hand to her cheek, as if to wipe away her tears, but then quickly lowered his hand onto his lap. He'd never had to deal with a crying girl before, and affection wasn't his strong point.

"Talk to me," Asher said. "I can't help you if you close yourself off."

"It's nothing," Jen said, trying to hide her face with her hands, but Asher reached up and took her hands in his own. "Let go."

"Not until you tell me what's wrong," he demanded.

"I don't know. I just...need to cry. I just need to let it out. It's all so overwhelming."

"That's exactly why you need to stay here tomorrow."

"No," Jen argued. "It's exactly why I need to go. If I sit around here, I'll be forced to think about it. I'll be crying all day. Asher, please. I'll stay out of your way. I'll hold my own. Lark can stay here where he can't escape. He's loyal to me. Just let me go."

Asher sighed, a sound that sounded like defeat. He looked away from her with lowered brows, contemplating the pros and cons of bringing her along with him. Finally, he let go of her hands and turned back to her. "I need you to be safe, not brave, even if that means you'll spend most of your day crying. I'm only doing what's best."

Jen groaned and pushed Asher away from her. "You're so stubborn."

"Don't forget headstrong," he teased.

"I hate you," Jen said, standing up. "I really do." She made her way to the wall and waited for the door to appear.

"By the way, the waterworks were almost convincing," Asher said, as Jen walked out of his room. She turned around to throw a sarcastic remark at him, but the door had already disappeared. She huffed and puffed the rest of the way to her own room. That insensitive jerk, Jen thought. I'll show him.

CHAPTER TEN

Mr. Burns

Asher awakened before the sun had the chance to bless the morning sky. He wanted to be gone before Jen woke up and started hounding him about tagging along. He had his reasons for not allowing her to join him. The whole mission of finding her father had proven to be quite a challenge, and he didn't want her risking her life in a city that showed no mercy. Asher had a bad feeling about meeting with Clint Burns, even though he didn't explain this to Jen.

It was a familiar deep pain in his stomach, as if he had a sixth sense that told him something was sure to go wrong. He'd been having the feeling quite often now, the first time being the day Jen came through the portal and the second time the day he broke into Gunner's factory to get Lark. That time he had ignored the feeling, and bad karma had followed. He couldn't risk Jen getting hurt, knowing ahead of time that something would probably go wrong. He also couldn't explain his true reason to her, knowing it would only worry her more. He had to say no.

Asher drove a half an hour north of Blue City to a small gated community that sat away from most of society. He was able to get past the guards with ease, having chosen to wear his military uniform, knowing it gave him authority and respect. Once inside the gates, it took him two minutes to find the house, which sat a good distance away from any other house in the community. Asher found that detail strange. He decided to park a distance away and walk to the house, not wanting to draw too much attention to his personal hover.

The sun had finally broken through the sky as Asher approached the door, giving him light as he peeked into the window closest to the front door. He saw nothing but a dark, unoccupied living room. Asher moved to the door and knocked. He waited a few minutes before knocking again. No one seemed to be home.

His hand moved to the door knob to open it and was surprised to find it wasn't locked. He could get into a lot of trouble breaking into someone's house, but he didn't care much about trouble. He'd already come this far, so he might as well find answers.

Asher walked inside the dark house, softly closing the front door behind him. He felt around on the wall for a light switch when he heard the floorboards behind him squeak. He froze in place.

"Don't move a single inch," a deep voice said from behind him. Asher obeyed and stayed as still as possible as he listened to the man behind him walk by. The living room light came on, making Asher blink his eyes rapidly to adjust to the change. "Who are you and what are you doing in my house?" The man had an Irish accent.

"Sir," Asher began, wishing he could turn around and face the man. Although he couldn't see it, he could almost feel the energy radiate from the shooter pointed at his head, and one false move could cost him his life. "I need to speak with Clint Burns." The man's silence seemed to drag on for an eternity.

"What do you need with him?"

"I have to ask him some important questions about an event that happened several years ago. I'm told Clint Burns may have the answers."

"I knew this day would come," the man slowly muttered. "I knew the Enforcement would come for me for knowing too much. I won't let you take me alive!"

Asher felt a sharp pain explode in the back of his head. He stumbled forward, leaning face-first against the wall. He quickly touched the wound in the back of his head. He brought his hand into view and found his fingertips were covered in blood. His head felt fuzzy as he tried to keep his footing, but he collapsed on the ground within seconds. He closed his eyes, drifting in and out of consciousness. The last thing he remembered was looking up, opening his eyes, and seeing an elderly man standing over him with a scornful expression. Asher finally understood why he'd had such a bad feeling in his stomach before he left his house. He closed his eyes again and welcomed the darkness.

A half an hour passed, and Asher began to awaken. Once he was fully alert, he took in his surroundings, noticing he'd been tied to a metal chair. He pulled against the ropes, testing their durability, and knew he wouldn't be able to escape. Whoever had tied the knot was skilled. He had a challenge ahead of him.

"You've finally come to." Asher heard a familiar voice to his right. The man walked into the room, pulling a chair behind him, and took a seat adjacent to Asher. He had a long, crooked nose and balding hair, and was missing two top teeth. "You've got questions? Well, I do too. You will play by my rules, Commander Moore." Asher instantly regretted wearing his uniform and name badge. He'd thought his position would help him, not hinder him, but it seemed as if the man in front of him didn't take well to the military.

"I'll play along, but you'll answer my questions as well," Asher said through clenched teeth. His head wound was causing him a great deal of pain. The man laughed.

"I've already told you. You will play by my rules, and my rules means you answer questions, not ask them," the elderly man said. "First question, why are you here?"

"To question Clint Burns," Asher said. It took everything in him to remain conscious. He could feel the blood trickling down his neck from the gash in the back of his head.

"Why?" the man asked, stomping down his foot.

"Because I need answers."

"Bloody h—?" the man started to laugh, but it was far from an amused sound. "You can be more specific than that. Don't give me crap answers anymore. If you do, I'll hurt you."

It was then that Asher noticed the table to his right, where different knives and instruments of torture were displayed. Even then, Asher wasn't one to give in so easily. He'd dealt with worse from his own father. The only reason he decided to play along was that the truth would set him free. He wanted this man to know that he was not the enemy.

"I'll ask you again, why are you here?"

"I've come to find Clint Burns," Asher began. "He knew my

friend's father, George Kallis."

"Your friend's father? You're lying. George doesn't have any children here."

"So you do know George Kallis. Where is he?"

The old man fumed. "You tricked me, huh?" He stood up, walked over to the table, and picked up a sharp knife. "I warned you. I said I would be the one questioning you." The man walked over to Asher and held the knife an inch from his face. "I'll slice you open if you try that again."

"I'm telling the truth. His daughter is here and she's trying to find him."

"Then where is his daughter? Why isn't she here?" the man asked. "How do I know you aren't trying to see how much I know about George Kallis so you can report it back to your commander? How do I know you aren't the enemy?"

"You don't know, Mr. Burns," Asher said, and watched the old man's face fall at the sound of his name. "I know you're Mr. Burns. I know you can also help me."

Mr. Burns lowered the knife and smacked Asher across the face with his free hand. "I've had it with you. I want answers now!"

"I told you already," Asher slurred. His head was ringing from the impact. It didn't help that he already had a head injury. "I'm not the enemy. His daughter is looking for him. Help me."

"Listen here, lad," Mr. Burns began, raising the knife back up to Asher's cheek. "This knife is sharp enough to slice into your skin like butter. I won't hesitate to cut your pretty face next time. Why did the Enforcement send you here?"

"I'm not here on military business."

"Then why are you wearing your uniform?"

"To get past security," Asher told him. "You have to believe me. Mr. Kallis' daughter traveled through the portal two days ago in search of her father. I offered to help her."

"Why would a government official, who knows the law, help a complete stranger who'd broken the law by coming through the portal? See, Commander Moore, your story isn't adding up. I've given you quite a few chances to come clean and you've refused to. Maybe this will help you talk." Mr. Burns lowered the knife and jammed it inches deep into Asher's side in the exact location his previous wound had been. Asher screamed out in pain, gasping for air.

His vision doubled, and he feared he was on the verge of passing out again. He'd already lost a lot of blood from his head injury. He couldn't suffer more blood loss. He was panting, trying to get as much air as possible, but felt as if all the oxygen in the world wouldn't be enough. Sweat began beading down his face as he tried to think of a way out.

"Are you ready to comply?" Mr. Burns asked Asher.

"I already am," Asher said, his head sinking low.

"Why are you here?"

"To help me," a familiar voice said from behind him. Asher lifted his head long enough to see Jen standing near the door, pointing a shooter at Mr. Burns' head. "I'm George Kallis' daughter. I'm here to bring him home."

Mr. Burns dropped the knife and straightened. Guilt immediately washed over his face as he studied Jen. "Well, I guess I can't deny that claim. Even though your skin is much darker, you do resemble the lad." Mr. Burns looked down at Asher. "I take it he was telling the truth."

"He was, and you just stabbed an innocent person. You'll repay your crime by telling me everything you know, or else I'll shoot," Jen said, walking farther into the room.

"Ah, you even sound like your father." Mr. Burns laughed, as if he didn't have a shooter pointed at his head. He clapped his hands together. "Very well then. Shall I make tea?"

"If you think I'd trust you to leave us to make tea, you have another thing coming," Jen said. "Take a seat, Mr. Burns. We have a lot to discuss."

"As you wish," Mr. Burns said, sitting back down in his chair. He looked at Asher, appearing guilt-stricken, and tsked softly. Jen touched the cross around her neck for strength and quickly moved to Asher to remove the ropes that enslaved him. She noticed Mr. Burns had stabbed him in the exact spot his previous wound had been. You must have a death wish, Asher, she thought. His head dangled as a few drops of blood and sweat dripped onto his lap. Jen could tell he was close to passing out. Her heart raced as she thought about him dying. She rushed to Asher's side, pressing her free hand against the wound while keeping the shooter pointed at Mr. Burns.

"Tell me everything you know about my father and his whereabouts."

"Well," Mr. Burns began. "I haven't seen your father since I left Burdock seven years ago. However, he did reveal some things to me during his stay. George told me he had been taken from his daughter's bedroom three years earlier by some men who'd opened the portal. He said these men kept him imprisoned for three years until he managed to escape. George never gave many details for fear of getting people killed if they knew too much. Toward the end of his stay, he started to become paranoid, thinking everyone was out to get him, even the nurses.

"I used to work for a man who robbed high-end banks. I'd come up with the blueprint to help them get in, get the money, and escape. George knew this. He asked for my expertise in getting him out of Burdock. I didn't understand why he'd even want to leave or why he felt he couldn't just walk out, but George had his reasons. A week before I left Burdock, I drew up a plan for him and wished him luck. I'm not sure if he ever got out, since I haven't heard from him since then.

"It wasn't until much later that I began to piece certain things together. Even though George was secretive, he'd talk in his sleep. He used to shout out a name in a fit, tossing and turning wildly as if he was fighting someone in his sleep. The man's name was Frank Hoggs. George would also mutter things about a corrupt government and how he didn't trust them.

"I did research and found out about a sergeant named Frank Hoggs. It seemed as if there was some truth to the things George used to mutter in his sleep. I knew then that he had strong reasons for never telling me why he'd found refuge in Burdock. What I found interesting was that Burdock was run by the same government George was stating he couldn't trust. I realized then that was the reason he wanted to escape. When I learned I'd helped him run from the government, I moved out of Blue City and found this place. I knew if he was serious about everything, someone would one day come knocking on my door for answers."

Jen remained quiet for a while, taking it all in. Finally she nodded, lowering the shooter and fitting it inside the large pocket of her liquid blue jumpsuit. "Thank you. I appreciate your cooperation. Are you sure there's nothing else?"

"I am sure," Clint Burns assured her. "And I do apologize for stabbing your friend."

Jen remained tight-lipped. "We'll be leaving now." She tapped Asher and waited for him to lift his head. Instead, his head dangled even lower. Jen lowered herself, put his arm over her shoulder, and stood straight. His weight against her was enough to make her stumble, but she forced herself forward. "Come on, Asher. Try to walk."

Asher was coherent enough to try to put his best foot forward, but he ended up collapsing on her. Jen was forced to carry most of his weight against her as she made her way to the front door. Between his head and his side wound, he hadn't lost a lot of blood and Jen knew it wasn't enough to severely harm him. However, he was still injured enough to need help. She ignored Mr. Burns' attempts to help her as she left his house and began nearing the hover with a new worry. Who was going to drive the hover back to his condo?

Jen sat Asher down in the passenger seat and softly smacked his face. He looked terrible. She wondered if she should take him to the nearest hospital but then thought against it. Doctors would probably report back to his commander that he'd been injured, and he'd have more to deal with than he needed. She'd take him back to his house and get Lark to help nurse him back to health. "Asher, I need to you try to stay awake."

"How...how did you...get here?" he asked, barely lifting his head to look at her.

"I'll explain everything later," Jen said. "Right now, I have to figure out how to drive this thing because obviously you can't." Asher said nothing as his head began to hang. "Asher," Jen called. Asher didn't even try to lift his head again. She groaned, pushed him farther into the seat, and reached over to snap his seat belt in. She walked around to the driver's side and got in the hover.

"There has to be some sort of manual," she said, thinking out loud and trying to find a glove compartment, but coming up empty-handed. She racked her brain for information that she may have gathered while being in Blue City. She thought back to the buttons Asher had used to start the vehicle, remembering that he had pressed a green button first, and so she mimicked his action. The hover roared to life. "Okay, nice job, Jen," she said to herself. "Now we need to figure out how to lift this baby." Jen closed her eyes, picturing Asher's hand, and instinctively touched an orange button. She shrieked as the hover lifted off the ground and stabilized. "It isn't so bad."

"Blue," Asher muttered from the passenger seat. Jen saw a blue switch and flicked it. The hover moved forward, causing her to laugh in excitement. "Steee..."

"What?" Jen asked.

"Stich..." Asher started coughing in a fit and then collapsed against his seat.

"Stich," Jen repeated, trying to figure out what he was trying to say. She glanced down at the stick next to her. Bingo. "Stick! The stick shift. That's how you maneuvered it. I remember now. Okay, Asher, pray we don't die." Jen's hand shook as she lowered it to the stick and softly pulled it back. The hover rose in the air at a slow pace, and it took everything in Jen to remain calm.

"Blue streets," she said, looking at the gravel road ahead of her. At some point, she was supposed to glide onto the neon streets, but she saw none. "Where are the streets?" Jen floated past houses until she reached the gate. She was thankful to see that the security guard was busy assisting another hover that was trying to enter. She drifted past, undetected. The neon blue street started just ahead, and Jen slowly lifted the hover until it was just above the street lines. "So far so good."

Jen drove a few minutes before she noticed traffic at a stop up ahead. She needed to figure out how to brake or she'd slam into the back of the other hover. She began to panic as she got closer. "Asher," she cried, letting go of the stick to shake him. The hover tilted to its left, causing Jen to slam into her door. She quickly grabbed the stick, straightening it out before it crashed. The commotion was enough to make Asher raise his head. "Asher, how do I brake?"

"Foot," he mumbled. Jen was inches from crashing into the hover in front of her and slammed her foot down on a small peg on the floor of the hover she hadn't noticed before. The hover jolted to a stop, and Jen straightened, taking deeps breaths to calm herself.

"I can't do this," she said, feeling tears threaten to spill from her eyes. Out of everything she'd been through since arriving in Blue City, she hadn't been half as afraid as she felt now flying the foreign vehicle.

"I...told you to...stay," Asher said, tilting his head to look at her. He managed to find enough energy to give her the coldest stare.

"I just saved your life," Jen argued. The hover behind her beeped its horn, letting her know that it was time to go. She lifted her foot off the brake and began drifting forward. She drove for five more minutes before another thought occurred to her. "Where do you even live? Is there a built-in GPS system? Siri?" Jen cleared her throat, preparing to speak to the hover bug the way Asher had spoken to his condo. "Car, take me home." She waited, but nothing happened. "What do you call this thing? Oh! Hover, take me home." Again, nothing happened. Jen let out a frustrated sigh. "Asher, where do I go?" Still silence. Just when Jen was about to give up, Asher lifted his head. He slowly reached toward the dashboard and pressed a purple button. The car made a ringing noise and then zoomed into the air. Jen was forced to let go of the stick as the hover began to drive itself. She was flabbergasted.

"It drives itself? You mean to tell me I could've pushed that button a long time ago?" Jen turned to Asher, who seemed to be hiding a smile behind a pained expression. "You did that on purpose."

"You needed to learn a lesson," Asher said, pressing against his waist to keep his wound from bleeding. "You're too inexperienced to be my sidekick."

"Jerk," Jen barked. "I saved you. I'm the best sidekick there is." She heard Asher chuckle and looked over just in time to catch a glimpse of a brilliant smile. How he managed to still look beautiful with blood dripping down his face was a wonder to Jen. She preferred the sight of his smile over the sight of the futuristic, alluring buildings on either side of the street, but she turned back around and watched the hover drive them to Asher's condo.

Twenty minutes later, they floated into Asher's garage. Jen helped Asher out, making sure he was secure around her shoulder, and walked him toward the front door. She lifted his hand and held it up to the sensor and waited for it to turn green. Moments later, the door clicked open. It didn't take long for Lark to rush to her.

"W-what happened?" he asked with wide eyes and messy hair. "The two of you just l-left me here by myself with no explanation." Lark gasped and covered his mouth when he saw Asher's bloodstained shirt. "I-is he okay?"

"I don't really know. Help me get him to his bedroom." Lark obeyed, taking Asher's other side and relieving Jen of most of his weight. Once they had laid Asher on his bed, Jen ran to his bathroom and grabbed the first aid kit from under his sink. When she returned to the room, Lark had removed Asher's shirt.

"He's been stabbed," Lark said. "And he has a head wound. I don't know which is worse."

"Should we take him to the hospital?" Jen asked.

"No," Lark said, grabbing the first aid kit from her. "They don't call me boy genius for nothing. I can patch him right up. Just leave us alone for a while."

"What? No, I stay."

"Go!" Asher shouted at Jen from the bed. She blinked in response.

"I can handle it. Just give me room, Jen," Lark said. "I'll let you know when everything is okay."

Jen sighed. She stalked out of the room, angry with Asher

over his rude attempt to get her to leave. She paced back and forth in the living room, blaming herself for Asher's injuries, and then decided to take a warm shower, wanting to wash away all of her anxieties. It seemed to work for a while, but then she found herself in the living room, doing pushups and squats, knowing exercise helped some people relieve stress. That didn't work, either. She finally decided to drift off on the couch, only to find herself tossing and turning while moaning uncontrollably.

"What's my problem?" she asked herself, after her fourth failed attempt at sleeping. "I'm going crazy." She jumped up from the couch and walked to the window, allowing the unique view of the city to distract her. Different color hovers zoomed past on brilliant, azure streets. Signs appeared on buildings, advertising casinos and hotels. One of the advertisements depicted a man running across the building, and when he got to the edge, he disappeared and reappeared on the next building. He then stopped and turned forward as if looking directly at her and smiled. A sign appeared above his head that read:

The Running Man
Olympic Champion
Donald Gemsie

Jen was amazed. She had never imagined technology would come to the point where an advertisement could jump from one building to the next. It was a true work of art.

"He's patched up," Lark said from behind her. Jen spun around, thankful to finally know something. "He'll live, although he shouldn't try anything risky for at least a week."

"My father—"

"Will have to wait," Lark said, cutting her off. "Another week. Maybe two."

Jen sighed and nodded. She definitely understood that Asher was injured, but she was angry that he hadn't allowed her to accompany him. Sure, it was her fault he was even in the situation in the first place, but if she had tagged along, he wouldn't have been hurt.

"Thanks, Lark." She walked past him to sit on the couch. "I'm exhausted."

"What all happened?" Lark asked, sitting next to her.

"Asher wouldn't let me tag along, so I snuck into the back of his car and slept there all night. I watched him as he walked up to Clint Burns' house and let himself in. It didn't look as if anyone was home, so I expected him to come back out, but he never did. At that point, I got worried and went inside.

"I heard arguing in one of the rooms and overheard how Clint Burns didn't believe Asher was who he'd said he was, and so I intervened. If I hadn't been there, Asher would've died. He should be a lot more thankful for my bravery and stubbornness. He should be falling to his knees thanking me."

"That doesn't sound like something Asher would do." Lark studied Jen closely. "Are you okay?"

"For a kid, you sure are observant. I'm as okay as I'll ever be. Just exhausted and anxious, really." She cleared her throat and changed the subject. "We have a new clue. A guy named Frank Hoggs. He's a military sergeant who had something to do with my father. I wonder if Asher knows the guy."

"The military is extremely big. I doubt Asher would know the guy directly. But if anyone could find out about this guy, it would be Asher."

"From now on, wherever he goes, I go," Jen said. "I'm not letting him leave my sight."

"In that case, I'm not letting you leave my sight either, so we're going to be the three amigos," Lark crossed his arms and proudly lifted his chin as if his words were final. Jen couldn't help but laugh.

"You couldn't come up with a more original name?"

"I like the three amigos. It has a nice ring to it."

Jen laughed again, realizing that the worry she tried so hard to escape had naturally vanished on its own. It was good to have a friend, someone who actually seemed to care about her emotions. She felt bad for having questioned Lark's loyalty before, but she knew now that he was there on her side and would fight with her to the end.

An hour later, Jen jerked awake. She hadn't realized she'd dozed off on the couch. She sat up, rubbing her eyes and saw Lark sitting on the floor near the TV, playing a racing game. She found it strange that he had no controller. His hands were stretched out in front of him as he gripped an invisible stirring wheel. Jen didn't waste time trying to figure out how the game worked. She was more concerned with her grumbling stomach.

She stood and walked toward the farthest wall, waiting for a door to appear. Once it did, she stepped into a kitchen and marveled at the way the white walls morphed into skillfully carved wooden cabinets. The white, circular refrigerator came up from the floor, and had a built-in TV screen on the door that displayed a race between motor bugs that were going so fast Jen couldn't follow them around the track without losing sight of them. A kitchen island, which was made of glass and outlined in white, had risen from the ground in the middle of the kitchen, just as a fancy dishwasher clicked into place. Within seconds, the bare room transformed into an all-white kitchen more contemporary than Jen had ever seen.

Jen picked up an apple sitting in a basket, took a bite, and moaned as the sweet juices filled her mouth. She took another bite and walked to the kitchen sink. There were no knobs to turn the water on, but Jen guessed it had a sensor. She put her free hand under the sink and waited for the water to run. Nothing happened. Jen blinked a few times as she thought about a different way to approach it.

"Water!" Jen bellowed, and water began to shoot from the faucet. She smiled, proud she'd figured out how the faucet worked. "Water, off."

After the water cut off, Jen walked toward the refrigerator and opened it. She grabbed two bottles of water and tucked them under her arms. She closed the door and turned away, taking another bite of her apple.

"Anna, I want food."

"What would you like to eat, miss?" Anna responded.

"What is Asher's favorite dish?"

"That would be a grilled cheese sandwich, miss," Anna answered.

"Grilled cheese? He has the taste buds of a nine-year-old," Jen said under her breath. "Anna, can you make two grilled cheese sandwiches for Asher?"

"As you wish, but might I add that Mr. Moore usually eats four grilled cheese sandwiches."

"Okay," Jen said, looking up at the ceiling. "Make it four. And can you also make me a turkey avocado sandwich?"

"My pleasure, miss. Your wait time is three minutes."

Jen began hearing noises around the kitchen, but couldn't see anything being cooked. She wondered if there was another kitchen within the walls, where mechanical hands prepared food. The condo's technology was well beyond her limited understanding.

Exactly three minutes had passed when a hole in the island opened up and a rack with two plates of food arose. Jen removed the plates, placed her eaten apple on the rack, and left the kitchen. She made her way to Asher's room and set his plate and two bottles of water on the nightstand next to him.

Asher turned toward her, opening his sleepy eyes. His head was wrapped in white bandages, making him look fragile and innocent. Jen smiled at him, although she didn't want to be nice. "I brought you food." Asher shifted to his right and looked at the food sitting on his nightstand. He groaned and turned back on his left side, where he hadn't been wounded.

"I don't have an appetite."

"You need to eat regardless." Jen set her own plate of food down on the nightstand. "Try to sit up."

"I said I'm not hungry," Asher stated.

"And I said you need to eat regardless. Do you have to argue about everything? It would help if you learned to listen every once in a while." Jen flopped down on the side of the bed and picked his plate up, placing it on her lap. "I will feed you if I have to." Asher groaned but didn't turn to face her. "Asher, don't think I won't. Do you really want melted cheese all over your face? Huh?"

"Better my face than my mouth," Asher replied.

"That's it!" Jen placed the plate on the nightstand and

gripped Asher's shoulder, forcing him onto his back. She quickly seized one of the grilled cheese sandwiches from the plate and brought it to Asher's face, trying to shove the food into his mouth. Asher grabbed her wrist, managing to keep the sandwich at a distance. It became a power struggle as she tried to force the sandwich closer and he tried to keep it away. He was obviously stronger and flung her arm away, causing the sandwich to fly out of her hand and slam into the nearby wall. Jen ground her teeth in frustration as she looked down at Asher. He was staring back at her with a challenge in his eyes. If she hadn't known better, she'd have thought he was enjoying the little battle. "It's okay," Jen said. "There are three more sandwiches."

Jen picked up a second sandwich on the nightstand. She placed one knee on either side of Asher so that she straddled him, hoping to gain the upper hand. Asher grabbed onto her waist and tried to push her off him, but she stayed planted, trying to avoid brushing against his wound.

"What are you doing?" he asked. "Get off of me. It hurts."

"Liar! It doesn't hurt. You're just saying that to get me off of you!" Jen used both hands to try to stuff the sandwich into his mouth. Asher caught her wrists just as the sandwich touched his lips and pushed. He made a pained sound and faltered, causing Jen to fall forward and smash the sandwich against his mouth. "Eat!"

A noise came from the door. Jen and Asher paused and stared at Lark, who stood in the doorway, his mouth hung open. Lark looked at the sight of Jen on top of Asher with a sandwich pressed to his mouth and blinked.

"Right." Lark turned his back on them and walked away. The door vanished into the wall, leaving the two of them alone. Jen stared at the wall a moment longer and then returned her attention to Asher.

"Well, that wasn't awkward," Jen said sarcastically. She lifted off Asher and sat on the side of the bed. She looked back at Asher's pouty and defiant mouth and sighed. "Asher, please, just eat. It'll make you feel better."

Asher groaned and pushed himself into a sitting position. "Fine. But I'll feed myself."

Ten minutes later, he had devoured the remaining three sandwiches and sat back against his headboard. "Happy?"

"No," Jen began, swallowing the last bite of her sandwich. "I'm not happy at all. You wouldn't even be in this position if you hadn't been so stubborn about me going along with you to Clint Burns' house!"

"So it's my fault that I wanted to keep you out of trouble by telling you to stay behind?" Asher scoffed. "You are unbelievable. Here I am, on my deathbed, and you choose this time to point fingers at me."

"You are not on your deathbed!"

"Sure feels like it. What a way to show comfort, Jen. You climbed on top of me and dug your knee into my wound as you tried to force feed me. Then, after I actually managed to eat the food, you still scolded me for not taking you along. Have some sympathy for a dying man."

"You're not dying," Jen argued, but then softened, knowing he had a point. She'd chosen the wrong time to be mad. He needed her support, not her attitude. "I'm sorry."

Asher blinked in surprise. "Come again?"

"I'm sorry," Jen said, too stubborn to meet his eyes. She didn't want to see the victory written all over his face.

"Say that ag—"

"I said I'm sorry, okay?" Jen cut him off. "I should've waited until after you healed a little more before I started hounding you. But you deserved the sandwich in your face. I won't apologize for that."

Asher chuckled. "Apology accepted. So tell me, how did you follow me to Mr. Burns' house?"

"I hid in the back of your car...your hover."

"Didn't think you were that smart."

"Don't insult my intelligence. I'm very smart. And my saving you just proved why you can't leave me out of any more dangerous missions. Lark and I came to an agreement, and majority rules. We're the three amigos."

"The what?" Asher tried his hardest to hold back a laugh, but it escaped through his mouth in a loud grunt.

"The three amigos. Lark came up with the name."

"Figures."

"I like it. It completely grew on me," Jen said with a soft smile. "It makes me feel like we're a team now. We aren't going to sit back and watch you do everything by yourself. "

"Okay," Asher agreed, which made Jen snap her head in his direction.

"You're not going to argue?" she asked, studying his unreadable expression. Asher shrugged.

"I'm not happy about it, but I can't force you guys to stay put, especially when you'll just find a way to follow me anyway."

Jen looked away and smiled. For the first time, she felt at ease with the mission they had in front of them. She was starting to get the hang of things and knew, with a little help from Lark, that she would make it. They were getting closer and closer to finding out what happened to her father. After a week or so, they could begin searching for him again, and once they found him, she could return home to where her mother waited...to where things were normal. Jen glanced at Asher and found he'd been staring at her lips, as if he wanted a kiss. If she had a lighter complexion, her cheeks would have flushed scarlet.

"What?" she asked.

Asher blinked.

"I was wondering when you were going to get out of my room. I'd like to sleep."

"Right." Jen quickly stood and grabbed the empty plates of food, feeling embarrassed for automatically thinking he'd wanted a kiss. They barely knew each other and couldn't stand each other. That would have been the last thing on his mind. So why was it the first thing she'd thought when he'd looked at her that way? She shook the thought out of her mind and began walking toward the door.

"Jen?" Asher called, and she spun around, almost too quickly.

"Yes?"

"You forgot to pick up the sandwich." Asher pointed to the spot on the floor where the grilled cheese sandwich lay.

"Tell Mary to do it. Oh wait, she can't! She's broken. Well, I guess it'll have to stay there and rot since I'm no maid." Jen

turned back toward the door that had appeared and left Asher's
room before he could mutter a clever response.

CHAPTER ELEVEN

Pizza Parlor

Asher's holo-phone buzzed on his nightstand, slowly pulling him away from his dreams. The drowsiness caused by the painkillers Lark had given him still hadn't fully worn off as he pulled himself into a sitting position. Judging by the amount of light reflecting into his room from the outside, Asher figured it to be late evening. He painfully reached onto his nightstand and grabbed his holo-phone. The caller ID read: Commander Moore.

Asher quickly removed the bandages wrapped around his head, knowing the second-in- command—his own father—would be suspicious of his injury. He tucked the bandages under his covers and sat up as straight as he could. He hit the talk button and allowed his holo-phone to float away from him as it picked up his image. The holo-phone shone a yellow circle onto the carpet and within seconds Asher's father began to materialize from the ground up.

Commander Thomas Moore stood as regal as ever in a metallic uniform that cast its own light in Asher's room. He glared at Asher, who stared back, giving off his typical indifferent vibe. Asher reluctantly saluted the commander. "How are things, sir?"

"Things could always be better," Commander Moore began, with a calculating gaze. "There is still no lead on the criminal who came through the portals. However, witnesses in a nearby building reported a biracial girl who seemed out of place on the twentieth floor near a hover rental store. An investigation was done at the rental store, where authorities questioned the robots working that day. Unfortunately, those robots weren't programmed to store facts about customers, as they needed to be able to store data about the rentals and other work-related issues. They weren't able to give the authorities accurate events of the people who had rented that day."

"And why are you telling me this, sir?" Asher asked.

"As I've stated, I want you to keep an eye out for any suspicious activity."

"I have, sir, and I haven't come across anything out of the ordinary. Is there anything else you'd like to discuss? I was in the middle of a nap."

"You will report to me, whether you're napping or dying," the commander barked. "That attitude of yours is what holds you back from being promoted."

"With all due respect, I'm not interested in being promoted, sir," Asher said, which caused the veins in Commander Moore's neck to protrude in anger.

"I could stay on this call and argue with you, but I actually have work to do. I'd suggest you start doing some work of your own. I expect more of you." Commander Moore gave Asher a disapproving grunt and then turned away. The image before Asher flickered, and his holo-phone drifted back into his hand. He wanted to throw his phone across the room but decided against it. His bedroom door began to materialize, and he sighed in frustration. He was in pain and drowsy and didn't want to be bothered.

Jen walked into his room, carrying a bowl of soup. She set it down on his nightstand and took a seat next to him on his bed. Asher had to admit, the soup smelled marvelous, but he wasn't in the mood for more food. It felt as if he'd just eaten his last meal ten minutes ago. However, he decided not to give Jen a hard time since she wasn't above force feeding him, which would result in hot soup spilling all over his face and bed.

Asher studied Jen as she picked up the soup bowl and stirred. His eyes went to her locks of curls, and he fought back the urge to reach out and pull a strand of her hair to see if the curls would bounce back. He liked the color of her eyes, the way they weren't quite green yet weren't quite brown, either. She was an exotic mix of two races, which seemed to complement her well. Even though she had attractive qualities, she also had some bad ones that annoyed him, like her stubbornness. It almost matched his, and two people who bumped heads would never get along.

Jen finally met his eyes, but only for an instant. Her eyes

traveled up to his head as wrinkles formed in her forehead. Asher knew that look all too well. She was about to throw a tantrum. "Asher," she began, "Where is your bandage?"

"I took it off," Asher said, purposely leaving out why he'd done it, just to get a rise out of her. He wouldn't admit it, but he liked being the reason Jen got so worked up.

"Why did you take it off?"

"Because." Asher's tone suggested that he hadn't planned to say anything further. Jen closed her eyes and took a deep breath. Asher tried his hardest to fight back a smile, having been thoroughly entertained.

"Do you have a death wish? You have a gash in the back of your head. It could easily get infected. Not to mention how hard Lark worked to patch you up, and you just removed it. You're inconsiderate."

"Am I?" Asher smiled.

"Wipe that smirk off of your face," Jen fumed. "Yes, you are. Very."

Asher looked away as if he were thinking. "That would explain a lot. So, I guess I was being inconsiderate when I decided to help you escape the day you came through the portal. And I guess I was being inconsiderate when I saved you from being killed by Gunner. And I was most definitely being inconsiderate when I let you stay here and provided you with all of your necessities. Wow, Jen. You're right. I'm very inconsiderate." Asher looked down at the bowl in her hand. "Soup? Looks yummy."

"I don't even know what to say to you right now." Jen sighed and looked down at the soup in her hands, deciding not to argue with him. It was obvious that he wanted to get a rise out of her. "Yes, I have soup. Chicken noodle soup to be exact."

"Are you going to try to feed it to me like you did earlier?" Asher asked, not caring to hide the amusement in his voice.

"No." She wouldn't allow him to get under her skin. "You can feed yourself."

"Hmm." Asher raised a hand to his chin and began stroking it as he thought. "I think I'd rather you feed me." Jen's face fell.

"Fine," she said, noticing the confusion in his eyes, which he quickly tried to mask. Jen lifted the spoon to his mouth. "Open wide."

Asher quickly took the spoon from her hand and then reached over, grabbing the bowl out of her lap. "I expected you to object."

"I caught on to that, so I decided to play along," Jen said, feeling victorious. She'd realized Asher was deliberately giving her a hard time and she didn't appreciate it one bit. She glared at him as he took the first sip of his soup. He made a face and spit the soup back into the bowl.

"Are you trying to kill me?" he asked, bringing a hand up to his mouth. "This is too hot."

"An extremely hot soup for an extremely hot tempered boy," Jen said with a pleased smile. "Eat up before it gets cold. Looks yummy."

Asher shook his head and raised a spoon full of soup to his mouth, blowing before taking the bite. Jen glanced down, seeing his bloody bandage hanging out from under his covers. She grabbed it, raising it up to examine it.

"Did it fall off while you were sleeping? Is that what happened?" Asher set the bowl of soup in his lap and swallowed the contents in his mouth.

"I'd gotten a call from my commander and needed to look as if I was in perfect condition or he'd become suspicious," he confessed.

"Why didn't you just say that to begin with?"

"I don't always have a reason to my madness."

"I'm not going to argue that. I'll just patch you back up." Jen stood and disappeared into his bathroom. She returned with his first aid kit and sat back down next to him. "I guess it needed to be cleaned anyway."

She dabbed some rubbed alcohol on a piece of cloth, which she placed on the gash in the back of his head. He tensed but didn't make any noises as she cleaned his wound and then wrapped his head with the bandage. Asher scooted back so that his back was resting against the headboard.

"I still have to clean your side," Jen said. "Sit back up."

Asher obeyed, moving closer to Jen, and lifted his shirt over his head. She had to look away, not wanting to stare at his abs. "Okay," he said, flinging his shirt onto the floor. Jen cleared her throat and turned back toward him, focusing intently on the bandage wrapped around the bottom half of his waist. She slowly removed it, regretting having to reach around to his other side to continue unwrapping it. It made her feel as if she was hugging him when she really wasn't.

As Jen cleaned his wound, she fought the urge to glance at his chiseled chest and his muscular arms that flexed as he winced in pain. She'd never been so close and intimate with a guy, especially one who had a perfect body. She didn't know how to handle it.

"When I was a little girl, I'd gotten hurt really bad in a bike accident," Jen began, deciding to focus on a distant memory versus the guy in front of her. "I was riding down a hill, going really fast, and I got scared. I slammed on the brakes, which only caused my bike to lean forward, and I ended up flying off it and landing on the concrete. I scraped the whole side of my leg pretty badly and completely removed the first layer of skin.

"I remember limping home and crying the whole way. When my dad saw my wound, he scooped me up in his arms and took me to the bathroom. He was adamant about cleaning it himself instead of taking me to the hospital. My dad was a hands-on kind of man. I remember how he and my mom argued over this the whole time he cleaned my wound. I ended up not going to the hospital and healed just fine." Jen paused, picturing the memory in her head, seeing her father's concerned and focused face. "I can see his face so easily, as if it just happened yesterday. It's funny how even the most unpleasant memories can mean so much more than they did at the time. When I look back, I don't see a stubborn father refusing to get his daughter the right care. I see a father who wanted to be the one to make his daughter whole again. I see a loving, concerned father." Jen smiled at the memory in her head.

"My mother didn't believe me when I told her that my father had disappeared into my closet that night the portal opened. She, along with everyone else, tried to convince me that my father had left, as if he'd stopped loving us. But my dad, he wasn't that type of man. He was the kind of father who cared about his family, sometimes too much. He didn't care that my mother was a black woman; he loved her with no restrictions. He didn't know hate and he didn't judge a soul. That kind of man doesn't walk away from his family.

"When I think about the pain and torture my father must have gone through being here, how crazy he must have gone at times—the nightmares, the scars, and the blood—I feel sick inside. It breaks me. I wonder how he slept each night being away from us and the pain it caused him. Until I got here, I never thought about how he must feel being separated from us. I'd always thought I was the only one who missed him. But now that I think about it, he had it worse. He's still having it worse.

"It drives me crazy just sitting here, not doing anything. I can't sit still, I can't relax, I can't sleep, and I can barely breathe. I'm always on edge, and I'm sure I'm really difficult to deal with. I'm sorry about that, I just—"

"Don't apologize," Asher said in a voice barely above a whisper. Jen looked up at his face, trying to read his expression; however, his face was masked as usual. Even then, she'd heard all she needed to in his voice. He was touched by her story. She hadn't meant to touch him; she'd only meant to distract herself, but he was touched nonetheless. "I should apologize for being so hard on you sometimes. You must be going through a lot."

"I think that's the most sincere thing you've ever said to me," Jen said, having finished wrapping up his wound.

"Yeah? Well, here's another sincere statement." Asher turned his head in Jen's direction, giving her the evil eye, although not a very convincing one. "You wrapped my bandage too tight."

"Sorry." Jen blushed, and began removing the bandage. "I guess I got a little carried away."

"Most girls do when they're in such close proximity to my abs," Asher said matter of factly.

"That's it." Jen let go of the bandage. She stood up, trying to hide her laughter. "Wrap it yourself."

"Hey," Asher called to Jen as she made her way over to his

now-materializing door. "You can't leave a dying man to fend for himself."

"Good thing you aren't dying." She gave him her most mischievous smile and left his room.

Jen took a seat on the living room sofa and entertained herself by watching Lark dance along to a video game he was playing. Once he'd discovered Asher's video game collection, he hadn't stopped playing. Jen couldn't help but laugh at how Lark tried to keep up with the beat as his lanky arms and legs flapped in the air. He didn't have much hand-eye coordination and what made it worse was his terrible sense of rhythm. Lark didn't look like he was dancing; he looked like he was having a seizure.

Eventually, Lark became frustrated and gave up on the game. He noticed Jen sitting behind him and smiled nervously. He quickly turned the video game off and awkwardly walked toward Jen.

"H-how long have you been sitting there?" he asked, plopping down in the chair across from her.

"Long enough," Jen smiled, feeling amused. "There's some soup in the kitchen if you want to eat."

"I was thinking about going out for pizza."

"How? We don't have a car."

"It's easy." Lark pushed the brim of his glasses up his nose. "We take Asher's hover and go find a pizza place."

"Asher won't let us take it, and even if he did, who's going to drive it?"

"I have a license."

"You're fourteen!"

"That's legal driving age. Even kids know that you don't even have to know how to drive hover bugs. If you hit the purple button, it'll just drive itself."

"Okay, well, that still doesn't eliminate the major thing stopping us—Asher."

"That's easy, too," Lark said. "He's due for another pain pill. It'll knock him out and he'll most likely sleep through the rest of the night. He won't even know we left. So, shall I do the honors?"

"This is crazy," Jen said. "But I think I'll die if I stay locked up inside this condo. Let's go."

Ten minutes later, Lark and Jen flew through the night's sky in Asher's hover. Asher had passed out within minutes of taking the pill. Jen had to give Lark credit for his cleverness and had to admit to herself that she'd much rather be viewing Blue City than sitting in Asher's condo all day.

She marveled at the street signs and advertisements that colored the night. Her attention didn't stay on one particular thing for too long, as there was always a new sight to view. She turned around and looked at Lark, who seemed unfazed by his surroundings as he drove. She couldn't imagine there ever being a time when she'd be so used to Blue City that it would lose its appeal. A part of her wanted to stay there forever.

Lark parked the hover on the Bottom Ground and got out. Jen was so busy looking up at the 3D graphics on the pizza sign that she hadn't noticed Lark standing near her door. He knocked on the window, making her jump. She quickly opened the door and got out.

"Pretty cool, huh?" Lark said, looking up at the sign that seemed to move toward them, luring them into the building. "I was thinking about being a graphic designer when I grow up, but that's impossible."

"Why won't you?" Jen asked, following Lark to the front entrance of the pizza parlor.

"College is only for rich kids. People like me can't afford it. If you ask me, the government wants it that way. That's how they control people. Keep the poor, poor and the rich, rich. The only way to get rich when you're born poor is to go to college or be extremely talented. Well, they make it impossible to get into college."

"It's not like that where I'm from. Sure, college is expensive, but people can get loans or scholarships."

"Lucky for you," Lark said, opening the front door for Jen. "Must be nice living in a time where the government isn't so corrupt."

Jen's attention was stolen from Lark the moment a blue-haired male robot strolled toward her and led them to a booth in the middle of the pizza parlor. She couldn't help staring at the other guests eating at nearby tables, such as the family of four seated to her left. The father, mother, son, and daughter each had a different color Mohawk. The son looked around six and the daughter around twelve, and each had shaved sides and pointy hair that resembled their parents'. If Jen had been at home, such a family would have been looked down upon.

Another interesting family sat a few tables behind the Mohawk family, although their appearance was more normal. Jen watched as each of their pizzas floated in front of them as they ate. Lark followed her gaze to the family and laughed.

"Floating pizza. Try one?"

"How did they get it to float?" Jen asked, still eyeing the family.

"There's a little plate underneath the pizza that floats. Pretty cool, huh?" Lark asked. "When I was a kid, I didn't order anything that didn't come with a floating plate."

A female waiter glided over to where Jen and Lark sat. Jen could tell by her tight smile and hover board that she was a robot. "May I take your order?" the robot asked.

"I'll have two pepperoni pizzas and an orange soda," Lark said. The robot turned to Jen, giving the same, tight smile.

"I'll do one floating pepperoni pizza and a chocolate milkshake. Oh, and I want it to float, too."

"Is there anything else I can get you?" the robot asked.

"No, thank you," Jen responded, and watched the robot glide away.

"This feels like a date," Lark said teasingly.

"Don't get your hopes up, boy."

"I'm joking. I'm sure you'd rather date Asher."

Jen gasped. "No way."

"Why not?" Lark leaned closer to Jen, as if he couldn't wait to hear what she said.

"Why not? That's like me asking if you'd date Asher. That's how repulsed I am by your question!" Jen retorted. Lark smiled, but it quickly faded as his eyes darted past Jen.

"Uh oh."

"What is it?" Jen turned in her seat and watched two boys

around her age walk into the pizza parlor. One guy had spiky blond hair and a face covered in tattoos. The other had a face full of piercings and a shaved head. The first guy surveyed the parlor and spotted Lark. His eyes darkened as he smiled.

"We should leave," Lark said, but it was too late. The two guys made their way over to them.

"Look who we have here," the tattooed guy said, resting a hand on Lark's shoulder. "Long time no see, old friend. Keith, remember Lark?"

"Yeah, I do," Keith said with a very deep voice.

"Mind if we take a seat, old friend?" the tattooed guy asked, but he didn't wait for Lark's response. He flopped down in the seat next to him and then looked at Jen for the first time. "Well, hello there, beautiful. Am I interrupting a date?" He turned his head back to Lark. "She looks a bit old for ya."

"She's my friend," Lark said, quickly glancing at Jen before lowering his eyes. She noticed how he hung his head as if afraid to meet the tattooed guy's stare.

"Like how we were once friends," the guy said. He still wore a smile on his face, but Jen could tell he was anything but happy. "Yeah, but then ya stole from me. Remember that Keith?"

"Yeah, Roger," Keith said. "I remember it very clearly."

"How about you, Lark?" Roger asked. "Do you remember what ya stole from me?"

"No," Lark said, barely above a whisper.

"Well, let me remind you." Roger leaned over and punched Lark in the gut, causing Lark to double up and cough violently. No one else in the pizza parlor noticed. Jen jumped up, wanting to defend him, but she didn't know what to do. "Ya stole a thousand dollars from me."

"I'll p-pay you back," Lark said, clutching his stomach.

"Oh, really? How do ya plan to do that? Ya work for some big-time drug lord now? He's paying ya well? Ya paying for this date, too?" Roger laughed, glancing briefly at Jen. "It's not money I want, Larky boy. I want ya girlfriend here to give me a big, fat kiss." Roger shifted his eyes to Jen and smiled. It was then that she noticed his decaying teeth. She fought back the urge to make a disgusted face. "What do ya say, babe?"

"I'll tell you what you can kiss," Jen retorted.

Roger laughed, turning back to Lark.

"She's a witty one, yeah? Just how I like them. So, Larky boy. Gonna let me kiss her?" Roger asked.

"No," Lark responded, after the robot zoomed away. "You can't kiss her. Keep her out of it."

"Aww, no kiss? Well, then, I'll have to get creative." Roger leaned over and punched Lark again. Jen clutched the table, trying to keep herself from doing something stupid. Roger looked around the parlor, making sure no one had been watching him, and then reached into his pocket and set a twenty dollar bill on the table. "Food's on me. Now let's take a trip outside.

CHAPTER TWELVE

Rogue

Lark and Jen reluctantly followed Roger and Keith out of the pizza parlor. Jen's heart raced as she wondered what Roger had in store for Lark. Even though she and Lark had only recently met, their circumstances had brought them close together, and she truly cared about his wellbeing. He was almost like a little brother, so she felt she had to stand up for him. If not her, then who?

Leaving the condo for pizza had been a stupid idea. If something bad happened, Asher would know that they took his hover, and he wouldn't trust them ever again. It would ruin any chance of them proving they were worthy to stand next to him as they searched for her father. This one mistake could cost Jen a lot and was why she needed to prevent Roger from doing anything harmful. She was angry at herself for not agreeing to the kiss.

Roger guided them into a dark alley, away from street lights and prying eyes. Jen lifted a hand to the cross on her neck and said a silent prayer. She believed in a God who always watched over her and knew He'd never forsake her. Whatever they were about to go through, they'd get through it.

Roger abruptly stopped midway through the alley and turned toward them. He smiled down at Lark, the shadows spilling over his face in weird angles, making him look haunted. Jen instinctively took a step back and bumped into Keith, who she hadn't realized had been standing directly behind her. She tilted her head back to look at him and met his wicked smile.

"Tell me, Larky, what do you think would be a good way to repay your debt?" Roger asked, looking down at Lark who was doubled over in pain. "More pain? A thousand dollars' worth?" Roger's fist collided with the side of Lark's face, knocking him off balance. Lark fell to the ground, landing in a puddle of dirty rain water.

Jen moved forward to help him, but Keith grabbed her waist, keeping her pressed against him. She hated the feel of his chest against her back and told herself she'd smack him for it the moment she got loose. Lark tried to stand, but Roger moved in close, kicking him in his stomach.

"I'd say that kick was about twenty dollars' worth of revenge. Wouldn't you agree, Keith?" Roger asked, glancing behind Jen to where Keith stood.

"More like fifteen," Keith responded. Roger looked upward in thought and then nodded.

"I'd agree." Roger kicked Lark again, causing blood to spray out of his mouth.

"Stop it," Jen screamed. "You're going to kill him."

"Kill him?" Roger laughed. "No, we're just having some fun. Right, Larky boy?" Roger bent down and grabbed a fist full of Lark's red hair, forcing him to look Roger in the eyes.

"R-right," Lark managed to say through his panting.

"Now, where was I? Oh no! I lost count of how much money I've already beaten out of you. Oh well, guess we have to start all over." Roger lifted his foot to kick Lark, but Jen broke away from Keith long enough to cause commotion. Roger lowered his foot and turned toward Jen.

"At least be fair," Jen said. "Give him a chance to fight back. Only punks fight dirty. He's a kid, for crying out loud, and you're nothing but a bully."

"Yeah?" Roger laughed, walking away from Lark. "I suppose ya want to step in for him, then? Take his punishment?"

"Don't," Lark said, trying to stand before collapsing on the ground again.

"Yes," Jen said. She couldn't stand watching Lark get beaten for something he did as a kid. She didn't care about the money he stole or why he stole it. She was sure it was for a good cause, knowing he'd been on his own after his mother left him. If Jen had been in his situation, would she have acted differently? Possibly not. Roger looked like the type who deserved to have something taken from him.

"Is that right?" Roger stood inches from Jen and flashed his rotting teeth as he smiled. "I might enjoy this even more." He forcefully grabbed Jen's face, digging his thumbs into her cheeks, and caused her to cry out. "I'll make ya regret your bravery."

"Don't even think about hurting her," a feminine voice called out from the farthest end of the alley. Roger let go of Jen's face and turned toward the sound.

A young woman, a couple of years older than Jen, walked toward them. She wore thick black combat boots that echoed as she walked. Her hair was cut into a short black bob, and she wore dark, edgy makeup. Her clothes were also black, and a thick chain hung from the front of her belt and connected to the back of it. She wore black gloves with the fingers cut off, and held a cigarette loosely in one hand. She looked like the type of girl who could take on both Roger and Keith with one hand tied behind her back. She reminded Jen of Daniela.

"Who are ya?" Roger asked, momentarily forgetting Jen.

"Do I need a name?" the girl asked, flicking her cigarette on the ground.

"I...I'd suggest ya get out of here. This don't have nothing to do with ya!" Roger bellowed.

"From what I overheard, it has nothing to do with her, either," the girl said, pointing at Jen. "One of my biggest pet peeves is men who put their hands on women. You've got two-and-a-half seconds to get out of this alley."

"Or else what?" Roger asked, taking a few steps toward the girl.

"Your two seconds is up." The girl sprinted toward Roger, who started to back away. He reached into his pocket, pulling out a knife just as the girl reached him. She wasted no time dropping to the ground and kick spinning, knocking Roger off of his feet. He fell onto the ground with a loud thud.

Keith pushed Jen aside and charged toward the girl, but she was quicker. She turned toward Keith and kicked him in the stomach. Keith was bigger than Roger and only staggered a few feet. He growled and charged at the girl again. He managed to grab her shoulders, trying to slam her to the ground, but she rolled under his weight, connecting her elbow with his jaw. Keith was forced to let go of her, and she elbowed him again, making him fall to the ground.

Roger had gotten back up on his feet and kicked the girl in her back, making her stumble. He used her weakened state to his advantage and grabbed a fistful of her hair, pushing her up against a building. He quickly banged her head into the brick wall, making her collapse on the ground. Lark sprung to life and jumped onto Roger's back. Roger spun around in a circle, furiously reaching behind him to grab Lark. Once he had a piece of Lark's shirt, he leaned forward and threw Lark over his head. Lark fell to the ground and went still.

Roger turned toward Jen and smiled. He took one step toward her, but the girl was already back on her feet. She'd picked up a beer bottle from the ground and smashed it into the back of Roger's head. Roger blinked three times before collapsing on the ground.

The girl looked up at Jen and sighed. She took a few wobbly steps backward, grabbing onto her head, which was bleeding from the impact with the building. "Didn't see that one coming," she laughed.

Jen quickly rushed to Lark's side, helping him sit up as he groaned.

"Are you okay?"

"I'll be fine," Lark grunted, allowing Jen to help him stand. Once he straightened, he looked at the girl, who watched their interaction curiously with folded arms. "Who are you?"

"Apparently I'm the person you should be thanking for saving your life," the girl said in a sarcastic manner that reminded Jen of someone, although she couldn't put her finger on who it was.

"Thank you," Jen said, truly meaning it. If the girl hadn't been there...Jen didn't even want to imagine what would have happened. "We appreciate it."

"No worries," the girl said, still eying Jen curiously. "You're not from around here, are you?"

"What makes you say that?" Jen asked cautiously. She tried

to blend in as much as possible and didn't know what would happen if anyone knew who she was.

"Your accent, your mannerisms seem...of a different time," the girl said, walking toward Jen and Lark.

"No, I'm from here. Blue City."

"Don't lie to me after I went through so much to save your life," the girl said, looking annoyed. "I saw you come through the portal three days ago."

Jen felt as if her heart had stopped beating. She studied the girl's face to see if she planned any ill will against her. When Jen had come out of the portal, she'd been sure no one except Asher had seen her, but everything happened so quickly it was possible someone else had witnessed it. Even then, if the girl planned to turn her in, she would have done it already. Jen hoped her reasoning was sound.

"You were accompanied by a soldier," the girl continued. "I was sure you two would get caught, but later that day I saw on the news that you escaped. They still don't have a lead. Seems as though I'm the only one who really knows what happened that day. They're offering a lot of money to the person who finds you."

"Is that why you saved us? Just to turn me in?" Jen felt her heart beating out of her chest. No, she couldn't be caught like this. She'd only stepped out for pizza.

"Do I look like the type of girl after money?" she asked. "I'm just stating facts. You're the most wanted girl in the world right now. I kind of admire you. My name's Rogue, by the way." Rogue stood close enough to reach her hand out for Jen to shake. Jen hesitated but then took it.

"Rogue? What kind of a name is that?" Jen asked.

"It was given to me in the military, but it stuck after I AWOL'd. I have a rogue soul, I guess." Rogue looked at Lark and smiled. Jen thought she seemed genuine enough, even though she looked like a tough girl who had most likely been shaped by the military. In that moment, Jen decided to trust her. "There's something I want from you," Rogue said.

"What?" Jen asked, thinking she may have decided to trust her too soon. She glanced behind Rogue and noticed Roger stirring. Any minute, he was going to wake up. Rogue looked behind her but shrugged, not seeming to find Roger's movements threatening. She turned back to Jen.

"I want Asher," Rogue said matter of factly. Jen looked at Lark, who seemed just as puzzled as she was. She turned back to Rogue with questions in her eyes. "The soldier who helped you escape was Asher. I didn't save you tonight because I was interested in you; I saved you because I knew you'd take me to him."

"What do you want with Asher?" Jen asked, hesitantly.

"I didn't ask you why you came through the portal or what you were doing out in this alley with that kid, so please don't ask about my motives," Rogue said firmly.

"Then I won't be able to take you to him. You may want to kill him," Jen argued, which caused Rogue to laugh.

"I can assure you, I'm not skilled enough to kill my commander, nor do I have the desire to do so."

"Your...commander?" Jen was staggered. "Asher was your sergeant?"

"Indeed he was." Rogue's eyes glazed over as if recalling a distant memory and smiled. She returned her gaze to Jen. "Will you take me to him?"

"Here's the thing," Jen began. "Asher doesn't know we left. If we come back with you, we're busted."

Rogue laughed. "Scared of what Asher will do? He's a big softy. Take me with you and I promise my presence will make him forget all about you."

"W-we'll take you," Lark spoke up. Jen gave him an evil look. "What? H-he'd most likely find out anyway. It's Asher." Lark turned to Rogue. "It's the l-least we can do for a f-friend of Asher's."

"Friend," Rogue repeated, smiling to herself. "Yes, friend."

"Well, I guess...follow us." Jen swiftly turned away and walked out of the alley, slightly annoyed.

Twenty minutes later, Lark pulled the hover bug into Asher's garage. Lark was able to trick Asher's sensor by rewiring it, and within minutes the door clicked open. Jen entered first, expecting an empty living room. She was surprised to see Asher sitting on the back of his couch with an arm lightly pressed against his wound, burning holes into her with his eyes.

"Where have you been?" he asked in a deadly slow manner. Lark walked past Jen, oblivious to Asher's presence. "Stop right there, Lark."

Lark stopped and slowly met Asher's eyes. "A-asher."

"Why did you two take off with my hover? Didn't think I'd find out? Thought I'd sleep through the sound of my sky door opening?"

"We just wanted pizza," Jen said.

"And you couldn't have it delivered?" Asher shouted, incredulous. His voice echoed throughout the room, making Jen's ears ring. She had never seen him so angry and shrunk back in fear.

"Cut them a break," Rogue said from behind Jen. She walked farther into the room and stood next to Jen. Jen watched as Asher's eyes first lowered in disbelief and then widened in surprise as he recognized Rogue. His mouth hung open as he blinked rapidly, momentarily forgetting his anger.

"Hello...friend."

Jen wondered why Rogue exaggerated the word friend and instantly regretted bringing her back with them. Could she be an enemy? But the look in Asher's eyes made Jen wonder if he and Rogue may have been more than just friends.

"Sergeant Hills," Asher said, barely above a whisper.

"I'm not deserving of that title. I go by Rogue now. You know, the nickname you gave me."

Asher smiled softly. "I guess that's fitting. Why are you here? How did you know—?"

"I saw you in the pub the day the portal opened. I spent the whole time trying to work up the nerve to go up to you. I wanted to catch up and apologize for leaving the military so abruptly. When you left the pub, I followed you to the portal and watched as you questioned her. You took off with her so quickly, I couldn't keep up, and I lost you. Tonight when I saw her, I knew it wasn't a coincidence. I knew I had to see you again."

Just as Rogue had predicted, it was as if Jen and Lark no longer existed. Asher took a few steps toward Rogue and then rushed to bring her into his arms. Jen didn't know how to feel watching Asher be so intimate with a girl right beside her. She stepped away, allowing them to have their privacy. She glanced at Lark, who watched her suspiciously, and she hoped she hadn't worn her distaste on her face.

"I'm going to shower," she told him, looking away. "It's been a long night."

Ten minutes later, Jen stood under the hot shower, still not feeling relaxed. Images of Asher rushing to hug Rogue made her uneasy. Was she jealous? But how could that be when the only thing she'd ever felt toward him was irritation? And yet she'd rushed off, not being able to stand the two of them holding each other as if they were having the sweetest reunion.

Hugging wasn't the way a commander greeted his soldier. It was the way two people, who had deeply cared for each other and had been separated for a long time, reunited. Had Jen's instinct proven to be true? Were Asher and Rogue once lovers?

"No way," Jen said to herself. Rogue looked more like a guy's girl, someone who watched football and drank beer and joined "men's night." If Rogue had longer hair and dressed feminine, she would have been beautiful, but Jen couldn't picture her being Asher's type. "Maybe she's just like a sister. That has to be it."

A man and a woman could hug the way they had and still be completely platonic. They'd probably had close bonds that had come to an abrupt end when Rogue left the military. Jen felt better as she stepped out of the shower and dried off. She looked in the mirror at her wet curls sticking to her forehead and then noticed that she had marks on her cheek from where Roger had grabbed her. At least she was grateful that Rogue had helped fight them off. Jen would have been covered in bruises otherwise.

Jen walked out of the bathroom, dressed in a new gray jumpsuit. She found Asher, Lark, and Rogue all sitting in the living room, laughing at some joke. Lark was first to notice her join them. He waved her over to sit on the couch next to him.

Jen sat down, studying Asher as his eyes stayed trained on

Rogue. Even though he was still injured, he seemed completely healed, as if Rogue's presence had cured him. Or maybe she was just seeing things.

"Rogue was telling me funny stories about their experience in the military," Lark told Jen. He seemed to have forgotten his own bruises.

"Ash, you tell the next story," Rogue said, sounding alive with joy. It was completely different than how she'd acted in the alley.

"Okay." Asher smiled. "Umm...here's one." He stopped to laugh. "So, Rogue was the only girl in her squad. She'd always try to outdo the men, and most times she succeeded. But this one time—"

"Not that story!" Rogue covered her face in embarrassment.

"You told me to tell a funny story," Asher said with a brilliant smile. Jen couldn't help notice how beautiful he was when he smiled like that. It wasn't often that he flashed Jen with such a smile. He was a different person with Rogue, obviously. He was open and free and the pain and darkness usually hidden behind his eyes had vanished. It was nice to see him happy, so why was she still unsettled?

"Ash, tell them about how we first met," Rogue said, glancing at Jen and smiling.

"Well, back then, Rogue had long, blonde hair. She was one of those girls who didn't even know how beautiful she really was. I mean, Rogue had every guy in her unit turning their heads as she passed by on that first day. I was standing with her troop, and she'd marched right up to me and said, 'Are you the man I'm going to spend the rest of my days here hating?'"

"I didn't say that." Rogue laughed.

"Yes, you did." Asher chuckled, beaming brightly. "And I said, 'You'll actually spend the rest of your life hating me.' Rogue looked at me with horror, but then she smiled and said, 'I like you already.' If you ask me, the reason Rogue worked harder than others was to impress me. She was in love with me from the beginning."

"I think it was the other way around," Rogue corrected. "Asher always tried to find some reason to pick on me, even when I'd gotten the best scores. But whenever the guys tried to intimidate me, Asher was right there, defending me. He'd always sit with me when we ate, and always made sure I was on his team whenever we did challenges."

"So, you two dated?" Lark asked. Rogue and Asher smiled at each other.

"We weren't allowed to date," Asher said. "A commander and his soldier? It was the worst thing one could possibly do." Jen let out a breath of relief, a breath she hadn't realized she'd been holding.

"So instead, we didn't label it. We'd sneak around when everyone else was asleep. Stole kisses when no one else was looking," Rogue said, but her eyes had turned sad. Jen noticed a change in Asher as well as he shifted in his seat.

"I'm getting tired," Asher said. The dullness in his eyes had returned as he sat back in his chair. It was as if a dark cloud had rolled into the room, turning Asher's happy mood into one that was solemn and grim. Whatever happened between Asher and Rogue wasn't good.

"Asher, can we talk in private?" Rogue asked. Asher nodded and stood. "Follow me to my room."

Jen watched them leave, and the only thing she could think about was how Asher hadn't glanced in her direction.

Not even once.

CHAPTER THIRTEEN

Nightmare

It wasn't like Jen to eavesdrop on a private conversation, but she found herself far enough away from Asher's door to keep it from materializing and close enough to hear what was being said. For a while, neither Asher nor Rogue spoke. Jen began to wonder if they planned to just sit and stare at each other. Rogue finally spoke, just when Jen was about to walk away.

"What happened to your head?"

"Long story," Asher said. "I'll be okay in a few days." More silence stretched on. "You look different."

"A lot has happened since the military," Rogue admitted.

"Why did you go AWOL?"

"I—"

"Why did you leave me?" Asher asked, cutting her off.

"If I hadn't, we would've gotten caught. You could've gotten kicked out of the military. You worked so hard to get to where you got—"

"I would've thrown it all away for you," Asher said, raising his voice. Jen almost felt his pain, like his heart had shattered a thousand times over in that moment.

"That's why I left," Rogue whispered. "I couldn't be the reason you failed. I couldn't be the reason I failed either. What is a relationship when you can't be open about it? It hurt, knowing I couldn't just fall into your arms when I wanted to. I suffered as much as I loved. If I would've stayed, we would've eventually hated each other. I didn't want my first words to you to come true."

Jen thought back to what Rogue had said to him the first day. Are you the man I'm going to spend the rest of my days here hating? She understood what Rogue meant; she understood why Rogue left.

"Why did you come here today?" Asher asked, disguising the

hurt in his voice, trying to become nonchalant, but Jen could tell he didn't quite pull it off.

"Curiosity," Rogue said. "I missed you. I wanted to know that you were okay, that you'd moved on."

"Have you? Moved on?"

"No," Rogue said. "I tried to. I tried to forget everything. I created a new image for myself, took myself off the market. Look at me. Do I look like the kind of girl men chase after? No, they all stay away, and that's how I prefer it."

"You're still beautiful to me," Asher said. "No matter how much you tried to change your image, you're still Rose Hills." More silence filled the air.

"Do you like her?"

"Who?" Asher asked.

"That girl, Jen," Rogue said. "Why is she here? Why did you agree to help her?"

"I don't know. I was bored with life and wanted an adventure. It's not every day that someone comes through the portal saying they're from the past. She was a damsel in distress. What can I say? I took the bait."

"You never answered my first question," Rogue reminded him. "Do you like Jen?"

"Why does it matter? You left."

"I left to protect you, because I loved you. I still do. It's why I'm here."

"What is it that you want from me, Rogue?" Asher asked, and the familiarity of his impatience comforted Jen.

"I just want to see how the cards will fall, since we have no restrictions, nothing to keep us in hiding," she said, and Asher sighed deeply. "Look, I know it's a lot to take in. I know you probably feel you can't trust me, and that's okay. I'm not looking for an answer right now. Just let me stay around for a while. Let me prove that I want this: us."

"You want to stay around here, as in live in my condo?" Asher asked.

"I could stay in one of your guest rooms," Rogue said, sounding cheerful. "I could even be of assistance with whatever you're helping Jen with. You're injured; I could help you get better. And in the meantime, I'll give you time to decide what you want to do about us."

"Us," Asher repeated as if testing the word out. "Fine, Rogue. Prove to me why you belong here. In my heart."

"I will," she said, and the promise was clear as day in her voice.

Jen heard all she needed to. She backed away from the wall and almost screamed at Lark's close proximity. She hadn't realized he stood next to her with his ear pressed against the wall. He looked up at her and tsk'd.

"Asher's got it bad," Lark said. "Did you here that? She's got it bad too. I bet they'll get back together."

"He won't take her back," Jen told Lark, walking away from the door. Her words hadn't come out very convincing, and she wondered if Lark could hear her doubt. "If there's one thing I learned about Asher, it's that he's headstrong. He would've cut ties off from her after she broke his heart. He wouldn't let her back in."

"Did you see how he looked at her? Like I said, he's got it bad."

Jen wanted to change the subject, feeling annoyed that she was like a columnist in a gossip blog talking about Asher's love life. "How are you feeling? You did get beat up today."

"Surprisingly good," Lark said. "I cleaned myself up and took some pain pills. I've been a lot worse."

"Well, get some good sleep so you'll feel better. And Lark, I'm glad you're okay. Things could've been a lot worse," she said, and stalked off to her room.

Jen went to sleep that night with a heavy heart. She couldn't wrap her mind around the way Rogue had randomly popped up in their time of need. It seemed too much of a coincidence that she just happened to be at both the portal and the pizza parlor. Jen couldn't get a good read on Rogue. One minute, she was kicking butt in the alley and the next she was girlish around Asher. Either Rogue had multiple personalities or she was just really happy to be reunited with him.

Jen had a feeling Rogue was going to slow down their mission, and a part of her feared Asher would give up on their mission altogether. Asher didn't need a distraction—he needed to stay focused. Rogue was already trying to fit herself back into his life. She offered to help Jen and the mission, but that was Jen's decision, and she didn't want Rogue to tag along, even if she could fight.

Maybe she was jealous and that's why she was trying to find something wrong with Rogue, even though she couldn't figure out why she was jealous in the first place. But not wanting Rogue around without a good enough reason made her feel selfish, as if she wanted to keep Asher and Lark to herself to help find her father and once the mission was complete, she would return to her normal life without one look back. She didn't know why she had reservations and wanted to just forget about it all, even if it was only for a night. Jen lay in bed, tossing and turning, until she was finally able to push away her confused feelings and focus on sleep. Only then, was she able to drift off into a deep slumber.

Jen was walking down a dark hallway. The lights above flickered in and out, creating shadows in corners, making the white walls look dark and haunted. She heard weeping down the hall and was trying urgently to see who was making the noise.

Jen reached a closed wooden door, one that looked exactly like the one to her bedroom. She felt as if she was having déjà vu. She hesitated a second before opening the door and was surprised to see her room materialize before her. Jen's father sat on her bed, holding the old fairy tale book he used to read to her as a child.

"Daddy?" Jen called. She couldn't believe her eyes. Her father looked different from how she remembered him. Specks of gray colored his dark brown hair, and wrinkles had formed around his eyes...eyes that looked hopeless and desperate. He turned around to her and his face lit up at the sight of her.

"Jen," he said, standing up with a pained expression, as if his heart almost stopped at her sight. She rushed into his arms, taking in his familiar scent. He pulled away first, cupping her face in his hands. "Where are you?"

"I'm right here," she said, holding onto him as dearly as he had with her.

"No, you aren't," he said. "You're not really here."

"Yes, I am, Dad." She pulled him into a hug again. Glancing down at her bed, she saw the fairy tale book. It had flipped open to a page Jen barely remembered. The page looked like a drawing of a floor plan, something completely unique. She didn't know what it was, but she knew it wasn't part of the original book. Had her father shown her that page as a child? "What is that?"

"There was a reason I read you the same fairy tale over and over. Do you remember what I told you to never forget?" Mr. Kallis desperately searched her eyes. "Jen? Can you hear me? You're starting to disappear."

"What?" Jen didn't know what he meant. She was still there with him, holding onto him.

"Listen closely. The book I used to read you. Remember what I told you. It's very important." Her dad sighed and cupped Jen's cheek affectionately. "I can't feel you anymore."

"Dad, I'm right here, I'm—" Jen began, but her words were cut short as she watched her father start to fade out. His hands were the first to completely disappear, followed by his arms, and then his shoulders. Jen tried to hold him even tighter, but it felt as if she was holding air. She now understood what he meant. "Don't go, Dad. Tell me where you are. Tell me how to find you!"

"Jen—"

"Please help me find you," Jen cried, but the last of her father had disappeared, leaving her to deal with her pain alone. She collapsed on the floor, panting and crying hysterically. It was the second time her father had disappeared on her.

"Jen!" She glanced up, still hearing his voice. She quickly stood, looking around her room for the source of the noise.

"Daddy!"

"Jen!"

The dream vanished as if it had never been. Jen felt hands around her shoulders, shaking her awake. She sat up in a fit, pushing the hands away while gasping for air. She tried to get out of bed, but those same hands pressed her back down. Jen opened her eyes and found Asher standing over her with concern written on his face. Lark stood behind Asher, with a similar expression, and then she saw Rogue, who stood in the background watching quietly.

Jen was at her breaking point. She pushed Asher away with as much force as possible. She couldn't breathe and needed air. She felt as if her lungs were collapsing inside her chest. The only thing Jen could focus on was getting home and finding that book. It was more important to her than the air she barely breathed in. She had never had a panic attack, but she was sure that was what she was experiencing. She was trying to remember what her father frantically wanted her to know. What had he told her as a child? Images of her childhood came rushing back, momentarily distracting her from Asher and the others in the room...

She was six years old again, and her father had just finished reading her the last part of the story.

"Come on, Daddy. One more chapter!" little Jen begged, earning a smile from her father.

"How about I tell you the story about why this book is important, and then afterward you go to sleep," Mr. Kallis said, laughing as Jen furiously nodded her head. "There once lived a book that held the secrets of a thousand worlds, and it was entrusted to a smart little girl named Jen to guard for all of her days to come."

"Why is she guarding it?" Jen asked.

"One day, her daddy is going to need her to bring him that book and she has to be ready. Only then, will she fully understand the importance of this book."

"Is she a warrior princess, Daddy?"

"She's my angel." He smiled and tucked Jen into bed. "Never forget, my love. Never forget."

Jen snapped back to reality, having finally understood what her dad needed. She tried to push against Asher, who kept her pinned down on the bed.

"Stop fighting me," Asher grunted, keeping her restrained.

"Calm down. It was just a dream."

"No," Jen cried, caught between her dream and reality. She fought even harder to break away from Asher. "Daddy...the book."

"Jen, calm down!"

"I need it," Jen continued. "I need to go back. He needs it!"

"That's it." Asher picked Jen up from the bed and carried her to the bathroom. He sat her in the shower and turned the faucet on. Jen cried out as the cold water began to soak through her hysteria. At first, she fought to get up, but Asher kept her planted firmly on the ground, getting himself wet in the process.

Jen hated him—hated how he yelled at her so harshly and then ignored her for Rogue and yet tried to come to her rescue. She'd rather it was Lark showing concern, not him. She knew Asher didn't care about her. She was only a burden to him.

"I hate you! Why do you care?"

"Jen—"

"Just go!" she screamed over his voice. "Lark can help me. Just go. Leave me alone."

Jen crawled to the farthest corner of the bathroom and brought her knees to her chest, shaking wildly. She could see the hurt in Asher's eyes, but she didn't care. She didn't need him to comfort her. Lark gently pushed Asher aside and kneeled down to where she rocked back and forth.

"Are you okay? Can you tell me what happened in your dream?" Lark's concern made her cry even more. She shook her head.

"Make them leave first. I only want to see you."

Lark turned around to where Asher stood, staring at Jen helplessly. Rogue stood quietly in the doorway, watching with an unreadable expression. "Can you two leave?" Asher nodded, breathing deeply and closing his eyes. When he opened them, the hurt look had gone, and he nonchalantly followed Rogue out of the bathroom.

Lark waited until the door disappeared before turning back around to Jen. "Talk to me."

"I had a dream, but it felt real. My father was in my room, holding this book he used to read to me as a child. He'd aged; he looked how he would look now if I'd seen him in real life. How is that possible?" Jen paused, catching her breath. "He had to be there."

"The brain is a powerful organ. It can make dreams seem real, and it can certainly age a person, based on what you think they'd look like older."

"But he told me to bring him this book he used to read to me as a child," Jen argued.

"Did he ever say that to you?" Lark asked. "As a child?"

"Yes," Jen began. "When I was a child. He told me to protect it."

"So then the dream was an actual memory being played out. Your father wasn't really there."

"But I'd noticed something about the book I hadn't seen before. There was strange writing on one of its pages. I couldn't make out what it said and don't even know if I can now. How could I see something I'd never seen before?"

"Maybe you had and just don't remember. You were a kid. Maybe these recent events triggered something inside of you to begin to remember the importance of this book," Lark continued to explain, trying to console her.

"Lark, I need to get that book. I need to time travel go back to 2016 and get that book!"

"That would require opening a portal, and we don't have a way to do that."

"But you're a genius."

"Even if I could, it would be risky. Opening the portal would be like telling the Enforcement, 'Hey, we're over here, come get us!' They'd be able to trace the exact location the portal had opened up to. We'd light up like Christmas lights on their radar. We'd be caught within minutes."

"But I need to get the book."

"Jen, it's just a book, and you were just having a bad dream. You've gone through a lot. Now I know a lot about everything, and I know for a fact that your dreams are just your subconscious trying to work its problems out. Who's to say that the writing you saw is even in the book? It doesn't even make sense.

Your father doesn't know you're here. Don't allow a dream to make you delusional."

"Let me guess, you got that straight from a phycology book. These things really happened. My father told me to protect that book," Jen argued.

"Why would he be so concerned with a book?"

"I don't know, but I'm going to find out, with or without your help." Jen sighed and relaxed her head against the shower walls. Her heart rate had finally started to become normal, and she felt sleep wanting to settle in, again. The fit she'd thrown was wearing her down by the second. Lark noticed and helped her get to her feet. He handed her a towel and began walking her back to her bedroom. As Jen exited the bathroom, she saw Asher to her right, who had most likely been eavesdropping on her conversation with Lark. She didn't even bother to look him in the eye as Lark led her to her room. She'd had enough of Asher for one day.

Once Jen was alone in her room, she stripped out of her soaking wet jumpsuit, clumsily dried off, and threw on a nightgown. She looked over at the alarm clock on her bed and saw it was only three in the morning. It meant she had enough time to sleep off all of her stress, and she could only hope she'd feel better by the morning. Sleep overtook Jen the moment her head hit the pillow.

"I figured you'd be eavesdropping." Lark walked toward the living room couch, feeling Asher follow behind. Rogue wasn't with him and must have gone to the other guest room to go back to sleep. It didn't bother Lark that Asher hadn't offered him the guest room on the first day; Lark didn't mind sleeping on the couch.

"What is this book she's talking about?" Asher asked.

"So you were eavesdropping," Lark said.

"Wouldn't you?" Asher said, looking tired. He rubbed his eyes in frustration. "Did you see how she just rejected me like that?"

"What did you expect?" Lark asked, pushing his glasses farther up on his face. "The first thing you did when we came back was yell at her, and then you completely ignored her. You thought she'd open up to you first?"

Asher sat back in his chair in defeat. Lark had a point. He had been hard on her lately. Not to mention how preoccupied he'd been with Rogue when Jen was the one who was helping nurse him back to health, even if her methods were torturous. A part of him began to wonder if Rogue played an even bigger part in Jen's attitude toward him than what he'd originally thought, but he quickly dismissed the idea. Jen wasn't the jealous type. She couldn't care less that his ex-girlfriend had popped back in the picture when he'd dedicated himself to helping her.

Rogue came out of her guest bedroom and smiled at him. "You should get some rest, Ash." She was right. Asher had a head injury and a stab wound. He needed to be careful so that he could heal properly, but he was on edge. There was something about seeing Jen so defeated and broken.

He went back to his bedroom and tried to force himself to sleep, but it was difficult. He lay awake, wondering what he was going to do about the situation with Rogue and also questioning his relationship with Jen. It was apparent she'd put some distance between the two of them. Asher only hoped the distance would fade as her dream had faded. He hoped tomorrow would tell a different tale. Eventually, he put his worries to rest and fell asleep.

In the morning, Asher heard the clinking sound of a plate being set down on his nightstand. He rolled onto his side, opening his eyes to see a pair of hands and a bowl of oatmeal. He smiled, glad that Jen had snapped out of her bad mood and decided to bring him food. He could get used to her feeding him every day.

"Good morning."

Asher froze and slowly lifted his eyes to meet Rogue's smiling face. He'd almost forgotten she was there. His mind raced, seeing her staring down at him with love and admiration. His Rogue, the girl he once had loved more than anything in the world—she was with him. She was familiar and warm, and yet he was disappointed. He'd been expecting Jen. Asher hid his disappointment as he sat up, smiling warmly at her as she sat on the edge of his bed.

Asher wasn't too happy with her black cropped hair. He preferred it long and blonde, the way he remembered her, but he also appreciated her way of expression. She wasn't innocent anymore. Whatever she'd gone through had changed her.

Asher did, however, like the blue shirt and skirt she has chosen from the guest wardrobe. He had always kept standard size men's and women's clothing in case he had overnight guests. The outfit she'd chosen reminded him of something her old self would have worn. It was probably why he had picked it out to begin with. The only thing missing was her long blonde hair.

"How did you sleep?" she asked, pushing a loose strand of black hair behind her ear.

"Good enough," Asher said, stretching. He took the time to study her soft features, familiarizing himself with her again. He'd never thought he'd see her again, and there she sat, almost the way he remembered her. It had been a year and a half, but it felt as if only two days had passed since they'd last stolen secret kisses behind the military tank.

Rogue handed Asher the oatmeal and watched him silently as he ate. After a few bites, he looked up at her and laughed.

"What?"

"I miss watching you eat," she said, batting her eyes angelically.

"I miss you watching me eat, except I don't have to scarf it down like I used to."

"Have you thought any more about what we talked about yesterday?" Rogue asked, changing the subject. "About us getting back together?"

Asher sighed, setting his bowl on his lap. "You came at a difficult time," he admitted. "I've committed myself to helping Jen and—"

"You never really answered my question about that. Last night, I asked if you liked her."

"I barely know her."

"You don't rush into a girl's room after her nightmare and play knight in shining armor when you barely know her."

"Are you jealous?" Asher asked cockily. "Because I have another girl in my house that I'm helping out?"

"If she's one of the reasons you're hesitating about getting back together with me, then I'm concerned, but not jealous."

"You walked away from me, you went missing from the military, and you expect that the moment you show up I'm going to drop everything and be with you? It doesn't work that way, Rogue."

"Fine," she sighed. "I'll continue to wait for you. I'll continue to "I haven't kicked you out, have I?"

Just then, Asher's farthest wall started to shift and his door materialized. Jen walked in, carrying a plate of food. Asher could make out his favorite, blueberry waffles. He chuckled to himself, knowing Jen had figured out how to ask Anna about his favorite foods. First it was exactly four grilled cheese sandwiches, then his favorite soup, and now blueberry waffles. He admired the way she paid attention to detail, but he was surprised to see her bringing him anything after last night's episode. This must be her way of making up.

Asher watched as Jen looked up from the waffles and paused. He started to feel weird as she looked from him to Rogue sitting on his bed and back to him again. Jen looked down at the plate, seeming unsure of herself.

"I...umm," Jen began. "I thought you'd be hungry, but I see you've already eaten."

"Blueberry waffles are my favorite," Asher said, trying to make light of the situation. He didn't want to upset her, seeing how fragile she was. Rogue snapped her head in his direction, but he ignored her.

"I'll just set this on your nightstand then." Jen walked over to his nightstand and put the plate down. Her eyes glanced at the bandage on his head. "Do you need me to change your bandages?"

"I'll do that," Rogue spoke up, not giving Asher the chance to answer. Jen nodded and walked out.

Asher had to bite back the urge to call after her. He was still concerned about Jen's nightmare and wanted to talk to her. He didn't like hearing about her dream secondhand and wanted the full details.

Rogue began laughing the moment Jen had left. "Did you see how pathetic she looked? Do you even like blueberry waffles or were you being nice?"

Asher set the half-eaten bowl of oatmeal down and grabbed the waffles, stuffing his mouth just to prove a point to Rogue. If she really knew him well, she'd know he loved blueberry waffles and had only eaten her oatmeal out of kindness. Rogue frowned and stood up, grabbing the bowl of oatmeal.

"Well, I'll leave you to your waffles."

She quickly left the room.

Jen stood in the kitchen, eating two plain waffles while leaning against the island. She'd still been shaken up over her dream, but the sight of Rogue sitting next to Asher on his bed made her momentarily forget it. She didn't even know why she'd brought him food. He was always rude, and mean. And his ignoring her after Rogue showed up had been the cherry on top.

Rogue entered the kitchen with the bowl of oatmeal, and even though she was dressed in feminine clothes, she still looked rough around the edges and walked like a tomboy. She placed the bowl of oatmeal in the sink and turned toward Jen. Jen could have sworn she'd seen something menacing cross over Rogue's eyes before she smiled.

"Thanks for being concerned about Asher," Rogue said. "I'm not sure why you felt the need to bring him food when he's obviously quite capable of walking around his own house."

"Then why did you bring him the oatmeal?" Jen asked, annoyed by Rogue's hypocritical comment. Rogue smiled again, but it looked forced to Jen. The true Rogue was the girl back in the alley: the one dressed in black, the one with a killer right hook. The Rogue that stood before her now was dressed in a cute blue shirt and skirt, smiling sweetly as if she were running for Miss America. But Jen was catching little moments where Rogue's true colors came out. Something wasn't right about her.

"I'm his girlfriend," Rogue said, mimicking Jen by leaning against the island in the same way.

"I thought he hadn't given you an answer," Jen said, regretting her words as soon as Rogue frowned.

"That was a private conversation. Were you eavesdropping?" Just then, Lark walked into the kitchen, stopping Rogue mid-sentence with his presence. He was completely oblivious to the tension in the kitchen as he looked at them with a goofy expression.

"Good morning. I'm hungry," he said, walking to the sink. His eyes lit up as he saw the oatmeal sitting there, and picked the bowl up. Lark lifted a spoon full of oatmeal to his nose, sniffed it, decided it was good, and took a bite. He then moaned and left the kitchen with the bowl in his hand. Jen would have laughed had her mood not been dampened by Rogue's presence. She also didn't want to discuss eavesdropping on their conversation, so she quickly changed the subject.

"You should really go clean Asher's wound," she said, meeting Rogue's eyes with a challenge. "Or should I?"

"Thanks for reminding me," Rogue said with a harsh tone that contradicted her smile. She swiftly turned and marched out of the kitchen, leaving Jen alone with her sour mood. Jen decided in that moment that she really didn't like Rogue. Not one bit.

CHAPTER FOURTEEN

Distant Memories

Y ou don't see it?" Jen whispered to Lark as they sat on the couch. "There's something off about Rogue."

"You're imagining things," Lark said.

"She's a completely different person now than she was back in the alley," Jen stressed, trying to get Lark to see her point.

"Love can make you do crazy things. Look at how Asher's acting. It's like he turned into a big mush in less than a day. That's love for you."

Jen felt sick to her stomach. "Love doesn't just walk away without an explanation. I overheard how she just left the military."

"You must not know anything about the military. Relationships aren't allowed there. If Asher and Rogue got caught...who knows? But it wouldn't be good. I think she left to save him from being discharged. And, you know, m-maybe she cracked from the pressure of it all and just left."

"What do you know? You're fourteen. You've never even been in love," Jen said, but even her own words sounded stupid to her. Lark may have been fourteen, but he was one mature kid. Sometimes, he seemed even more mature than she was.

"I-I've dated before...possibly...maybe." Lark looked away with reddened cheeks and cleared his throat. "And I'm surprised. Last night, you were so concerned about this dream, and now this morning you can't keep Rogue off your mind. If I didn't know any better, I'd say you were jeal—"

"I've been avoiding the dream," Jen admitted, cutting Lark off. "Every time I think about it, I feel like I'm going to have a panic attack. When I woke up this morning, I lay in bed for half an hour replaying the dream over and over in my mind. I feel helpless and don't know what to do. Lark," Jen turned toward him, watching him stare back at her with raised eyebrows.

"What if my dream was real? What if my father needs me to get that book? I need you to help me open a portal."

"I've already told you, even if I opened it, we'd get caught. You can't just open portals around here."

"I have to try. I just know, somehow, deep inside, that there's something in that book and my father needs it."

"Okay," Lark said, looking uneasy. "I'm sure I can find a portal and figure out a way to open it. But I won't do it unless we have a bulletproof plan and won't get caught."

"That's where I come into play," Asher said.

Jen almost jumped out of her seat, not realizing Asher was standing behind them. She wondered how long he'd been standing there and if he'd overheard the conversation about Rogue. Asher took his usual seat in his plush chair and studied Jen.

She felt awkward as he assessed her and wondered why he was looking at her so intently. Then it dawned on her how she had shunned him after her dream last night and then brought him breakfast as if the night before hadn't happened. He was probably trying to see which side he was going to face. Jen didn't really know herself.

"I helped you escape when you came through the portals the first time," Asher said. "I can help you escape again. If anyone knows how to outsmart the system, it's the person who's close to the top of that system."

"Asher has a point," Lark agreed. "We need to figure out the best location for this to happen and map it out. We need a place where the police will be thrown off. I can find a good location. Asher, you just need to make sure you're healthy enough for this."

"I'll be fine," he said. "I've had tougher challenges in worse conditions. I actually know a spot we can go to. It's deep in the subways of New York. Some of those subways are so deep, it'll take minutes for the portal opening to pick up on any radar, and even when the police pick it up, they'll have a challenge getting to the location. It'll buy us at least five minutes, which is all we need. Leave the details to me, Lark, and worry about opening the portal."

"How do you open it, anyway?" Jen asked.

"The portal is a cubed puzzle. It's one of the most complicated puzzles there is, and that's why many people can't open one," Lark said.

"A cube?" Jen asked. "I don't understand."

"It's a metal cube that opens up when you adjust it. If you open it correctly, it transforms into a large metal frame that becomes the portal. It's like the ancient movie Hellraiser and how they open the cube to hell. I'm pretty sure whoever invented the portal was a big Hellraiser fan." Lark laughed. "It's genius actually. But the key is to opening what's inside the cube, which is too complex to explain. It's like opening Pandora's box. However, once the portal closes, the cube dissolves into nothing. There were only a few hundred cubes made, making time travel a rarity. Eventually, thieves got their hands on a lot of the cubes. I've heard there are only a few left."

Jen nodded, understanding what he meant. "So how do we get this cube?"

"I know a man who owns a pawn shop. He came to me one night and said a strange man dropped a cube off without an explanation. The man must not have known what it was. Anyway, he decided not to sell it, knowing it was a portal. He reached out to me to see if I knew how to open it. Of course I said no. I wasn't going to do anything so openly illegal.

"His name is Larry Wright. He's a big, powerful black man and is someone we shouldn't cross. He has a lot of valuables in his pawn shop and a top security system to protect those valuables. I should be able to dismantle the security system, but then we'd have to get past his dogs."

"Dogs?" Jen swallowed hard.

"He has three pit bulls, all trained to kill," Lark said.

"I can take care of them," Asher said with a cocky smile.

He must be healing, Jen thought. Back to his usual cocky self.

"Planning something without me?"

Jen snapped her head to her left as she watched Rogue walk out of the guest room. "Asher, you should invest in soundproof walls. You can hear every conversation being held. Even the whispered ones." Rogue looked pointedly at Jen, which made her wonder if she had overheard her conversation with Lark.

"We were discussing opening the portals," Lark said, scooting over so that Rogue could sit on the couch.

"As I've heard," Rogue said, taking a seat. "It's a stupid idea—too risky, especially if you're doing it based on a dream."

"No one even invited you, so I'm not sure why you feel the need to add your two cents," Jen spat, which made Rogue smirk.

"Trust me, Jen, my opinion is worth more than two cents. And I can assure you that you'd want my help."

"How so?" Jen asked.

"I'm a fighter, or have you forgotten that quickly?" Rogue asked. Jen wondered if it was obvious that the two girls didn't like each other. She looked at Lark, who didn't seem to notice the animosity. She was too afraid to meet Asher's eyes for fear of what they'd reveal. She looked back at Rogue. "You'll need both Asher and me to protect you. What happens if you run into the police after opening the portals? What if something goes wrong? You think the three of you could fight off a few dozen trained men? You've got to be kidding me."

"She's right," Asher said.

Jen kept her eyes trained on Rogue, not daring to even look in Asher's direction. She wondered if he knew how hard she was trying to avoid eye contact. Jen wanted to punch him for agreeing with Rogue. Rogue's presence wasn't part of the plan; she wasn't supposed to be a factor.

"We need as many people on our side as we can get, and there aren't very many people you can trust in Blue City," Asher continued. "If you want to find your father, you have to stop being so stubborn. Rogue goes with us."

"Fine," Jen said, not willing to argue it. She'd lose in the end anyway. In her eyes, Asher was doing exactly what she feared. He was putting Rogue before her by including her in their mission and taking her side in their debate. It was only a matter of time before he forgot Jen completely.

Jen told herself it didn't matter; she'd be leaving soon anyway. She'd be home with her father and mother, living her life, and forgetting all about Blue City. Even as she thought it, she knew it wasn't true. How could she ever forget those who helped her find her father? Okay, so maybe she wouldn't forget all about Blue City, either. But she needed to stop thinking about the future and worry about the "now." The mission was what she had to focus on, not her own childish thoughts and jealousy. None of that really mattered in the end. She shouldn't have been so concerned about Asher and his ex-girlfriend, and yet she had been.

Why? Did she like Asher? Asher, who was cocky, egotistical, rude, apathetic, and extremely militant? And yet he was the same Asher who had offered to help her, even if it would cost him his military position. He was the one who had been beside her the moment she woke up from her dream. He was the one who had chosen her blueberry waffles over Rogue's oatmeal, and yes, she'd noticed that fact when Rogue had entered the kitchen with a defeated look. Asher was also going to get Jen to her father, and that was the icing on the cake.

Jen realized she'd turned his negatives into positives. Sure, Asher had his flaws, but he also had those very same qualities that had made her begin to like him in the past four days. I do like him, Jen finally admitted to herself. A weight lifted off her chest as she allowed herself to accept that fact. She liked Asher, and it was a complicated, crazy kind of thing. She liked him in the midst of chaos and fear. She liked him even when he liked someone else. I must be crazy. Liking Asher is pointless. I'll be going home soon.

Jen absentmindedly allowed her eyes to drift up to Asher and found him staring at her with an unreadable expression. She didn't pull her eyes away once she realized she was staring back at him. Instead, she took in the sight of his buzz cut, thick, fierce eyebrows, long lashes, full lips, and dazzling blue eyes. She'd never allowed herself to get lost in his looks, for fear that she'd never find her way back out, and in that moment her fear came true. She couldn't look away from him.

How would she be able to leave Blue City and never see that face again? How could she return to her normal life as if he didn't exist? Jen wanted to have more fights with him. She wanted to force him to eat more meals. She wanted to bump heads with him and get angry. She wanted to wake up next to him after a bad dream. It was those small things that made her like him, and as she stared at him, she knew she couldn't walk away that easily.

Asher's lips twitched, as if he was fighting back a smile. Jen realized how silly she must have looked, staring at him the way she had been. She quickly looked away, trying to hide her embarrassment.

"Asher, I want to see how far you've healed. Then I'll be able to determine when we can make the trip. My best guess would be a week, but I have to see the wound," Lark spoke up, and Jen was thankful that he broke the silence.

"Okay, but I think it'll be a lot sooner than a week," Asher said. Jen dared to glance at him and noticed he still stared at her with that same unreadable expression.

"Asher," Rogue called, stealing his attention away from Jen. He looked up to where Rogue stood by his side and smiled. "I'll need to leave for the day. I have to go home and grab some equipment that I'll need if we're going to do this soon. Can I take your hover?"

"Sure," Asher said, absentmindedly handing her the keys in his pocket. Jen noticed that his mind seemed to be in a different place, even though he spoke to her. Rogue smiled down at him appreciatively, bent down, and kissed him on the cheek. When she rose, her eyes spotted Jen and she smiled innocently. "I'll see you guys later."

Asher's eyes followed behind Rogue as she headed out the door leading to his garage.

"Well, we have a plan," Lark said, continuing the previous conversation. "Get the cube, open the portal, get the book, and then find Frank Hoggs for answers. Sounds harder than it looks." Lark laughed and then looked at Asher. "Well, are you ready for me to clean the wound?"

"I can do it," Jen said. "I'm familiar with his wounds; I can tell how far it's healed. You can just start working on the plan with the portal." Jen stood up, signaling for Asher to follow her to his bedroom.

Asher followed Jen into his bedroom and took a seat on his bed as Jen went into his bathroom, grabbing his cleaning supplies and first aid kit. She returned quietly and took a seat next to him. Asher noticed how she avoided his eyes, the way she always did when she had something on her mind. He could see right through her. It wasn't like Jen did a good job of hiding her feelings.

Especially how she felt toward Rogue. Asher wasn't naïve. He could tell Jen was slightly insecure and felt intimidated by Rogue's presence. He was beginning to wonder if she liked him. He'd first wondered it when she started acting differently toward him once Rogue showed up and then he'd noticed the way she'd been staring at him in the living room as if she wanted to declare her love right then and there.

Asher had to admit, it was very cute. She was cute. But she shouldn't be falling for a guy like him. His heart still hadn't healed from Rogue. In fact, he still loved her very much. He was seriously contemplating taking her back. Not only that, Jen would be leaving soon, and Asher couldn't risk liking a girl who was only in his life temporarily. It was his duty to remind Jen of this, before her feelings got too deep.

Jen removed Asher's bandage around his waist and examined his wound. "Wow, this is healing really quickly."

"The military gives us a shot that makes us stronger and also helps us heal from injuries quicker. It's actually hard to get a hold of here, but being in the military has its perks. We're not supposed to talk about it, but I guess it doesn't matter if you know, since you're leaving soon."

"Right," Jen said, as she began to clean his wound. Asher had gotten used to the sting of the alcohol and didn't flinch when she pressed the cloth to his raw skin. The stab wound was now an inch deep and only hurt him when he moved a certain way. His head injury only gave him a slight headache from time to time. He was sure one more night of sleep was all he'd need.

Asher watched Jen as she cleaned his wound. She really was beautiful. Her brown curls fell in her face, masking her eyes; her nose had the cutest point; and her lips were full and pink. In another life, he would have fallen for her, helplessly, but they weren't in that life, they were in Blue City. He had to tell her that she shouldn't like him.

"So, I was thinking—" Asher began.

"You and Rogue look nice together," Jen said, cutting him off.

"Excuse me?" Asher lowered his eyes in confusion. He tried to see Jen's expression, but her curls masked her eyes. He wished she'd lift her head.

"I think you two should work it out," she added, which continued to surprise Asher. She was definitely a woman of many faces. Was it a front? Was that really what she wanted? "I can tell you love her. That kind of love can't be ignored."

"Oh," Asher said. He definitely didn't expect that, and her declaration put him on edge. It was okay for him to tell Jen not to even think about falling for him, but for her to tell him to date Rogue? It felt like a slap in his face. She'd rejected him first. "Well, how do you even know she's what I want?"

Jen looked up at him, smiling sincerely. "It's all in the eyes, in the way you look at her. She's the only one who can pull your attention away from whatever you're focused on. She's the one who you'd help without a moment's thought."

"I helped you," Asher pointed out.

"And why? Because you genuinely wanted to or because you wanted the challenge?" Jen laughed. "And what do I have to do with it anyway? It's almost as if you're arguing against what I'm saying, that you should be with her." Asher was at a loss for words. Jen continued cleaning his wound, not minding his silence. "She loves you. The girl I saw in the alley, she changed the moment she saw you. At first I thought it was because she was a fake person, but I understand now. Losing love makes people dull; it kills something inside of them. Rogue, she was dead in that alley. You were dead too, Asher. When I first met you, I saw something sad and terrible in your eyes. I didn't understand why until now. You were hurting, and so was she in that alley. But now, you both have bloomed.

"I must admit, I was a bit concerned about her, but I realized I was just jealous. I was afraid you'd break your promise to me and run off with her into la-la land. I was being selfish, only worrying about myself and my mission, and not what you or even Rogue needed. So I figured I'd check your wound and give you some good advice. It's the least I can do for you helping me. Anyway, you should tell Rogue that you'll take her back."

Asher pulled away from Jen, turning his back on her. Why did she say such things? Things that confused him about his own feelings? Did he truly want Rogue? Sure, he loved her, but was she what he truly wanted? He turned back toward Jen, staring into her soft, hazel eyes, and he felt the urge to kiss her. Kiss her? Asher tried his hardest to mask his confusion. Kiss Jen? Jen who was ancient meat? Jen who was probably friends with his great, great, great, great grandmother in the past? Jen who knew nothing about his world and who was naïve, jealous, entitled, and headstrong? No. No way...just no. And yet, he felt something toward her. He wasn't quite sure what that something was, but it was something. But he couldn't afford to figure it out; he already was confused about Rogue. He closed his eyes and swallowed his feelings.

"Thanks," he told Jen. "I'll definitely figure things out with Rogue."

Jen nodded. She moved up to his head wound and examined it. She welcomed the silence, thankful to be left alone with her thoughts. She'd said the right thing. She wasn't going to be upset by Rogue's presence, and she only wanted Asher to be happy. She'd bottled in her own feelings in the process if she had to. She didn't speak again until she was done wrapping his head.

"Your head looks fine now," she said, and stood up. "I'm going to go update Lark." Jen quickly left before he could say anything. Asher sighed and flopped back down on his bed. His thoughts immediately went to Rogue and a distant memory...

Asher couldn't believe how beautiful Rogue was. She had the perfect athletic body; long, blonde hair; and was fearless against men. She was also witty, smart, and fought hard for what she wanted. He smiled as he watched her running with her troop in the field as the blazing sun beat down on her bare, tanned arms. Her eyes shifted toward him, as if she knew he'd been staring, and she beamed. Asher was what she wanted, and she'd let him know it the night before as they sat in the field, staring at the stars.

Asher's heart raced as he stared back at her. In fact, his heart had been racing since the moment she confessed her feelings to him. He'd been the idiot and said nothing, but Rogue wasn't insecure. She didn't need his declaration. She knew she had him.

After their drill, Rogue ran up to him, hitting him playfully on the arm.

"If you stand around staring at me during drill, people will know that you like me, sir," Rogue said, earning her his biggest grin.

"We can't have that happening, can we, sergeant?" Asher asked.

"I knew you liked me, sir," she said, catching on to his words. "Even though you didn't say anything."

"Well, sergeant, there isn't anything I can do about that, can I?"

"Yes, you can, sir," Rogue said, giving him a mysterious, sexy look that made him want to pull her close and kiss her. "Don't ask, don't tell. It could be our secret."

Asher smirked, liking the sound of that. "And what if we get caught?"

"We won't. I'm good at hiding things. Remember that."

"Oh, I'll remember," Asher said, loving her mischievous grin and the way she bit down on her lip before walking back toward her troop.

It was a sweet memory, one he'd never forgotten, but somehow sweet memories were always followed by bad ones. Asher began to recall the day Rogue had gone missing from the military when his holo-phone buzzed on his nightstand. He quickly picked it up, realizing his father was calling, and removed the bandage from his head. He hit the talk button, watching as the holo-phone floated in midair. His father appeared before his eyes, as regal as ever. Asher displayed his practiced emotionless expression as his father's cold eyes bore into him. Truth was, the emotions Asher really felt were fear and obedience to his father.

"I haven't spoken with you in almost a week," Asher's father barked. "You're to report to me twice a week."

"Sorry, Fath...commander." Asher almost forgot he was supposed to address his father formally. "I've been busy trying to solve the mystery of the portal opening."

"So I've heard," his father said, lowering his eyes. "You're doing a terrible job. The criminal has yet to be caught."

"I'm only keeping an eye out. It's the police's job to search for the criminal, not mine."

"First you stated that you were busy trying to solve the mystery and now you're saying you're just keeping an eye out. Your story isn't adding up," Asher's father said with lowered, fierce brows. "What is it you're really up to? Do I need to watch you more closely?"

"Father..." Asher corrected himself. "Commander, I've been searching. I only downplayed my actions because you were suggesting I wasn't doing a good job. I assure you, my duties as a commander come first, and I won't take advantage of the position."

"In three weeks, you will physically report to my office," his father stated, as if he hadn't heard Asher's previous words. "You will be commander over a new boot camp here in Japani. When we meet, I will give you more details. Understood?"

"Yes, sir." Asher responded immediately but felt a sense of panic rise in his chest. What if he hadn't found Jen's father within that timeframe? What would he do? "I will do as I was trained."

"Good." Asher's father lowered his eyes again, making Asher wonder what he was thinking. His father was a hard man to read, which taught Asher how to mask his own emotions. "You are dismissed," the commander said before disappearing. Asher's phone dropped into his lap as the screen turned black. Sighing, Asher lay back against his headboard and covered his face with his hands.

His brain was full of problems—portals, girls, geniuses, enemies, and now his job. He could only hope he'd get Jen and her father safely home within three weeks. If not, he'd have to tell Jen he could no longer help her. Asher didn't want to get ahead of himself, thinking the worse, so he sat up, pulled out a piece of paper and pen from the drawer of his nightstand, and began writing down their plan to get the cube from Larry Wright.

CHAPTER FIFTEEN

Larry's Pawn Shop

Larry's Pawn Shop sat on the corner of a dark and deserted road. The blue street lights ended a few miles away, stopping at the edge of the city's limits. The pawn shop had once sat in the heart of the city, but had suffered many burglaries, making Larry move it to the farthest corners. Many thieves wouldn't venture so far out to steal from his store. Due to the move, there were fewer burglaries, and he'd begun to loosen up on security.

Jen, Asher, Lark, and Rogue stood outside the pawn shop, talking quietly among themselves. It was Asher's idea that they all dressed in black to draw less attention to themselves. Asher wore black slacks, a black turtleneck, and combat boots. He wore gloves to prevent him from leaving fingerprints. Jen looked down at her own gloved hands and silently praised him for the idea. She'd worn a black jumpsuit, similar to the one Rogue wore; however, Jen's hips and butt filled her jumpsuit out, making her look sexy. She'd earned herself an appreciative nod from Lark, which she'd laughed off.

Lark resembled Asher in black slacks and a shirt, but his clothes were a bit too big on him, and he stood there, clumsily pushing up the brim of his glasses.

"Once we're inside, we need to split up," Asher whispered. His eyes were serious and his voice was commanding as if he were speaking to his troops. He stood tall and imposing, ready for the mission that lay ahead of them. "Rogue, you take Lark. Jen will come with me."

"Why in that order?" Rogue asked with a slight frown. Jen could tell Rogue didn't like the idea of her and Asher being teamed together.

"We're experienced, Rogue. Jen and Lark aren't. Would you prefer to have Jen as your partner?" Asher asked. Rogue's eyes cut to Jen quickly, but she said nothing. Asher took that as an answer and nodded. "Very well then, Jen goes with me, and Lark goes with you. Once we're inside, we'll split up and search for the cube. If something goes wrong, whistle loudly. It'll be our distress call. Rogue, you're to protect Lark. We will all make it out alive. Understand?"

"Yes, sir," Rogue answered, standing as rigid as possible and looking straight ahead as if she were still in the military. Jen wanted to laugh at her.

"Larry has a few security guards that patrol every twenty minutes. They should be south of the building and will be standing in this exact spot within fifteen minutes. That means we should get in and out in ten minutes. If we can't find the cube in that amount of time, we abort the mission and try again another day. Understood?"

"Yes," everyone responded. Asher turned to Lark.

"Can you disable the security code?" Lark nodded. "Okay, you have less than a minute to do so." Lark bobbed his head again and quickly got to work near a small box that stuck out of the building. He opened it, revealing different color wires, and started snipping some of them with a small knife-like object he'd had in his pocket. Lark accomplished the task in less than a minute, stuffing the knife in his pocket and giving a lopsided grin. "All done."

"Let's go," Asher said.

Asher grabbed Jen's hand and began pulling her toward the front door. Jen didn't have to look at Rogue to know she had been staring. Asher pulled Jen to the right, signaling for Rogue and Lark to go left. Asher led Jen down a dark hallway while Rogue and Lark took the front of the store.

"I thought there were supposed to be dogs," Jen said.

"Me too," Asher responded. "Maybe we got lucky."

Asher pulled out a small circular object and sat it on the ground. The ball rolled to the middle of the hallway and beamed a fluorescent light. The dark hallway lit up, but cast odd shadows along the wall. Jen stopped and marveled at the ball, but Asher quickly pulled her forward. He walked to the first door and tried to open it, but it was locked. He pulled out what looked like a small paper clip, twisted it, and picked the lock.

"We're going to search this room. Make sure you put every-thing back the way it was," Asher commanded as they walked inside.

"I'm not stupid," Jen said, walking to her right, seeing a filing cabinet she wanted to search. She heard Asher say something under his breath, but didn't ask what it was. Jen pulled the cabi-net opened and saw nothing but files. She closed it and opened another cabinet, seeing the same thing.

"There's only paper in there, Ancient Meat," Asher said, hav-ing begun searching another cabinet. Jen closed the cabinet and turned toward him.

"You never know." She rolled her eyes and moved over to a stack of shelves, housing different objects. Jen began searching through the shelves, studying objects she'd never seen in her life. She picked up a wooden box that made a beeping noise and quickly set it back down. She didn't really know what to look for, but knew its shape and what it was made of. She hoped that she'd be the one to find it.

"It's not on that shelf," Asher called out. Jen turned toward him, placing her hand on her hip in irritation over his bossiness.

"If you weren't so worried about what I'm doing, we could be halfway through searching this room."

"I'm done searching. It's not here," he said. "Let's go to the next room. We have about seven minutes left." Jen reluctantly nodded and began walking ahead of Asher, entering the hallway first. She walked up to the next door and leaned against the wall with her arms folded. Asher took one look at her and smiled. He shook his head and began working on the lock. Once he was done, he pushed the door open and stepped inside. Jen followed and bumped into his back.

"What the—" Jen looked past him to see why he had stopped, and heard the growl before she saw what made the sound. Jen gasped, grabbing onto the back of Asher's shirt. A few feet ahead of him stood a fierce-looking black pit bull. The dog's eyes were pitch black, and its vicious teeth clamped down in anger as sali-va dripped from his mouth. Asher reached back and squeezed Jen's hand.

"On the count of three, run," he said slowly moving a hand toward his holster. "One..." The dog started to bark as if understanding what they were about to do. "Two..." The dog took a step toward them and growled even louder, ready to attack. "Three."

Jen ran out the door. She slammed into the wall in the hallway and turned around, seeing Asher shut the dog inside the room, just before he slammed against her in the hallway.

Jen's eyes settled on Asher's chest, which was tightly pressed against her own. She looked up to find him looking down at her, breathing just as heavily as she was. Her eyes shifted down to his full, pink lips, which hung slightly open as he panted. She fought back the urge to kiss him and noticed Asher's mouth twitched as if he was fighting back a smile.

"You look like you want to kiss me," he said with a low and husky voice.

"I—" Jen paused as she watched Asher's face turn serious.

He placed a hand above her head to balance himself and began to lower himself toward her lips, as if he were about to kiss her.

Jen stopped breathing as her heart sped up in anticipation. He was now less than an inch away from her burning lips.

"We found the cube," Lark shouted with a light and happy voice. Both Asher and Jen snapped their heads in Lark's direction, seeing him and Rogue standing five feet away. Lark smiled at them, completely oblivious to what they had been about to do. Rogue, on the other hand, burned holes into Jen's eyes.

"What are you two doing?" Rogue asked, her voice deadly low.

"We..." Asher casually pushed himself off Jen. "...barely escaped a pit bull in that room. We ran into the hall and crashed into each other."

"Good thing you managed to shut the door," Lark said, holding a metal cube up in the air. "We got it!"

"Great," Asher said, walking toward him with a nonchalant tone to his voice. He took the cube from Lark and put it inside the backpack he'd been carrying. "Let's go."

Asher led the way back to the front door, keeping his distance from both Jen and Rogue. Jen stayed a few feet ahead of Rogue but could feel her jealous glare. Jen felt completely uncomfortable and wanted to be as far away from Rogue as possible. She tried to speed up, but noticed Asher had stopped again. She followed his eyes to the middle of the store where two pit bulls dogs playfully fought each other, completely unaware of the intruders standing a distance away. Rogue turned to Lark with lowered eyes.

"Oops," Lark said with a guilty laugh. "W-we saw these p-pits in one of the r-rooms too, but I t-thought I closed the d-door. I must've not s-shut it all the way."

The pits looked up simultaneously, having heard Lark's voice, and wasted no time jumping into action. Asher instinctively pushed Jen behind him and pulled out a knife. Rogue did the same, guarding Lark with her body. Rogue kicked the first dog that pounced at her and watched as it slid across on the floor, letting out a cry. Asher had done the same, kicking the dog away from him, readying himself for the next attach. Lark grabbed Jen's arm, pulling her toward the exit. Jen tried to protest, remembering that Asher had told them all to stick together, but Lark was stronger.

"Come on, they can fend for themselves," Lark said, and pulled Jen out of the building.

It was a terrible mistake. Two guards had been standing just outside the door, and turned toward them with raised shooters. Jen lifted her hands in the air, watching the guards' stunned expressions. Both men looked to be in their early thirties and had ugly, pale skin and angular, bony faces. They looked like criminals who hadn't eaten in days.

"How did you get inside?" one of the guards demanded. "Who are you?"

"What did you steal?" the other guard asked, shaking his shooter furiously at both Jen and Lark. Jen regretted allowing Lark to pull her out of the building. Lark was supposed to stay with Rogue and she was supposed to stay with Asher. Neither Jen nor Lark had any weapons, making them an easy target.

"We didn't steal anything," Jen answered, hoping to buy

them some time as Asher and Rogue fought off the dogs. "We're just a couple of stupid teenagers that thought sneaking into a building would be funny."

"Is that so?" the second guard asked. He took a step toward Jen and grabbed her by the arm, pulling her close to him. "You look legal to me." His eyes lowered to her breasts as he took the sight of them in. Jen gasped and covered her chest.

"I'm only seventeen," she told him, earning a laugh.

"That's pretty legal," he told her. Jen thought back to when Asher told her the legal age in Blue City was sixteen and she cringed. "You're too pretty to be a thief," he continued, sending chills down her spine, hearing the lust in his voice. "Let's say we settle this the easy way. I'll let you both walk if you do me a favor."

"What is that?" Jen forced herself to ask. She was anything but brave, but wouldn't let him see her fear.

"How about we go behind the building and have some fun."

"Get lost," Jen replied. The guard's eyes lowered as he squeezed her arm.

"There's the hard way, one you won't like much," he said. "See, we'd never let the owner of this store know that two kids managed to outsmart us and sneak into the store. We'd lose our jobs. Understand? So, instead of us killing you, like nothing ever happened, we'll spare your lives. That is, if you like my other solution."

"Kill me," Jen cried. "I'll never let you touch me."

The guard smacked Jen, making her stumble, and then pushed her to the ground. He hovered over her, laughing. "We'll make your friend watch, since you want to be so difficult."

"No," Lark said, jumping into action. He ran toward the man and was about to punch him, but the other guard quickly reached out and grabbed Lark, pulling him away. The guard standing over Jen laughed and returned his gaze on her.

"Now, where were we?" The guard began to lower himself onto the ground, directly above where Jen lay. She tried to hit him, but he grabbed her wrists, pushing them over her head. "Be still."

"Get off of her!" a familiar voice yelled. Jen angled her head so that she could see Asher and Rogue standing near the door, both pointing their shooters at the two guards. "Now."

The guard let go of Jen's hands and stood, laughing as if the whole situation was amusing. "I see you brought friends with you."

"Back away from her," Asher ordered, sounding more frightening than Jen had ever heard him. She looked up at him and saw how dark his eyes had gone. His hands shook as he pointed the gun at the man. Asher was doing everything in his power to remain calm. He watched as the man took a step away from Jen, raising his hands in submission, but his face held an evil scowl.

"My partner here will kill you first for raising that shooter at me, and then he'll kill the kid. And then I'll take this pretty piece of meat right here and rip her open."

Asher fired the shooter, knocking the guard back three feet. He quickly pointed his shooter at the other guard and shot him in the head, just inches from Lark's face. The man fell to the ground, taking Lark with him. Rogue rushed to Lark's side as Asher ran to Jen, helping her sit up.

Jen met his dark, hooded eyes and noticed that he was still shaking. She was afraid of him when he was in a volatile state and didn't know what to do to calm him. She slowly lifted a shaking hand to his cheek and rested it there. Asher closed his eyes at her touch and breathed in deeply.

"It's okay," Jen assured him. "I'm okay."

"I want to kill him again," Asher said, grabbing onto Jen's hand and pushing it away from his cheek. "When I heard what he said he'd do to you. I wanted to...I wish I could kill him again."

"Shhh." Jen tried to force a smile, bringing her hand up to his face again.

"I told you to stay with me," he said through gritted teeth. He pushed her hand away and stood. "I told you not to leave my side! You ran off anyway!"

Jen quickly got up, watching as Asher paced back and forth, trying to calm himself down. It didn't seem to work. Once again, Jen had done something to anger him. The last time had been when she and Lark snuck off with his hover bug. This time, he was even more furious.

"I'm sorry," Jen said, but her voice was so low she didn't know if Asher heard her.

"I just killed two guards," he continued. "I killed two guards because you were stupid enough to run off without me. How was Lark supposed to protect you? Huh? There was a reason I said for you to stick by me!"

"We were caught up in the moment," Jen argued softly. Asher stopped and spun around to face Jen.

"Stupid people make stupid mistakes, Jen," he yelled.

"I'm not stupid," Jen said, with a lowered head. She crumpled back onto the ground, feeling overwhelmed.

"Asher," Rogue said. She'd helped Lark up and now stood a few feet away from Asher. He turned toward her, breathing heavily. With one look at Rogue, he seemed to visibly calm. She walked closer to him and rested a hand on his cheek, just as Jen had done, but Asher seemed to melt in Rogue's hand. Jen had to look away. "It's okay. Calm down. We would've had to kill the guards anyway. Let's just go before someone else shows up."

Asher sighed and then nodded. He stalked off, leaving Jen, Lark, and Rogue behind. Lark followed behind him. Rogue watched them stalk off and then walked up to Jen and extended a hand. Jen hesitated but took it, allowing Rogue to help her to her feet and meeting Rogue's harsh glare with wide eyes.

"I saw what took place back in that hallway," Rogue said. Her grip on Jen's hand tightened. Jen tried to pull her hand away without success. "Let me remind you of your place. You only do things to piss Asher off and make him more upset. I'm the one who can soften his heart and make him happy again. You only confuse him, while I bring him peace. You're just a burden to him, while I'm his saving grace. Asher will never love you the way he loves me. He will never allow you to affect him the way that I can. Let's face it, Jen, you'll never be me. You better start learning your place now."

Rogue released Jen's throbbing hand and walked away, leaving Jen standing by herself, panting heavily. Tears streamed down her face, and she frantically wiped them away. Her body felt numb as she looked down at the dead bodies. She'd almost been raped, and Asher had killed two men because of her. Rogue had been right. The only thing she'd done was complicate Asher's life. She thought about opening the portal and just returning home. Maybe her father hadn't even wanted to be found. Maybe he was already dead and she was searching in vain.

Jen wanted to disappear from it all. She hated herself for getting three people involved in her quest. So far, they'd been shot at, attacked, and almost killed on multiple occasions. She was done allowing people to hurt because of her. She was giving up. She just wanted to go back home and lay her head in her mother's lap and cry until her mother made her feel better. She couldn't handle it anymore—she'd made up her mind. Once Lark opened the portal, Jen would go through and never come back. It would be better that way.

"Jen?" She looked up to find Lark standing quite a distance away. He'd come back for her. His concerned expression made Jen want to cry even harder, but she did her best to hold it in. "Are you okay?"

"Just a little shaken up over everything." Jen forced a smile and wiped away the last traces of tears. "Let's go."

They made their way back to Asher's hover and quickly got in the back seat. Jen turned toward the side window and stared out it as they began driving home. She refused to look in Asher's direction. Halfway home, her resentment toward herself turned into hatred toward Asher.

How dare he tell her off after she'd almost gotten assaulted? How dare he blame her for killing those two guards when he could have found another solution? How dare he not console her and tell her everything was going to be all right? Hadn't he tried to kiss her back in the hallway? Maybe Jen had imagined it. It was clear that Asher detested her.

She couldn't wait to tell him off, but all she did was keep staring out the window while focusing on not crying. Their argument could come at a time when Jen felt emotionally stronger. For now, she was barely able to keep from crying.

Jen was the last to enter Asher's condo. She trailed behind, watching as Lark walked over to the couch and flopped down. She saw Rogue rub Asher's shoulder before heading off to the guest bedroom, and she watched Asher linger outside his own bedroom door before sighing and going inside. Jen went to the bathroom and took a hot shower, which seemed to be her go-to method to relax, although it hadn't really helped her much in the past. Still, the warm water running down her body did something to clear her mind so that she could think.

Jen wrapped a towel around her body and made her way to the bedroom. She headed straight for the dresser, picking out a pink sleepsuit, and was about to drop her towel to the ground. She shifted slightly and out of the corner of her eye saw a person sitting on her bed. She yelped and dropped the sleepsuit on the ground.

"W-what are you doing in here?" Jen asked, slowly reaching down to pick up the sleepsuit. Asher watched her intently, but his expression remained in its usual unreadable state.

"I wanted to talk to you," he said matter of factly.

"I think you've said everything you needed to say." Jen's voice was dull and lifeless.

Asher got up and walked toward Jen with slow, calculated steps. His eyes never left hers until the moment he stood a few inches from her. His eyes then drifted downward and took in the parts of bare, caramel skin that weren't covered by her towel. His eyes lifted back to her curious, guarded stare. He had to have noticed the puffiness around her eyes from crying. He should've been able to   sense how rigid she was and that she was uncomfortable with his presence.

"I'm sorry," he said with a voice soft enough to make any girl melt, but Jen didn't budge; her quiet demeanor remained. "I shouldn't have yelled at you like it was your fault. Lark told me that he grabbed you and brought you outside. I know we don't always think when we're in life-threatening moments. None of us expected the guards to be outside. We still had minutes before we needed to be out of the building.

"When I saw how the guard looked at you, as if you were nothing but a piece of meat..." Asher paused, closing his eyes as if trying to block out the memory. "When I saw you lying on the ground with him lowering himself onto you, I snapped."

"Why?" Jen asked. She wanted to know exactly why he had been unsettled. Was it because of jealousy? Did he not like the idea of another man hurting what he loved? Or was it all out of protection? Duty? For the sake of friendship? Jen had to know. It would make all the difference in her decision whether to stop her mission. Asher met her eyes with confusion coloring his already broken expression.

"Why?" Asher blinked a few times, trying to figure out how best to answer. "I feel a sense of responsibility for your life. I feel as if it's my duty to protect you. If anything happened to you, I'd blame myself."

"So, in other words, I'm just your burden, your pity party that you've agreed to help until the end."

"That's not what I said."

"No, I understand, Asher." Jen laughed, but she wasn't at all amused. "There were no real emotions tied to seeing me lying on that ground except your sense of responsibility and duty. I'm just part of a mission you took on, a mission you've got to keep intact in order to see it through."

"I—"

"I like you, Asher. And I'm probably in love with you, even though I hadn't admitted it to myself until now. Is it sad that I wanted you to say the thought of another man's hands on me made you jealous? That you wanted to protect my body because it was sacred to you? Because you actually like me?" Jen looked up to the ceiling, trying to prevent her tears from spilling. "I raised my hand to your cheek to calm you, but it only made you angrier. And then I had to watch Rogue place her hands on you and see you melt into them. I was the only one sickened by the thought of another person touching you. Rogue was right. You two were meant for each other, and I'm only getting in the way.

"I came here to find my father and ended up letting my feelings get in the way. My mind is clouded and I...I just want to go home. I want to open the portal back up and return to where I'm from. That way, I'll never have to see your face again. That way, you and Rogue can live happily ever after and—"

Asher wrapped his arm around Jen's waist and pulled her close. Before she could react, his hand cupped the back of her neck, and he kissed her, deeply. He kissed her as if the world around them was fading and they'd only have a few seconds to express their love for each other. He kissed her as if she was the only girl who had ever existed in his life. Not even Rogue was able to penetrate that kiss. There was nothing more powerful than what they shared in that moment, and when Asher pulled away, they were both left panting.

Jen searched his eyes and the raw passion there as he stared back. He didn't have to say anything. For the first time, Jen saw what he'd tried so hard to keep hidden, the reason he'd closed his eyes and pushed her hand away when she'd cupped his cheek. He'd wanted her, maybe even more than she'd wanted him. He'd only been trying to deny it, but he could no longer do so.

"You had me the moment you came through that portal," Asher said, holding her face in his hands. "You were so beautiful and innocent, and I slammed you against that wall just to feel your closeness. The night we went to the Pink Flamingo, I picked out your dress because it pleased me to see you in it. I let you change my bandages instead of Lark just to feel your touch on my skin. I purposely fought against eating the grilled cheese sandwich to see your reaction, and when you climbed on top of me, I fought so hard not to lose control and pin you underneath me.

"Yes, Rogue means a lot to me, and I was so surprised and shocked to see her that I unintentionally ignored you. But I forced myself to crave her touch so that I didn't crave yours. She'd be the one to stay when you returned home. So, I fought hard against my feelings toward you, knowing we could never be together. After all, you are ancient meat." Asher smiled, sweetly, making Jen swoon. "I didn't melt in Rogue's hand tonight. How could I, when I'd already melted in yours? Knowing I'd done so, I jumped up and started to attack you. Not because I was angry with you, but because I was trying to hide how raw I'd felt, how much you'd opened me up in that moment. I did it all because I like you...because I'm in love with you too."

Asher kissed Jen again, this time softer, as if he was afraid her lips would fall off if he kissed her any harder. He pulled back, searching her eyes with a pained expression.

"Tell me, Jen, how does this change anything? You're still from the past and will return to your life. Knowing my feelings, how will that make you sleep any better at night, knowing you left me behind?"

"We could find a way to be together," Jen said, desperately clinging to his shirt. She felt as if she was in a fragile dream and wanted to stay there forever. The pain from her hands tightly clinging to his shirt was proof that she was awake and facing one of the hardest things she'd ever experienced.

"That would require one of us giving up our home. That would mean you'd either have to stay here, or I'd have to come with you. I wouldn't ever ask you to stay here, Jen."

"I wouldn't ask you to leave," Jen said, understanding his point. It didn't matter how they felt about each other. The truth remained the same, and they'd never be together. It wasn't the natural order. They both had separate lives to live and they weren't meant to live them together. Jen understood why Asher had tried his hardest to keep his feelings at bay. Those feelings didn't matter in the end. The only thing that truly mattered was their mission.

Jen pulled away from Asher and walked toward her bed. She'd been chased by two police hovers; almost killed multiple times by Gunner; and had saved Asher from a crazy, old man. She'd narrowly escaped Roger and Keith in the alley; emotionally battled with Rogue over Asher; had been threatened by two pit bulls; and was nearly raped by a guard. Even with all that, she hadn't felt as defeated as she did right now. They'd admitted their feelings to each other, but in the end nothing had changed.

Jen flopped down on her bed, wanting to crash onto her pillow. She heard Asher's footsteps as he walked toward her. He lifted her legs onto the bed and softly laid her back against her pillow. Jen looked up at him with tears in her eyes.

"Don't go," she said. "If we only have a small amount of time together, I want us to spend as much of it together as possible. Come lie with me."

Asher gave Jen a kind smile, walked to the other side of the bed, and lay down next to her. She rested her head on his chest and began to relax as she listened to the sound of his heartbeat while he traced small circles on her bare back just above where her towel began. She couldn't believe Asher's revelation; she couldn't believe they lay in her bed, so close and intimate, as if everything was right in the world. She knew she should feel happy, but there was one thing pressing on her. She lifted her head to meet Asher's eyes. He smiled down at her, warmly. His blue eyes seemed happy and content just to be laying there with her.

"What about Rogue?" Jen asked. Asher sighed and shifted so that he could see her better.

"What about her?"

"Are you going to tell her how you feel about me?"

"If I do, she'll more than likely abort the mission."

"I never wanted her to be a part of this mission to begin with," Jen said with a frown. If that was the only reason Asher wanted to keep Rogue in the dark, it was ridiculous. "You, Lark, and I held up just fine."

"You're right," he said, continuing to trace circles on her back. "I'll tell her tomorrow."

"What exactly will you say?" Asher smiled and pulled Jen closer so that he could kiss the top of her forehead.

"I'll tell her that I'm madly in love with you," he said, barely containing his joy. Jen blushed and shyly buried her head in the nook of his neck.

"Say it again."

Asher outright laughed. He lifted her head and studied her face.

"I'm madly in love with you, Jen."

"Say it again," she giggled.

"Let me hear you say it."

Jen sat up on her knees, looking down at Asher lying against her pillow. He was so handsome and masculine. So refined and strong, just the way an alpha male should be. Jen knew she wouldn't be able to stay with him for long, and wanted to tell him over and over again how she felt about him, until they fell asleep.

"I'm in love with you, Commander Asher Moore," she began. "I'm in love with your self-assuredness, which can sometimes be too much. I'm in love with the sweet side you rarely show and yet you're showing it now. I'm in love with your concern for my overall wellbeing. I'm in love with your strength and your pride. And I'm in love with your smile, the one on your face right now." Asher smiled even wider.

"You're too cute." He pulled her back down so that she lay on his chest, and he held her there, enjoying one of the only moments of peace they'd experienced since Jen had arrived in Blue City.

Jen felt right to Asher. He didn't usually move fast with a girl, completely opening up to her in a matter of a couple weeks, but Jen was different. He felt she was meant for him, even though it made absolutely no sense how two people, from two different eras, could be soulmates. He didn't understand it, but he believed she was his soulmate, the way her heart beat against him, matching the rhythm of his own perfectly. He allowed the sounds of their entwining hearts to soothe him until they were both fast asleep.

Asher feared his father most after he came home from working long hours, tired and grouchy. The best way for his father to blow off steam was to take it out on Asher by finding whatever object he could to discipline him with. Asher had accidentally knocked over his father's favorite mug, and it completely shattered on the ground. Asher knew a beating was coming his way as soon as his father found out.

Asher heard the garage door open and he readied himself for what lay ahead. Commander Moore walked into the house, looking dangerous and proud, which was his normal demeanor. He spotted his thirteen-year-old son sitting on the couch with his head in his hands. His eyes then traveled to the broken mug lying on the living room table. It was his favorite mug, and it was broken. Commander Moore slammed his fist into the wall.

"You broke my coffee mug?" His voice was low and deadly.

"I-it was an a-accident," Asher stuttered, afraid of what his father would say. "It slipped from my hand."

"Why did you even have it?" he shouted.

"I wanted to make you some coffee for when you got home," Asher admitted, letting his head hang low. Commander Moore slammed his hand into the wall again, causing the paint to chip.

"Do you know how old that mug is? I acquired it when I traveled to the year 2030. They don't make coffee mugs like that anymore, and with the portals being prohibited, how would you suggest I go about getting another mug like it? It's irreplaceable!" Commander Moore yelled, causing Asher to jump in his seat. "Stand up."

Asher raised his innocent eyes to his father. "Sir?"

"I said, stand up."

Asher quickly stood, not wanting to get accused of not moving fast enough. "Don't cower like a lost puppy. I didn't teach you to fear anything. Stand straight." Asher obeyed as Commander Moore walked toward him. Asher did his best to stand still, knowing what was going to happen next.

Commander Moore's fist connected with the side of Asher's face, making him stumble. Asher quickly stood straight again, looking ahead as if he hadn't just been hit. It was how his father trained him to take his beatings. Commander Moore punched Asher again, knocking him off balance once more.

"Fight back," Commander Moore said, confusing his son. Asher raised his head to his father, holding onto his bloody mouth. "Don't look at me like you're stupid, boy. I know you want to fight back, and one day you'll try to. I'm going to let you know right now that you'll fail. If you ever try to fight me, I'll overpower you. Come on, fight me."

Asher had heard his father say countless times that one day he'd rebel and try to fight him. Asher wasn't stupid enough to do such a thing and definitely didn't want to hit his father right now. But his father had given him an order. If Asher disobeyed, he'd be in a worse position than if he actually managed to hit his father. Asher mustered up enough courage to swing his fist at his father. Commander Moore dodged his son's attack with poise and laughed.

"You can do better than that."

Asher put all of his anger and fury into the next punch and barely missed his father. Commander Moore grabbed Asher's hand midair and swung it around to his back, pinning him against the wall.

"Is that the best you've got? I raised a girl who likes to make coffee and break one-of-a-kind coffee mugs." Commander Moore laughed. "When I let go, you better defend yourself as if you were fighting for your life. You just might be."

Jen felt rough movements beside her, which woke her up. She turned over, seeing Asher's silhouette in the dark as he tossed and turned next to her. She quickly sat up, watching him in horror.

"No," Asher panted. "Please don't. Ahhh!"

He twitched in the bed, scaring Jen to death. She clapped her hands twice, and the light turned on. Asher's face was covered in sweat, and he wore the most pained, vulnerable expression Jen had ever seen. "Dad...Commander, please don't. Ahhh!"

"Asher!" Jen tried to shake him awake from his nightmare, but his eyes wouldn't open, causing her to panic. She shook him harder and slapped him in the face. "Wake up!" she cried. Eventually, Asher's eyes popped open and shifted to where Jen stood over him with an arm in the air, ready to slap him again. In one smooth motion, Asher had pinned Jen to the bed and sat above her with his hand at her neck, tightly squeezing. Jen fought against his locked grip, slapping at his shoulders while trying to gasp for air. "Asher...please..." she pleaded, barely able to breathe as he choked her. She stared up at him as he pinned her down, half aware of what he was doing, as if he were still in his dream. Tears started coming out of her eyes as her vision blurred. "Asher..." Jen's body went numb. "Ash..."

Asher blinked rapidly, momentarily confused as he looked down at Jen. It finally registered to him that he was choking her, and he quickly let go, jumping up from the bed and moving over to a corner where he was able to put as much distance between them as possible. Jen coughed frantically, holding onto her throat as she watched Asher collapse on the ground, putting his head in his hands in shame. His body shook as if he was crying uncontrollably.

Once Jen's coughing fit ended and she was positive she was no longer hurt, she slowly stood and began walking over to where Asher sat.

"Don't," Asher warned, keeping his face hidden. "I just hurt you."

"You were dreaming," she said, ignoring his warning. Her throat was sore and her voice raspy, but she wouldn't let him know just how bad she felt. "It's okay. It doesn't hurt. I'm fine now." Jen sat on the ground next to Asher, but he turned away from her. She sighed and slowly brought a hand up to his chin, turning his face toward hers. It was stained with tears. "You had a nightmare."

Asher finally allowed himself to meet her eyes. "I have it almost every night."

"Why?" Jen asked, hoping she wasn't pushing him for answers. She didn't want him to close back up. However, Asher grabbed her arm and pulled her into his lap, wrapping both arms around her waist in a hug.

"I'm sorry I hurt you. I thought you were my father."

"Why would you think that?"

"Because..." Asher paused, taking a deep breath, "...of my dream. I had dreamed about a time when he'd given me one of my worse beatings. I'd broken his favorite coffee mug and as punishment, he made me fight him. I was only thirteen, but he beat me like I was his worst enemy and left me there in my blood for a whole day before he took me to a doctor.

"He told me to fight him as if I was protecting my life, and I did. And yet I still wasn't able to hit him a single time. It was like he enjoyed knowing he could overpower me. He wanted me to remember that I would never be able to beat him. It was as if he'd thought there would be a day where we'd face off, and he wanted to put fear in my heart. He wanted me to know that when that day came, he'd win. He'd always win."

"Asher, I'm so sorry to hear that," she said. "I thought I had it bad, with my father gone most of my life, but you spent your life wishing you didn't have one. It's a worse fate."

"I admired your dedication to your father. It was another reason why I helped you escape from the police. I wanted to meet the kind of father who raised a daughter like you, one who loved him so much that she'd risk her own life to bring him home," Asher admitted. "I never really had anyone that loved me. My mother left us when I was three. She's somewhere in this world, living a great life while I had to suffer every day." Asher absentmindedly ran a hand through his buzz cut.

"My father used to tell me she didn't love me, that I was unworthy of anyone's love, and that it was the reason he was so hard on me. He'd tell me he was going to make me a great man, though—one who would take his place as Chief Commander of the army. He said men like me didn't need love. We only needed to know how to fight and survive. I spent most of my years justifying his abuse toward me as a way of teaching me how to be a man."

"He was wrong," Jen said, leaning her head back against his chest. "A man like you does need love." She turned toward him, searching his sad eyes. "Asher, I won't leave you. I'll stay here in Blue City and spend the rest of my life showing you just why you deserve love."

Asher smiled warmly. "I'd leave this place and go back with you before I let you stay here, Ancient Meat. Blue City isn't for lovers."

"My mother would kill me if I returned home with a boy from the future." Jen cackled.

"That wouldn't be a problem. I could use a special gadget that would influence her brain waves and make her submit to my will."

"Are you serious?"

"No." Asher laughed. "Science hasn't come that far."

Jen grinned, happy that Asher's mood had changed since his nightmare. He lifted his hands to her neck and gently massaged it. He lowered his head and kissed a sensitive spot on the side of her neck, making her squirm.

"I'm sorry for choking you."

"It's okay," Jen said, and stood up. She reached a hand out to Asher and pulled him to his feet. "Let's go back to bed."

Asher followed Jen back to the bed and lay beside her, pulling her as close as he could. She clapped and the lights went out, making everything dark again. Asher stared up at nothing but darkness, feeling a sense of relief for the first time in his life. He and Jen had admitted their feelings to each other. It didn't mean they were a couple, but it meant they would try to make it work out so that one day they could be together.

Asher started to feel weak in his stomach, the way he often felt when something bad was bound to happen. He began breathing deeply, hoping the feeling would go away, but instead his heart started beating faster, and anxiety weighed down his chest. Something bad was going to happen with him and Jen; his instincts told him so.

No, he thought to himself, pulling Jen closer. It's just my fears eating away at me. Nothing more. But even as he thought those words, Asher knew the truth. He didn't know what was going to happen, but he knew that loving Jen was going to be a mission harder than finding her father. At least for the night, they could lie in peace. Who knew what tomorrow would bring.

CHAPTER SIXTEEN

Laser Tag

Asher awoke before Jen and quietly tucked her under the covers before leaving her room. He planned to head straight for his room, but found himself standing in front of his second guest bedroom, watching the door materialize before him. He looked behind him at Lark, who slept on the couch with his head hung off to the side and his glasses hung from his forehead, seconds from falling off his face. One of his legs was elevated on the back of the couch and one arm dangled to the floor. His mouth was slightly opened and he snored loudly. Asher would have laughed, had his heart not been heavy.

Asher walked into his guest bedroom and found Rogue sleeping peacefully on the king-sized bed that floated inches from the ground. He looked around the room, admiring the décor. Baby blue paint covered the walls, plush white carpet with specks of baby blue covered the floor, and the carpet matched the white bedcovers and dressers that floated along the walls. This was Asher's elevation room: a room where every piece of furniture floated inches above the floor. This type of technology was extremely expensive, so he never had allowed company to stay in it before. Rogue was an exception.

Asher didn't bother walking quietly to her bed since he planned to wake her up anyway. He sat down on the edge of the bed but felt uncomfortable being so close to her when he had just been with Jen. At the same time, he wanted Rogue to know about his feelings as soon as possible. He watched as Rogue turned toward him, blinked twice, and smiled.

"Good morning. What time is it?" she asked.

"Six," Asher replied, refraining from smiling at her.

"You're up early," she said in the midst of stretching. The covers fell below her chest, revealing a very thin and flattering tank top. Asher looked away, not wanting to stare.

"The military does that to you," he said. "Of course, you'd remember."

"As soon as I left the military, I went back to waking up at noon every day," she admitted, making Asher laugh.

"Maybe it's also because my father never let me sleep in as a child."

"How is your father doing, by the way?" Rogue asked, sitting up and resting against the headboard.

"Same old." Asher looked down at his hands. "I'll be overseeing a new boot camp here in a few weeks."

"Just like old times," Rogue said, smiling at a distant memory. Asher cleared his throat, not wanting to talk about the past. He'd come to her room for a reason. He watched Rogue's watchful eyes darken as she frowned. "What's wrong?"

"I need to tell you something," Asher began. Rogue pulled herself off the headboard and quickly grabbed his hand.

"I was thinking about going back to blonde, my natural color. I know you love it most."

"You don't have to change your hair," he told her, feeling a little guilty. He'd always been the kind of guy who could tell a girl he wasn't interested without a drop of sweat. However, Rogue was different. Even though she'd once broken his heart, he couldn't find it in him to do the same to her.

"I want to," she said. "I'm tired of being something I'm not."

"And what is that?"

"This tough girl, one who doesn't care about anything. The kind of girl who laughs at danger," she confessed.

"You've always been that type of girl, though. It's what made me fall for you," Asher said, and instantly regretted his words. That wasn't going to help him explain why he didn't want to be with her.

"I guess I have, huh?" Rogue smiled to herself. "You like tough girls. Jen definitely isn't tough."

"What made you bring Jen up?" Asher looked confused.

"She's so naïve, and she's almost always getting herself in a situation that could get herself killed. Remember in the alley and how she took off with your hover without asking? And how she just ran out of that building with Lark? That was stupid. I'm surprised you're even still helping her."

"About Jen—"

"She's going to be leaving soon," Rogue said, cutting Asher off. "I can tell you care about her. But it would be stupid to get involved with her. Girls like that are selfish. Why care about someone who only cares about her father? I bet she'd tell you anything to convince you to continue helping her. Don't forget, she'll leave in the end as if none of us even mattered. And poor Lark.

"He likes her the most. His heart will be crushed when she leaves. Just imagine how he'd feel if he learned she was dating someone. He'd quickly abort the mission. Without Lark, we wouldn't even be able to open the portals and Jen would probably never find her father." Rogue paused and laughed. "Of course, I'm just speaking hypothetically. My point is, the mission comes first. Even I've committed myself to the cause. Jen, she's the type that's weak enough to get distracted. It's our job to make sure she keeps her eyes on the goal. I trust you can do that, Asher. Keep her focused on the mission, and only the mission."

Asher's shoulders had visibly sunken. However, Rogue's eyes had shifted to the window, watching the morning sun as it began to illuminate the sky. She was right, Asher thought. She'd just explained a perspective he hadn't seen before. His decision to admit his feelings to Rogue would have caused havoc, not only to her but to Lark. It was obvious that Lark had a small crush on Jen. Was it possible he'd abort the mission once he learned of her feelings for Asher?

Was Asher willing to risk it all for the sake of his heart? If there was one thing the military taught him, it was to put his feelings aside. Admitting them could ruin the mission. He found himself in a terrible position. How could he be so foolish to believe he'd find a way to be with Jen? He had to wake up from his dream and face reality. Soon, Jen would be gone, and all he'd have would be his job and Rogue. Asher sighed and stood up.

"Was there something you needed to say?" Rogue asked with innocent eyes. Rogue, his Rogue. Maybe he could live a happy life with her. Maybe he could truly forgive her for leaving him in the military. He reached down and rubbed her cheek with his thumb.

"Just wanted to say good morning." Asher quickly turned and stalked out of the room.

Jen stretched as she fought off sleep. She turned to her right and marveled at the clock on the nightstand. Its round, black base cast a green light into the air that formed into numbers. She lifted a hand and brushed through the floating numbers, feeling a bit of heat from the bulb in the base. It was nine in the morning.

Jen remembered that Asher was lying next to her and rolled over, barely containing a smile. Her smile turned into a frown when she saw the empty spot next to her. She quickly sat up, wondering where he'd gone. Maybe he'd decided to sleep in his bed and left her halfway through the night. Had she been snoring? Was she tossing and turning all night? Maybe he couldn't get back to sleep after the nightmare and wandered off into another room. She hoped it wasn't Rogue's. Jen got out of bed, slipped on the sleepsuit she'd meant to put on the night before, and made her way out of the bedroom.

Lark sat on the couch playing video games while staring up at the TV that filled the whole wall. He was playing another racing game, with his hands outstretched as if clutching a steering wheel. He was mumbling obscenities under his breath and was concentrating too hard to realize she stood behind him.

Just then, the door to the second guest bedroom materialized and Rogue emerged, fully dressed in combat attire. She wore a camouflaged jumpsuit and combat books, but what stood out was the head gear strapped across her forehead, an eyepiece covering her left eye. It was a piece of lens with a red line through it as if it were scanning the room. Jen hadn't realized she'd walked right up to Rogue until she stood a few inches from her face.

"What is that?"

"It's the RTG200, a device that allows you to see through objects," Rogue said blandly. "Watch this." She pressed a button in the collar of her uniform and her whole outfit became invisible. The only things remaining were her head and hands. Jen took a step back, gasping loudly. She heard Lark laugh behind her.

"It's standard military wear," Lark said.

"Can you believe Asher kept my uniform all this time?" Rogue mused, staring down at herself. If Jen hadn't known better, she would have thought Rogue was bragging on purpose.

"Why are you wearing it?" Lark asked, having put his game on pause.

"Asher and I are going shooting. To blow off steam."

"What? We should be working on the plan to use the portal." Jen's voice rang with a defiant tone.

"And we will, after we blow off steam," Rogue said, not at all fazed by Jen's attitude. Asher walked out of his bedroom, dressed in all-black combat wear. He paused when he saw Jen. She noticed how uneasy he looked as his brows formed a hard line on his forehead. Had something changed within a single night? Jen felt panic rise inside of her but kept a cool disposition.

"So you guys just planned an outing without us? What if Lark and I want to blow off steam, too? You think you two are the only ones who need to release some tension?" Jen asked, feeling her anger rise, even though she had been trying to be cool. Why had Asher chosen to take Rogue instead of her, especially after their night together?

"Can you even shoot?" Rogue asked, laughing lightly. Jen quickly stood, boiling underneath.

"Take me, and I'll show you how I shoot."

"I'm not letting you practice with a shooter," Asher said quietly, folding his arms in protest. Jen turned toward him, wanting to throw the pillow Lark had been sleeping on in Asher's face.

"Have you forgotten that I've used one already? I could use more practice," Jen said, taking a step toward Asher.

"You have a better chance at getting me to take you to play laser tag." Asher laughed, but his harsh tone was far from amused.

"Laser tag!" Lark roared, raising his hands in the air. "That's a great idea. Jen, this isn't normal, old school laser tag; this is laser tag on steroids." Lark turned to Asher. "We can team up. Me and

Jen against the two of you."

"What?" Jen was shocked.

"After the last incident with the guards, I'd say we have a lot to prove to them. They obviously don't think we're good enough to invite to the shooting range," Lark explained to Jen. "Catch my drift?"

"We'd kill you two at laser tag," Rogue smirked, and turned to Asher with a new challenge in her eyes. "Let's show them."

Asher's eyes left Rogue's and drifted to where Jen stood. He sighed and nodded his head. "You two have twenty minutes to get ready. Wear something comfortable." Asher turned and stalked out of the living room. Lark turned to Jen and shrugged.

"Maybe he just woke up on the wrong side of the bed."

"He was fine earlier," Rogue quickly chimed in. "When he came to my room this morning."

"He came to your room?" Jen asked, thinking back to waking up and finding Asher gone.

"You said that like it was a surprise." Rogue laughed. "We did date, Jen. We're trying to work on things."

Jen did everything in her power to smile neutrally at Rogue, but all she really wanted to do was ring her throat. Better yet, she wanted to ring Asher's throat. He'd just spent the night with her and had woken up early to go to Rogue's side. It was obvious he hadn't told Rogue that he was in love with Jen. Was he playing her? Asher did seem standoffish moments ago. Maybe he'd had a change of heart that quickly. Jen wouldn't let that happen. She'd finally admitted her feelings to him, and she wouldn't lose him due to his own self-doubt. She'd fight hard, and she'd start by proving herself during their game.

The laser tag setup was something Jen had never dreamt of seeing. As soon as she walked into the dark, she gasped as she took in the fluorescent neon lights that outlined every object in view. The neon lights trailed along big, black blocks that were randomly spread about the large space. The lights decorated floating shields meant for players to hide behind. Jen also noticed two hills on the east and the west sides of the large room that traveled past the second floor to the top of the roof. Different color mounts lined along the steep hill so that a player could climb up it. Large windows opened the second level up to the battleground so people could snipe their competition. Jen thought it would be a great hiding place.

She was the first to step onto the battleground, bouncing a few feet in the air and almost falling when she landed. With her mouth open in surprise, she held out both arms to steady herself. She heard snickers behind her and knew the others were laughing. Jen looked down at the floor, wanting to laugh herself. How hadn't she noticed it was made from the same material in trampolines?

"It's called a bounce floor," Lark said, bouncing into view. His lanky body looked odd as he landed nearby. "The floor was designed to allow you to quickly bounce out of your enemy's way. If you're really good, you can jump up to the second level and snipe." Lark pointed there and smiled.

"You also have more to worry about than just us," Rogue said, bouncing into view and landing beside Lark. She had a proud look on her face as she took in the battleground around her. "Everything comes to life when the game begins. There are built-in defense mechanisms meant to slow you down, so watch your every step."

"You mean, the room will fight back at me?" Jen asked with an incredulous expression. She definitely wasn't prepared for this.

"It's not so bad," Lark said, taking a small step and bouncing next to Jen. He leaned down and whispered in her ear. "I know this place like the back of my hand, so just stick with me and we'll win."

Lark straightened up at the sound of the instructor making his way onto the battleground. The instructor was an attractive black man in his late twenties. Accompanying him was a floating cardboard box that held all of their equipment. He smiled brightly when he saw Jen and bounced toward her first. He pulled out breast, knee, shoulder, and elbow pads and handed them to Jen. He smiled once more and took a step to his left, where Lark stood, repeating the same process.

"I'm going to assume that none of you have played laser tag

and will explain the game and rules thoroughly. Starting with the rules," the instructor moved to Asher, handing him equipment, but his eyes kept shifting back to Jen. Asher snatched his equipment out of the instructor's hand, but the instructor didn't seemed to notice Asher's irritation. Jen wondered if Asher also noticed that the instructor couldn't stop staring at her. "The object of this game is to take your opponent out before they do the same to you. You can kill your opponent by shooting them in three places: the chest, the stomach, and the back. The shooters sting once it zaps you, so you'll know when you've been hit. Do not shoot at a person's head or limbs, as it could result in minor injury.

"If you get hit by a laser, the lights in your equipment will go out and you will not be able to use your laser gun for twenty seconds. If you get hit three times, you lose. Each game, depending on how many players there are, usually lasts anywhere from ten minutes to an hour. First thing you should know is this game can get dangerous, and you've already signed a waiver stating you cannot hold us at fault for any injuries. Second, be aware of the room, as it has its own mind. Things will randomly move to change the dynamics of the game and make things more interesting. If you end up in a situation where you're stuck or are injured, there's a red distress button built into the chest plate that you can push, and the game will automatically stop and we will be notified. Any questions?"

"No," Asher said, eyeing the instructor ominously. The instructor was still unfazed by Asher's hostility and bounced back toward Jen, smiling once more.

"Go ahead and put your equipment on. Let me know if you need any help," he said, bouncing backward until he was in the doorway, watching her intently. Lark turned toward Jen, eying her equipment.

"Let me help." He put down his own equipment and picked up Jen's, snapping the pad around her chest and moving to her knee pads. She snapped the elbow pads into place. Lark finished with her shoulder pads and then moved away, so that he could put his own equipment on.

Jen took a few minutes to study her protected body. The pads were made of some sort of thin plastic but still weighed her down. She wondered what was actually inside them that made them so heavy. Her curiosity was satisfied as the neon lights on her armor began to shine. She had to blink and look away as she lit up like a thousand stars. She looked over to Lark, whose own armor lit up with the same whitish, blue light. Jen glanced over at Asher and Rogue and found them standing next to each other with red tinted armor. It was clear their teams were defined by the color of their armor. Seeing Asher and Rogue talking quietly angered Jen, and she found herself wanting to shoot both with a laser shooter. She couldn't wait for the game to start.

"Here," Lark said, handing Jen a blue shooter that matched her armor. "You dropped this. You're gonna need it. Trust me."

"All right," the instructor called from the doorway. "Blue team to the left; red team to the right. As soon as this door closes, the game begins. Good luck!"

"Come on," Lark said. He bent his knees and shot into the air, bouncing ten feet away. Jen couldn't believe how light he seemed while bouncing through the air, but she bent her knees and quickly jumped into the air, following toward him.

The air brushed past her face as she bounced, and she laughed midair, until she felt her body begin to rotate. She shrieked as she tried to level herself, but quickly crashed on the ground next to Lark. She was thankful for the bouncy floors, which allowed her to bounce right back into a standing position.

"Tough landing?" Lark asked with a laugh and pulled her behind a small wall. "Try to stay level or you'll land wrong. I would show you how, but we don't have enough time. Look around you, quickly. Stay behind these walls. The blocks help too, but they aren't as tall so you'll have to kneel. Stick with me, but if we get separated, try to make your way up to the second level and snipe. Let's show them that we aren't useless. We can win."

A loud buzz sounded, causing Jen to jump. She looked down at the rubber ground and noticed thick heaps of smoke beginning to cover its surface. The black block that shined next to her shifted and floated a few inches from the ground. The wall closest to her shifted five feet to the left, so quickly that anyone standing in front of it wouldn't have time to move out of the way. Something slammed into Jen's back, making her bounce in the air, but Lark grabbed her hand, pulling her toward him. When Jen stabilized, she looked behind her and noticed the wall that had smacked into her back.

"Watch out for those walls," Lark said. "Kneel down. The game has started."

"Okay." Jen quickly kneeled down behind a fluorescent yellow block to her right. She hadn't realized just how much her heart was racing until that moment. She really wanted to win, not against Asher, but against Rogue, to prove that she wasn't one to mess with. Jen held her shooter firmly, remembering the last time she'd fired a real one. She'd ended up killing an enemy. Never in her life had she imagined being brave enough to shoot a gun; then again, she never imagined being in the year 2222, playing futuristic laser tag. But even though she never imagined half of what she was going through, she was ready for all of it.

Jen heard the shot before she saw the red light flashing past, smacking into the wall behind her. Lark bounced to his right, dodging behind a neon red block. He peered over the edge of the block and fired two shots. Jen peeked around her own block and saw a glimpse of someone running past, hiding behind a green wall. Jen signaled to Lark, letting him know where the enemy was. He signaled back for her to move from her spot. She kneeled down further and put all of her weight into her jump. She quickly flew in the air, passing Lark and landing in the open. She hadn't adjusted to the amount of pressure she needed to get to a specific destination.

Jen was out in the open, an easy target for whoever hid behind the green wall. She began to panic and jumped and landed behind a purple block to Lark's left. Jen sighed in relief and turned toward Lark to signal that she was safe, but the purple block slammed into her side as it began to move away. Jen fell to her knees, once again exposed, and saw Asher as he leaned away from his wall, staring directly at her. He raised his shooter at her and shot, narrowly missing her right shoulder. Jen was frozen in place, until something hard smacked into her once again. Jen

flew into the air as a pair of arms wrapped around her. She landed on her back and bounced three times on the ground before
settling. She looked up and saw Lark, bouncing to his feet, turning away from her and firing his shooter. Once he was satisfied
that Asher had backed down, he turned back to Jen.

"What was that? You play like a toddler. You left yourself
open. Asher had a clear shot."

"And yet he missed," Jen said with a victorious smile.

"Asher told me the other day that he doesn't miss, so he was
obviously cutting you some first-time slack, but I wouldn't expect such kindness the next time. Only apply a little pressure if
you want to bounce somewhere near. I don't need you bouncing
to Mars, Jen. We need to win."

"Sorry." Jen frowned, turning away from Lark. She'd never
seen him so serious before and wondered why he was so anxious to win. "I'll buckle down."

"Asher has obviously taken the front line and left Rogue to
the back. I think we need to split up as well," Lark said.

"But you said—"

"Tactics change. I'll distract Asher while you jump up to the
second ground. Go toward the east side and look out. You'll
probably see Rogue kneeling behind a wall. Shoot her and run
back."

"Got it," Jen said, feeling excited about shooting Rogue. This
was a mission she was going to make sure she succeeded at. Lark
nodded and jumped from behind the wall and began firing away.
Jen peeked around the edge and saw Asher intently focused on
Lark, firing back his own shots.

Jen put all of her strength into her next jump and quickly
flew toward to second level. She grabbed the railing as she
slammed into the wall and pulled herself up. She collapsed on
the ground, surprised she didn't bounce back up. She knocked
on the wooden floor below her, thankful for its sturdiness and
peered over the edge, catching a glimpse of Asher hiding behind
a black block. Lark was only three feet away and couldn't see
where Asher lay hidden as he walked closer to the black block.
If Lark moved another inch, he'd be shot.

Before Jen could call out, she felt a huge pinch, followed by a burning sensation in her back. Jen fell to the ground, moaning in pain, and turned toward where Rogue stood, smiling down at her, as if she'd won the world.

"Does it hurt?" Rogue asked and then laughed. "You guys fell right for it. Asher knew Lark would send you to the second level. I've been waiting for you, my pretty." Rogue took a few steps toward the open window and laughed again. "Looks like Asher just took Lark out. That's one out of three."

Rogue walked away, leaving Jen sitting on the ground, panting as the pain from the shot wore off. She wanted to scream but stopped herself. This was all a game, and yet everyone was taking it too seriously. It meant there was some serious animosity and division happening. It made Jen even angrier at Asher for being distant the day after confessing his love. It hurt worse than the sting from the laser gun. The instructor said that it would sting, but no one had mentioned how much it would hurt.

Jen stood and flung herself over the railing, knowing she wouldn't hurt herself if she landed on the rubber ground below. Once she landed, she bounced a few times, trying to steady herself, and then searched for Lark. Jen's armor was now buzzing with blue energy as she ducked behind thin walls, looking for her partner.

She hadn't expected to find Asher a few feet away with his back turned against her. All of her anger seemed to leave her body and enter her shooter as she pointed it at his head. She faintly remembered hearing the instructor say not to shoot people in their head, but her shooter had a mind of its own. Jen rested her hand on the trigger.

Asher spun around, as if sensing her presence. Jen watched him tense at the sight of her. Finally, she had the upper hand. "You know the rules," Asher reminded her, seeing the shooter pointed at his head. Jen lowered it to his chest, burning holes into his eyes as she stared at him. "I see you got shot. There's a scoreboard up there. We have one point."

"It's about to be tied."

"We'd have two points if I hadn't spared you."

"No one asked for your pity," Jen shouted, too loudly. She

was sure the others heard her and would find their location in less than twenty seconds. "You've been avoiding me all day." Asher looked away from her with an uneasy expression. "You said you'd tell Rogue about us today, but instead you left my room and ended up in hers. Not only that, you've decided to ignore me, as if I have no feelings, as if yesterday didn't happen."

"It did happen," Asher said.

"Then why are you acting strange?"

"Because," Asher moaned, not wanting to have the conversation where they were. But he knew Jen wouldn't have it any other way. "Us liking each other will just make things complicated. Jen, can we talk about this after the game? Just shoot me already."

Jen obeyed and shot Asher in the chest. He flew back a few feet and landed on the ground with a deep grunt. Jen bounced toward him and kneeled down, staring at his pained face with no mercy.

The hope that sprung to life the night before as they shared their feelings had died almost as quickly as it had been born. They could never be a couple, no matter how much they wanted to. There were forces working against them, forces stronger than they'd ever imagined. As Jen stared down at him, she threw away the thought of loving him.

"You're a liar. You had the chance to tell Rogue about us and you didn't. Forget any chances of a romantic relationship. Obviously you can't figure out what you really want. It's best we just get this mission over with, so we don't even have to look at each other anymore. Jerk." Jen stood and bounced away, not daring to look back. It was no longer a game; she was far from games. She was filled with hate.

Twenty minutes later, the game was finished, and Lark jumped around the battleground in victory. Jen smiled as he flew across the room within seconds, just to repeat the process over again. After she had shot Asher, she was glad to hear that Lark had shot Rogue, making them even. After that, Lark and Jen stayed a step ahead and managed to shoot both Asher and Rogue one more time. Jen was sure Asher had given up, which would have been the real reason they'd won, but she wouldn't tell Lark that. She wouldn't tell Rogue that, either. It didn't matter how they'd won—they'd won.

Three long and uneventful days dragged on by as Jen made an effort to keep out of Asher and Rogue's way. She kept herself locked up in the guest room, watching the giant television she'd recently discovered behind the white wall near the foot of her bed. TV had definitely changed in the last two hundred years, which kept Jen's mind occupied as she learned about the newest fashion trends and culture on a show that aired daily.

The women in Blue City were really big on bright colors that clashed and stood out as much as possible. Pale women hosted television shows wearing gigantic blue afros, plastic-looking multi-colored dresses, and heels that looked to be at least seven inches tall. To Jen, the women looked like futuristic Barbies.

One woman had bright pink hair with streaks of glitter running throughout. Her hair had been molded into a cone-shaped horn, sticking up on her head. She looked like a human unicorn. Jen was starting to realize that it was a fashion trend in Blue City to resemble an animal. It was all hideous in her eyes, but she could see why the natives of Blue City liked the style. It was just what they knew.

When she was done watching TV, she turned it off and focused on the pitter-pattering on the wall-length window. It had been one of those dreary, dark, and rainy days that either soothed or depressed a person. For Jen, it was depressing as she studied the drops of rain desperately zigzagging down the window pane, trying to get to the pile of water on the seal. She wondered what Asher was doing at that moment. Was he with Rogue, lying in her bed, cuddling? Or was he just as down as she was, staring outside at a sad evening?

"Ugh," Jen moaned. "Why does it even matter if he's with her? It shouldn't matter. In fact it doesn't." She sat in silence for a while and then moaned again. "But it does matter. I wish Rogue would just go away."

Jen's door materialized, and Lark peeked his curly red head into the room, smiling as he spotted her.

"Can I come in?" he asked, hesitantly.

"Sure." Jen sighed. "The rest of your body may enter."

Lark took a seat at the edge of Jen's bed, looking around at nothing in particular. Jen wanted to wait to find out why he'd come in, but her curiosity won the best of her.

"How is Asher? I literally have been ignoring him for three days. Is he all over Rogue? Have you seen them kissing? Is he—?"

"Whoa, Jen." Lark laughed. "The fact that you care to the point that it's affecting you finding your father is bad. You have one mission, and that's to get him and return home. I know I'm only fourteen, but I'm smart, and I know you guys didn't steal me from Gunner just to sit around the house and mope. Both of you."

"He's moping?" Jen asked, hopefully. If he was moping, it meant he cared.

"Not only is he moping, he's moody. He snapped at me today just for playing a racing game on his TV. I always play that racing game. What else am I supposed to do all day?"

"You could be figuring out how to open the portal."

"With the help of Rogue, I figured it out two days ago."

"You've been working with Rogue?" Jen asked, disgusted.

"Who else was I supposed to work with since both you and Asher withdrew to your rooms? Rogue seemed to know a lot about portals. I know you don't like the girl, but she's a strong asset to this mission."

Jen ignored Lark's attempts to soften her up about Rogue. She would never approve of her. Instead, she allowed her spirits to lift as the realization that she was a step closer to finding her father sank in. Not only that, once she opened the portal, she'd be back home in her familiar room, around what she knew. She needed to fall onto her bed and wrap herself in her covers. She needed to run into her mother's room and tell her that she'd returned with her father. Just the thought of her mother's relief flooded Jen's eyes with tears.

"When are we going to do this?" Jen asked, sitting up as straight as she could on her bed.

"I need to talk to Asher first and make sure he mapped it all out. If everything looks good, we'll shoot for opening the portal tomorrow morning. How does that make you feel?"

"It makes me feel one step closer to finding answers."

CHAPTER SEVENTEEN

The Portal

The next morning came with a new challenge. Lark had gotten the okay for their plan to open the portal. Jen sat in the living room and quietly watched Asher as he fastened the last button of his all black liquid jumpsuit. Lark stood next to him, identically dressed, but he could never fill out the jumpsuit the way Asher did. Jen had to clear her thoughts, disappointed in herself for noticing how attractive Asher looked when he wore all black. It brightened the blue in his hooded, calculating eyes. Jen also wasn't supposed to catch the small glances he stole in her direction when he thought she wasn't looking.

Soon, everything would be over and she'd never see Asher again. A deep part of her didn't want to spend their final moments together mad at each other. Jen was about to speak up and clear the silence, but Rogue beat her to it.

"Your time is almost up here, Jen," Rogue began. There was a menacing look in her eyes, which let Jen know Rogue wasn't about to play nice. "I bet when you leave, you won't even look back. Not even at Asher."

Jen watched Asher shift, his hooded eyes growing darker. "That's not true. I'll miss Asher the most." Asher lifted his eyes and met Jen's steady gaze. "He saved my life." Jen's heart shuddered at the small smile that tugged at Asher's lips.

"Well, I can't say he'll be missing you much with me around," Rogue said, resting a hand on Asher's shoulder. Asher lowered his head again and didn't even try moving her hand. It tore Jen up inside, because she knew Asher would move on without her. When she left, Rogue was still going to be by his side, holding him and loving him. And by the looks of it, he would let her.

"All right," Asher said, moving away from Rogue to stand in front of everyone. "It's time to head out. You know your places, or do I need to remind you?"

"We're ready," Lark answered.

"I'll remind you anyway," Asher said, his strong jaw setting into a firm line. "Rogue and I will stand as guards as Lark opens the portal. Once it's opened, Jen will go back inside and grab the book. She has approximately three minutes to get in and out before we're caught. If anything goes wrong, follow the escape plan, even if it means leaving someone behind. We can do this, okay? Nothing is going to go wrong."

"What makes you so sure of that?" Jen caught herself asking as she looked up into Asher's unreadable eyes.

"Because I'm third in command; I get things done," he reminded her in a detached and cocky way. The old Asher had returned.

A half an hour later, the hover bug floated into a dome-like brown cave, just above old gravel under the tunnels of Old New York. Jen took in the sight of crumbled cement and trash scattered everywhere. Even the walls were cracked and looked like they were seconds from collapsing in on themselves. She understood why Asher chose the subway as the best place to open the portals. No one in their right mind would be caught in such a hazardous area.

The headlights of the hover pointed straight ahead, showing the faint image of an entryway that had crumpled in. Jen had noticed a lot of other entry points that were closed off as well, making it difficult for the police to successfully find an entrance that would lead them directly to where the portal would be opened.

Everyone jumped out of the hover and moved toward the subway, where the headlights still shone brightly. Lark kneeled down to the ground, pulling out the portal, which was wrapped in a white cloth with intricate silver designs on it. He moved away from everyone, finding a good open spot, and sat down on the gravel, not worried about getting dirty. Asher and Rogue also moved away and spoke in hushed voices as they ran over the plan. Jen stood awkwardly, not exactly sure what she should be doing. She decided to go sit next to Lark and watch him.

"Hey," she said, sitting down. Lark held the metal object in his hand, intently staring at it while running his hand along its surface.

"B-bored?" Lark laughed. "Or just nervous?"

"Nervous," Jen said.

"S-same here," Lark stuttered, then cursed under his breath in frustration as he studied the portal. "Whoever invented the p-portal was a genius. It was d-designed as a puzzle, and if opened c-correctly, it opens a n-new dimension, in which time travel b-becomes possible. All you have t-to do is imagine the p-place you want to go and it t-takes you there. They m-made the por-tals extremely h-hard to open because of the f-fear that they would get into t-the wrong hands and someone would rewrite h-history. Same reason why they only m-made a handful of these things. I heard s-scientists have tried to r-remake the portal but can't replicate it, not w-without the original blueprint."

"Well, where is the original blueprint?" Jen asked.

"I'm sure the p-person who invented the portal has it s-safely locked away, and for great reasons," Lark said. His hand twitched, and a side of the cube opened in a weird angle. Jen watched in amazement as the metal began to elongate and form into a large triangle because of Lark's calculated twists and turns. After about two minutes, he whistled and stood up, pull-ing Jen away from the portal. She stared down at the metal cube sitting on the ground, doing nothing. She looked up at Lark, con-fused. "Nothing is happening," she said, disappointed.

"Wait for it..." Lark told her, staring at the portal in amaze-ment. Jen listened and returned her attention back to the portal.

Seconds later, a loud ZAP made her jump back. She felt a hard body press against her and tilted her head back to see Ash-er staring down at her with a desperate expression. For a moment she was confused by his close proximity, but then his pain sunk in. The opening of the portal meant they were one step closer to never seeing each other again.

The portal stole Jen's attention as it began to shake and dou-ble its size. A strong, white light blasted from within, causing everyone to shield their eyes. Jen was the first to recover, slow-ly moving her hand away from her face and watching as the warm, white light began to swirl, revealing a small opening in the middle that grew wider until her bedroom became visible. Jen's heart beat faster as she watched everything familiar to her silently welcome her back, reclaiming her into its world.

Jen stared at her old bedroom in awe and then reached out to Lark and hugged him, with tears clouding her eyes. "You are a genius, Lark." She pulled away and reluctantly turned toward Asher and Rogue. Asher, who wore a guarded expression, moved toward Jen and leaned down to her ear.

"You have five minutes," he said, and as his lips brushed her ear, she squirmed in delight. Asher still had an effect on her, no matter how angry she was with him. She looked up at him, meeting his eyes. He was looking at her as if he cherished her, as if that moment would be their last.

Jen could decide to go home and never come back, and could he blame her? He hadn't made her feel very welcomed the last few days and it wasn't as if she hadn't thought about returning home in that moment. She had nothing to lose, really. Her father's disappearance would remain a mystery, and she'd never see Asher again. Even if she came back after grabbing the portal, the day was coming when she'd leave for good.

Jen took a step toward the portal, feeling a sense of dread fill her chest like a water balloon, seconds from bursting. It was a terrible feeling, and she had to shake her head to keep from allowing herself to think about the dangers of their mission.

"What's wrong?" Asher asked her, sensing her hesitation.

"Nothing," Jen said. "I'm ready."

"Less than five minutes," Asher said again, staring at her intently. Even though he said it, his hands still clung to her arms as if he had no intention of letting go. Jen nodded, pulled herself out of his grip, and began walking toward the portal.

"Hurry up! Stop wasting time!" Lark shouted. Jen nodded and took in a deep breath, preparing to jump through the portal.

"Here goes nothing," Jen proclaimed with determination. A second later, she closed her eyes and jumped.

Jen's feet landed on hardwood floor, which was a familiar sound to her ears. She opened her eyes and found herself standing in her room with a feeling of joy beginning to wash away all of her dread as she took in the familiar smell of her clean room. She wanted to jump on her bed and scream with joy, but she knew she only had about five minutes to complete her mission.

Jen turned back around and saw all three of her accomplices staring back, and it looked as if the only thing separating them was water. Jen turned away from the portal and took in the sight of her room. Everything was exactly how she left it. She looked at the clock on her wall and noticed that it was eleven at night. That meant her mother was home and was probably reading in her bedroom. Jen wanted so desperately to go to her mother and explain that everything was okay and that she was alive but knew she couldn't. She hadn't come back for her mother but for the book. Jen moved toward her nightstand to try to find the book.

"Jen?" She froze as she heard her name sounding from the hallway. "Who's in there?"

Jen knew that if her mother saw her, she'd need to explain everything, and she just didn't have time. She quickly ran to her nightstand, pulling the drawer open. She'd be able to grab the book and jump back through the portal before her mother even noticed. But the drawer was empty. The book was missing! Jen's heart sped up as anxiety settled in. Where had it gone?

Her door opened, and her mother walked into the room, first taking in the sight of Jen, and then the portal within her closet. Her mom raised a hand to her chest in shock.

"Jen..."

"Mom," Jen cried, running into her mother's arms, welcoming her warmth. A sound came from the portal, and Jen pulled away from her mother just in time to see Asher jump through. His fierce eyes connected with her as he walked toward her with determination. The sight of him made her mom cry out.

"What's going on? Who is he?" she asked, taking a few steps back in fear. "How is this possible?" Jen ignored her mother and focused on Asher.

"We don't have much time. Where is the book?" he asked.

"It's not where I left it!" Jen panicked.

"Think about it." Asher's voice was calm but full of authority.

"Where could it be?"

Jen nodded toward her mother. "Mom, where's the fairy tale book that was in my drawer? Have you seen it?"

Her mom held her chest in disbelief as tears poured from her face. "Yes," she wept. "It reminded me of you, so I took it to my room to read each night you were gone. Are you back now? Why did you even leave? What's happening? Jen, answer my questions!"

Jen shook her head, not having time to explain, and quickly ran from her bedroom to her mother's room. She began searching through her mother's things, finally, finding it under the bed in a wooden chest. She quickly grabbed the book and ran out of her mother's room, feeling as if minutes had passed and that she was too late.

"Thirty seconds left!" Asher yelled. "Hurry!"

When Jen returned to her bedroom, she saw Asher pacing back and forth as Mrs. Kallis sat on Jen's bed, still holding her chest.

"Momma, I love you, and I'll explain everything when I come back...with Dad."

"No! I've already lost you once. I can't see you go again."

"I'll come back...with Dad," Jen said, As Asher grabbed her hand and pulled her toward the portal.

"We have ten seconds," Asher said. The portal was quickly closing.

"Bring him back to me, Jen," her mom called out. "Please..."

Asher quickly pushed Jen through the portal and jumped through the narrowing hole, landing on hard debris. He stood and watched as the portal completely closed and vanished into nothing. Jen lay next to him, scrambling to her feet with the book in her hand. She was crying, even though she knew she should have been happy, but she couldn't shake the devastated look on her mother's face. She hated leaving her mother for a second time, but had to do what was needed. At least she knows I'm alive, Jen thought.

"You got the book?" Rogue asked, walking to where Jen was standing. Rogue snatched the book out of Jen's hand and flipped through the pages. "Exactly how is this book supposed to help you?" Jen snatched the book back.

"We aren't sure, but she's pretty sure her father needs it," Asher answered on Jen's behalf. "Now we have to go! The police are probably in the tunnels as we speak. Get in the hover, quick!"

Jen rushed to the hover and climbed into the passenger seat. She placed the black book in the glove compartment, shut it, and buckled her seatbelt. She remembered the last time they had been chased by cops and knew her seatbelt was a must. She closed her eyes and silently prayed they would make it out alive. Asher started the engine and the hover roared to life. Jen watched Asher's hand point at a large purple button and freeze. Confused, Jen looked up at his eyes and followed where they were staring. Straight ahead, two cop hovers pulled to a stop. At least seven different police robots jumped out and hid directly behind the doors, pointing shooters at them. The robots were different than the ones Jen had grown used to seeing. These were made of shiny, thick metal, and actually stood on two feet. They also had the word "Police" written on their breast plate and had a holster full of gadgets and weapons hanging from their hips.

Jen looked back at Asher and noticed the red light, about the size of a pen point, beaming on his chest. Jen didn't have to be from Blue City to know it was a laser pointed at him. "Oh my gosh," she cried out.

"Please step out of the hover with both hands up!" a voice blazed through the air.

"What do we do?" Jen asked Asher. "This wasn't planned!"

"We obey," Asher said, grinding his teeth in anger. "Just trust me."

Asher slowly opened his door and stepped out of the hover. Jen didn't need to look behind her to see if Rogue and Lark had done the same. She heard their doors close as they stood just outside of the hover with both hands raised. Jen was the last out.

"Turn toward the hover and place both hands on the hood," the officer shouted at them through his built-in loudspeaker. Everyone obeyed.

From the corner of Jen's eyes, she saw the robots rush forward and knew within seconds they'd all be handcuffed and taken to jail. Jen looked back at Asher, who watched her intently. Something glistened in his eyes, and Jen recognized it as determination and a bit of a thrill. The fear Jen had been feeling vanished as she stared back at him, understanding that Asher had already evaluated the situation and knew exactly what to do. It was as if it were a game for him, a very thrilling and dangerous game.

The first cop approached, pushing Jen against the hover with force, and began reciting words very similar to the Miranda rights. Jen kept her eyes on Asher, who now had a cop directly behind him.

Jen felt handcuffs snap too tightly around her wrists, and she cried out in pain. The sound made Asher jump into action. With one swift movement, he turned toward the cop holding him in place and tore its metal head from its socket. He quickly pulled the shooter from the robot as it fell to the ground, and turned toward Jen, blowing the robot behind her into pieces. Asher faced the other robots.

There were five cops left, but Asher knew more were on the way. He needed to create a barrier to keep the cops from finding the same entrance. But before he could do that, he had to subdue the other cops. Asher shot at the cop holding Lark and saw from the corner of his eyes that Rogue was fighting off the one who held her against the car. He didn't have to worry about her being able to defend herself, so he focused on the cop that hid behind the door of a hover, pointing a shooter in his direction.

Asher quickly threw himself on the ground, narrowly missing the shot, which hit fallen debris, causing dust to spew everywhere. He was on his feet again, firing his shooter at the cop, but it was no use; all of its energy had run out. Asher was at a disadvantage. The police officer was protected by the door, but Asher was protected by nothing except pure luck, as the cop lost interest in him and turned his shooter on the others. Fear coursed through Asher's body as his eyes landed on Jen.

"Get behind the hover!" Asher screamed, watching Jen sink

low to the ground just as the cop began to fire. He was angry now. He noticed another shooter lying near one of the robots and grabbed it. He kneeled down and positioned himself while pointing his shooter at the gas tank of the first cop car.

Asher hit the gas tank, but nothing exploded. He looked over to find his own hover damaged by the blast of the robot's shooter. Asher would be thankful if the hover worked after the shots it took. Asher lined his shot up again and fired at the tank, hearing the explosion before he felt it.

Hot fire shot toward him as the first cop car flew into the air, flipping over and over until it blocked the first entrance. The explosion was strong enough to send Asher flying back a few feet. He landed on the gravel and spotted the lifeless robot that had blown apart in the explosion. Yes, Asher thought. I got you. Two birds with one stone.

Asher ran to Jen's side and saw that she was still dazed by the explosion. He helped her to her feet and placed her inside the hover. He then turned to find Rogue limping toward the hover with Lark passed out in her arms. Asher moved to help, taking Lark from Rogue's arms, and sat him in the back of the hover.

"The explosion knocked him out cold. What were you thinking?" Rogue asked.

"I saved all of you with that explosion. Now get in the hover. We have to move!" Asher commanded, and Rogue followed orders, hopping into the back next to Lark. Asher quickly jumped into the driver's side and started the engine, thankful that it roared to life. He didn't hesitate as he pressed the purple button, causing the car to lift from the ground. He hit a few more buttons, and the hover took off into the empty, abandoned tunnel to his right.

Asher had spent the last three days locked up in his room, studying the tunnels, so that he'd know his escape plan like the back of his hand when the time came. Jen watched in fear as he zoomed through the tunnels, sharply turning left, then right, and left again. He'd been driving for five minutes and had gone down ten different tunnels. Jen wondered if he even knew where he was going, the way he was driving, but she reminded herself that she needed to trust him.

She tore her curious eyes away from Asher and screamed. They were seconds away from crashing the hover into a wall straight ahead, which would result in an instantaneous death. Jen let out a shriek and held onto her seat, saying a quiet prayer. At the very last minute, Asher shifted the stick and the car turned left down a new tunnel. Jen sat there, paralyzed and breathing deeply. She had just watched her life flash before her eyes.

A deep chuckle snapped her out of it. Asher was staring straight ahead, laughing at her as if it was all funny to him. Jen's eyes went wild.

"You jerk! How could you play at a time like this? Did you almost hit that wall on purpose?"

"Maybe," Asher said, still laughing. As hard as Jen tried to fight it, a small smile tugged at the edge of her lips. She hadn't seen Asher laugh in days, and it was a sight that lit up his whole face and would make any girl within eyesight drool. He was that beautiful, but he was also that cruel to play a joke on her in the middle of a crisis.

"There's something seriously wrong with you," Jen spat, but her anger didn't really come off as strong as she'd hoped.

"Again...maybe," Asher responded, and instantly went back to being serious.

They'd just had a moment, Jen thought. Although it wasn't really a cute moment, it was still a moment and it was still an improvement over the last three days when they hadn't spoken. Today he'd saved her life, multiple times, and he'd laughed out-right. He wasn't being mean and distant like he had been after they confessed their feelings to each other. Maybe he'd come back around. No. She was dreaming. Today reminded her how different their worlds were when she briefly stepped back in the year 2016 Soon this would all be over, and it would be like they never knew each other. Every time Jen thought of it, her chest felt heavy. She leaned against the passenger window feeling hopeless.

How was it possible that she could handle narrowly escaping death and yet want to die the moment she thought of life without Asher? She had only known him for a short amount of time and yet she'd experienced more life with him than she had with her actual friends. Her feelings for Asher were starting to outweigh her own feelings about finding her father. Jen needed to stop thinking with her heart and be logical. She had a mission to accomplish, and nothing was supposed to get in the way of that mission, not even love. She hated that she kept having to remind herself of this simple fact over and over again.

Jen closed her eyes as she fought back a round of tears. She wouldn't let them see her weak. She couldn't.

"Hey." Jen's eyes popped open at the soft sound of Asher's voice. She quickly sat up in her seat and saw the sun's glory as it began to illuminate the sky. They had managed to complete their mission before the break of dawn. "We made it out of the tunnels. We shouldn't have any other problems going forward. I don't want to speak too soon, but it's safe to say that we've succeeded in our mission."

"I thought it was impossible," Rogue said from the back seat, leaning too close to Asher for Jen's comfort. "But we did it, as a team."

"So what now?" Jen asked, trying to ignore Rogue, as she lifted a hand to rest on Asher's shoulder.

"We find Frank Hoggs who should lead us right to your father," Asher said, absentmindedly pushing Rogue's hand off his shoulder.

"And what if he doesn't cooperate?" Jen asked, earning herself a smirk from Asher.

"I'm good at making people talk," Asher said, in a tone that meant she shouldn't keep pressing the issue. Jen relaxed in her seat and stared out at the morning traffic as hovers zoomed by. She allowed herself to drift off to sleep for the second time that morning.

Jen rolled over, loving the feel of silk sheets caressing her face. Her bed felt even more comfortable than usual. It was as if she lay in a sea of clouds, with angels softly playing harps nearby. Then a thought occurred to her. The guest bedroom felt nothing like the bed she was lying in now. Jen sat up, first checking to make sure her clothes were on, and then looking around the familiar room at the dark walls and the black curtains barely letting any sun in. Her eyes finally rested on a pair of bare male legs stretched out next to her, and she shrieked.

"Calm down." Asher laughed, watching Jen nearly jump out of the bed. "You fell asleep in the car so I carried you inside."

Jen relaxed, looking back to see Asher resting against his headboard, wide awake. He held Jen's fairy tale book in his hand. "You could've carried me to the guest bedroom, you know?"

"Yeah." Asher grinned. "But it just felt right, putting you in my bed." He sighed and leaned forward. "Jen, I truly realized something today. It happened within the last few seconds of the portal closing." He paused and ran his hand down the side of his face in frustration. "I was so anxious watching you go inside the portal, wondering if you were going to come back to me, knowing how miserable I'd made you and seeing how happy you were to be back in your room. And then I saw your mother, and I knew the moment you saw her, you would have stayed there with her. I couldn't stand there and watch you not come back. So I jumped through the portal to make sure you came back, and if you decided to stay there, I was going to—"

Asher was interrupted as his door materialized. Rogue walked into the bedroom and took in the sight of them on the bed with a sour expression. Her eyes drifted down to The Book of Fairy Tales, and she visibly cheered up. "I was just coming to look at the fairy tale book."

"Not until I'm done looking at it," Jen told her firmly, not understanding why Rogue felt the need to see it. Rogue stood there, looking at Asher for the final answer. He sighed and waved Rogue away.

"You heard the girl," Asher said, tapping the book in his lap impatiently.

"Three days ago, you were all over me, Asher," Rogue fumed. "Can't you make up your mind? Now it's like you're pushing me away and inviting her back in. Remember that the girl who plans to stay around after this mission is right here. Me. Don't be foolish." And with that, Rogue turned around and stormed out of the bedroom.

Asher sighed. "Ignore her. Jen, I want to apologize for how I've been treating you. I know I'm not the most considerate person and I can be really stupid when it comes to my feelings, but I've never lied to you. I really do like you. That morning after we confessed our feelings to each other, I went to tell Rogue that I had no plans to ever take her back, but before I even got around to it, she started telling me how I'd never be able to truly have you because you didn't belong here.

"That's when it really hit me, that what we had would only be temporary. I decided in that moment that we couldn't have anything. I thought that the only way to get over you was to act as if you meant nothing to me, but I was so stupid because every second you were near me, I was on fire. What have you done to me, Ancient Meat?" Jen smiled as Asher raised a hand to her cheek, caressing the spot next to her lips.

Jen couldn't believe what she'd heard. This whole time she'd thought Asher had had a change of heart, and yet it had never changed, he'd only tried to make it change. He truly liked her, just as she liked him, and that meant there was still a chance for them. Jen was no longer angry or felt he was two-timing both her and Rogue. He was only trying to protect his heart, as she had been doing too. A thought occurred to her.

"Asher, you were about to say something else before Rogue walked in. What was it? If I had stayed behind in 2016, you would've what?" Jen asked, searching his eyes frantically.

"I was going to say, if you would've decided to stay, I...would've been really hurt."

"Oh," was all Jen said.

"I'm sorry..." Asher said, reaching out to grab Jen's hand and placing it in his own. He traced small circles in Jen's palm, which seemed to soothe her. "...for giving you hope in us and then removing that hope. Do you forgive me?"

"If I said yes, then what does that mean for us? At the end of the day, you're right. We don't belong together. We both have our own separate lives."

"It means I'll do whatever I can in my power to keep you

next to me for as long as possible."

"How can you say that? When I find my father, my family will be reunited. I'll go home and continue living my life. You know that. It's the reason I'm here. As much as I wish things were different, they aren't."

"But what if they could be different?" Asher asked. "What if we could find a way to be together?"

"That would mean you'd have to come back with me," Jen said. "And I'd never make you leave everything behind. I've told you this already."

"We'll see what happens when the time comes," Asher said cautiously. He watched Jen as her attention shifted to the black fairy tale book sitting in his lap. She reached over and picked it up, flicking through the pages in deep thought. Asher wanted to tuck a loose curl behind her ear but thought better of it. He loved how unruly her hair could be, and it reminded him of her defiant personality.

"My father would read this book to me every night. It never failed. Looking back, I see how strange that is. He never read me any other books, just this one. And after he was done reading, he'd always remind me of its importance. 'Keep this book close to your heart,' he'd say. 'This book holds the wonders of the world.' I never knew what he meant by that. Anyway, I always kept this book safely tucked away. It's the only thing I have left of him."

"Jen," Asher began, with crease lines stretching across his forehead. He looked deep in thought. "What if your father knew the future and made sure he prepared you for it? What if he knew he'd get kidnapped and that you'd end up on a mission to find him?"

"But how would he know that?"

"What if he traveled in time and saw the chain of events take place?"

"How would my father even know about time travel? It makes no sense."

"Think about it. He told you to bring him the book. He told you that it holds a thousand worlds. It sounds to me like there's something hidden inside. If I'm right, it shouldn't be hard to figure out why this book is so important. Here, let me see it." Asher grabbed the book from Jen and examined it. He then turned the book over and opened the last page. His hands brushed over the paper, and he focused on an imperfection in the seam. He pulled on a loose string, and the seam began pulling apart.

"Hey!" Jen cried out, trying to grab the book but Asher pulled back, continuing to rip the pages out. "What are you doing? You're destroying it!"

Asher ignored Jen and tossed the loose pages to the side so he could examine the hardback cover. He noticed a thin layer and peeled it back, revealing a complex document with numbers and equations off to the side as sketches of a square object took up the rest of the page. Asher held it closer, completely taken back.

"Your dad was hiding something all right. It's a blueprint." He finally allowed Jen to snatch the hardcover away from him and study it. It was definitely some sort of design similar to what an architect would draw. But what was it a blueprint of?

"Why would my dad hide a blueprint of something that seems far more complex than anything I've ever seen in my entire life? Only a genius could figure this out." Jen's eyes darted to where Asher sat with a victorious grin on his face. What did he know that she didn't? "What?"

"We have a genius."

Two minutes later, Jen and Asher sat on the couch next to Lark, who gazed down in fascination at the hardback cover, his glasses almost falling off his face. He sat up straight and pushed the brim of his glasses up on his nose.

"I can't believe it," Lark said in awe. His mouth hung open as he continued to stare.

"Well, what is it?" Asher asked with impatience.

"It's the blueprint to the portal. Do you know what this means?"

"The blueprint went missing over twenty years ago," Asher said. "There was a huge conspiracy about it. Some people said the government hid it from those who wanted to build their own portals and wreak havoc. Others said it was simply destroyed. My favorite theory was that an evil mastermind had stolen it and was planning world domination. But never in my life would I have guessed the portal blueprint was sent back to the year 2016 to go in a child's favorite fairy tale book.

"I think the question we should be asking is why," Asher said. "Why did your father have the blueprint and why did he hide it and make sure to send you subliminal messages as a child so that you'd eventually find it?"

"What are you guys talking about?" Rogue asked, walking into the living room as the second guest bedroom door disappeared into the wall.

"We found the blueprint to the portal," Lark shouted happily. Rogue frowned and took a seat next to Asher.

"So what does that mean?"

"We aren't sure yet," Jen said. "Hopefully we'll know why my father chose to hide the blueprint in my book once we find him."

"Oh my gosh," Rogue said, sitting up. "What if the portal opened up in your room when you were a kid because someone came looking for the blueprint and then took your father instead?"

"She's onto something," Asher agreed.

"Whoever has your father was after the portal. It all makes sense," Rogue continued.

"And we also know that the government may be behind my father's disappearance," Jen said, and then a sinking feeling hit. "But it just doesn't make sense. My father was born in 1962. How would he have even gotten the portal? How would anyone in 2222 know anything about my father? Ugh. I have a headache."

"How about we stop asking questions until we talk to someone with the answers," Asher said, rubbing Jen's back to calm her. "That means, next up we meet with Frank Hoggs."

CHAPTER EIGHTEEN

Blue City

Two more days passed as they prepped for their next mission. The atmosphere was tense the whole time. As Jen and Asher drew closer, Rogue's sweet-girl act disappeared and she was proving to be an even bigger pain than before.

Jen stood in Asher's grandiose kitchen as Anna prepared two cups of hot chocolate. This time, a machine similar to an advanced coffee pot clicked to life. Jen stood next to the counter watching as the hot water filled the pot and gasped when brown powder dropped into the water. A spoon lowered from within the machine and stirred the pot. A cabinet door by Jen's knees popped open, and a pair of robotic hands withdrew two cups from inside, set both down on the counter, and then retreated to its spot under the countertop.

Jen blinked.

"I swear, if I hadn't known you were from the past, I would've thought you were retarded," Rogue spat, walking slowly into the kitchen. Her eyes were low and her arms were crossed underneath her chest as she watched Jen. It didn't help that her dark eye makeup added to the "scary" effect.

"What?" Jen asked, trying to sound indifferent to Rogue's intimidating glare.

"You're standing there, staring at a hot chocolate maker as if it's the world's coolest invention."

"We don't have hot chocolate makers like this where I'm from," Jen said, watching Rogue with a frown.

"Go figure," Rogue said, bumping Jen as she brushed past her. That was it. Jen had had it with Rogue's attitude.

"What is it with you?" Jen asked, spinning toward where Rogue stood. "Do you have something against me?"

Rogue laughed, opened a cabinet, and pulled out a bag of chips. Then she turned toward Jen, opened the bag, leaned against the counter, and placed a chip in her mouth.

"I think it's you with the problem, Jen. You're selfish."

"What? How so?" Jen's mouth fell open.

"How much are you going to take from Asher? Was it not enough to just let him help you find his father? You had to go and take his heart, too? Live in his luxurious condo temporarily? Eat his food and wear the clothes he gave you? And what have you done for him? Nothing. You just take. And once you find your father, you're going to leave Asher here, without a heart, because you're taking it back to 2016 with you! So, yes, I hate you, because I'm watching you destroy the man I love."

"If you loved him, Rogue, you wouldn't have left him," Jen fired back. "You're accusing me of doing something I haven't even done yet, while you've already broken his heart, which is why he is the way he is now. Look in the mirror before you call someone else out. You're just jealous because you left something good and I'm here to take it."

"Do you plan to make him go back with you? You think he'd leave this all behind?" Rogue laughed, but it sounded filled with venom. "He's already made enough sacrifices for you. If you really liked him, you'd stay. You're already here, so is your father. So why not just stay, Jen? Wait, I know why." Rogue pushed off of the counter and walked toward Jen until she was standing directly in front of her face. Her closeness was enough to make Jen shiver, but Jen stood strong, her eyes never wavering as she stared back at Rogue's challenging gaze. "It's because you don't really love Asher. You just love that he's helping you. You're just using him, and as soon as you have what you came here for, you're going to toss him to the side. It's what I've been saying this whole time. Once you're gone, Asher will have me, and I plan to be the one to mend his broken heart. So, excuse me if, when I look at you, I'm reminded of your selfishness and I'm filled with hatred."

Rogue bumped into Jen as she passed, making Jen stumble against the counter. She reached a hand out to steady herself, but her hand smacked against the cup of hot chocolate, which spilled onto her hand. Jen jumped back, screaming as her hand got burnt, and watched the hot chocolate splash onto the floor.

"Crap!" Jen rushed to the sink and rested her burning hand under cold water. She couldn't believe Rogue's nerve.

"Are you okay?" Asher's deep voice instantly soothed Jen. She wanted to pull him into a hug, but then she remembered everything Rogue had said. There Asher stood, ready to save her again, but she wasn't going to let him. He'd helped her so much, and she had nothing to give in return.

"I'm fine," was all she said. She kept herself turned away from Asher as a single tear escaped. I wonder if his heart will burn as much as my hand when I leave him, she thought.

"You don't look fine," Asher said softly, and walked toward her. He stopped directly behind Jen, and the heat of his body rolled off his chest, making Jen even hotter. She shivered as soon as she felt his hand massage her left shoulder. "What's wrong? I saw Rogue storm out of the kitchen, and I heard you scream."

"It's nothing," Jen said, trying to make her voice even, but her tears were freely falling now. "Just spilled some hot chocolate and it burned my hand. I'm fine."

"Your voice is deceiving you." Asher spun Jen around and studied her wet face. He grabbed a napkin from the counter and dabbed at her tears. "What did Rogue say that upset you?"

"Nothing that isn't true," Jen said, trying to force a smile, but by the deepening crease lines in Asher's forehead, she could tell the smile wasn't working. She finally sighed and let her guard down. "Will you hate me when I leave?"

"If you leave," Asher corrected her. "And why would I?"

"Because I'm leaving what we could've had. I'm so torn. A part of me wants to stay, but I miss home so much and seeing my mother made me miss it even more."

"Is that what Rogue was hassling you about? This has been our plan from the beginning. I offered to help you find your father and get you home."

"And I can't even repay you."

"You have," Asher said, brushing a hand against her cheek. "You gave me an adventure and made me see that love is possible again. You've softened me. You've made me see the beauty in life again. Jen, I was just getting by day by day before you came. Now, I'm truly living.

"There's a strong possibility that we may not even find your father and make it out alive, so let's not worry about what's going to happen days from now. Let's focus on now. No hard feelings. No doubts. No sadness. Just us, enjoying what we have left. Can we do that?"

How he managed to make everything sound like it came straight from a romantic movie beat Jen, but she loved it. Asher wasn't the kind of man to utter sweet nothings, but obviously she was changing him. Maybe, in her own way, she had helped him fight his demons.

Asher was right—they had other things to worry about. They'd almost died multiple times and yet Jen was focused on the end. She needed to be focused on tomorrow, because it held all of the answers she'd been searching for. She snapped out of her thoughts as she felt Asher pull her into a hug.

"Who knows what tomorrow holds, but today I hold you," Asher said. "Can I take you on a date? A real one? I may never get another chance to do that."

Jen lifted her head, so that she could see his eyes as he stared down at her. "A date?"

"Yes. Somewhere you've never been before. Some place that'll always remind you of me and Blue City."

"I have a lot of memories already. But a new one would be great. And I'd love to go on a date. What are we going to do?"

"It's a surprise." Asher pulled away from their embrace. "Be ready in an hour, and find something comfortable to wear. I'll worry about this mess."

Jen rushed to the guest bedroom, forgetting the slight pain in her hand from spilling the hot chocolate. She had a date to get ready for.

A half an hour later, Asher's hover bug pulled up to a deserted beach. There was a small sign that read "Blue Ocean" that looked old and misplaced with such a stunning beach decorating its background.

The ocean was bluer than any ocean Jen had seen back at home. Even tropical oceans were nothing in comparison to the sea of aquamarine gems shining brightly in the early afternoon light. Even the sand looked whiter than it should have been. Jen felt as if she was in a vibrant painting that depicted what oceans looked like on other planets.

She didn't wait around for Asher as she slipped off her shoes and sank her feet into the sand, delighting in its warmth. After a few seconds, she ran toward the ocean with both hands outstretched. The waves crashed to the shore, filling the beach with the smell of seaweed and salt water. Jen walked a few inches into the ocean, allowing the waves that crashed to the shore to tickle her ankles. For the first time while in Blue City, she felt absolutely free.

"I knew you'd like it here," Asher said, catching up to her. He stood by her side, staring out at God's glorious ocean.

"I'm surprised more people aren't here."

"No one swims in the ocean these days, not when they have indoor water parks that keep people away from the sun."

"I'd prefer the actual beach over some manmade waterpark any day." Jen closed her eyes and lifted her chin so that the sun beamed down on her face. She could feel Asher admiring her, which made her smile.

"I knew you would. That's what I like about you. You're genuinely good. More than almost every person I've ever met in Blue City."

"What do you mean?"

"Everything here isn't natural, but you are," Asher began. "Let's take the ocean, for example. Ever seen water that blue before? They put a chemical in the water when they first built Blue City. A nonhazardous chemical dyed the water to give vacationers a picture-perfect beach feel. The water isn't naturally this blue.

"The food isn't real, either. It's all processed in a lab. And you can get any surgery done to look however you want for cheap. I'm sure there are about two hundred Michael Jacksons walking around Blue City due to plastic surgery."

"You know who Michael Jackson is?" Jen laughed out loud.

"Who doesn't? Sure, he was famous over two hundred years ago, but the tales of great legends never die, at least not his legacy."

"I'm impressed," Jen said, and lowered her eyes to a basket and large bag dangling from Asher's hand.

"I brought things for a picnic," Asher explained, and set the bags down. Jen watched as he unfolded a towel stuffed into the large bag. He then placed the basket's contents onto the blanket and began organizing it. Within minutes, their date had turned romantic.

Sandwiches on plates, nonalcoholic drinks in wine glasses, and a vase of roses in the middle of everything—Jen couldn't believe Asher had planned all of this for her. She smiled as his eyes met hers.

"Come sit," Asher said.

"Okay," Jen answered and took a seat across from him. She couldn't hide the silly smile plastered on her face or ignore the way Asher stared at her as if she was the most beautiful girl in Blue City. "This is so nice."

"It's just the beginning."

"What else do you have planned?"

"I'm not telling." Asher acted as if he was zipping his lips up. Jen giggled and picked up her sandwich. She hadn't realized how hungry she was until she took a bite. She moaned as the taste exploded in her mouth.

"Anna makes the best food," Jen said, taking another bite.

"I made the subs," Asher said and leaned toward Jen in a deadly sexy way. "I can't always let Anna take the credit."

"You should've been a chef, not a commander."

"It's just a sub." Asher's face had turned pink from her compliment.

"It's just the best sub I've ever had. Seriously. You should time travel to the past and create Subway."

"I just might," Asher joked. "What's your favorite color?"

"That was random."

"I want to know the little things," Asher stated. Jen nodded and put her sub down.

"Let's see," she began. "My favorite color is blue, I play the piano, although not that well, and I love tacos and Sloppy Joes. I also love all types of music, although Taylor Swift is my favorite artist. I once learned all of the dances in the movie Dirty Dancing. When I was a preteen, I had Jonas Brothers and Hannah Montana posters all over my wall. I hate cats, but I love dogs, especially little dogs like tea cup poodles, even though my mother would never let me have one."

"Tell me about your mother."

"My mom, she's amazing, although she hasn't always been that way," Jen said, feeling sadness tug at her heart. She didn't like to think of anything that made her sad, but she also wanted Asher to know the things that made her cry. "When my dad disappeared, she sunk into a deep depression and pretty much forgot to raise me. I spent a lot of holidays alone. It's..." she paused, taking a deep breath. "...it's in the past. She snapped out of it when I was around twelve, and I got my mom back. Since then, we've had a great relationship. Mom always dances to Michael Jackson in the mornings when she's making me breakfast. I have a huge feeling I'm going to do the same when I'm cooking for my children."

"I would love to see that," Asher said, smiling widely. It saddened Jen that he wanted to because he would never get the chance.

"I also love coloring. I know that's childish, but I love coloring pictures. I'm really good with kids and babies. I want a large family one day. I didn't have any siblings, but I want at least five kids. I already have their names picked out, but I won't tell you what they are."

"You really have the names picked out?" Asher laughed.

"Don't laugh at me." Jen reached over and playfully slapped Asher's knee. "Yes, I do. I live in a small town with barely anything to do, so my mind tends to wander. Anything else you want to know about me?"

"Yes." Asher's face grew serious as he contemplated his next question. "What made you keep faith that you'd find your father after all these years? Have you ever given up hope?"

"Yeah, a few times," Jen admitted. "Everyone used to say I was crazy for thinking he'd disappeared into my closet. When you have enough people telling you that your father just left you, at some point you do begin to believe it."

"I'm sorry you had to deal with so much," Asher said. That was when Jen noticed he hadn't taken a single bite out of his sub. "Eat!" she commanded. Asher picked up his sub and took a large bite. "And I didn't deal with anything I couldn't handle."

"You're shhrooong," he said with a full mouth.

"The fact that you're admitting I'm strong means a lot. For a while there, I thought you and Rogue thought of me as a burden. Especially with all the trouble Lark and I put you through." Jen paused, thinking about Lark and his curly, red hair, and over-sized, thick glasses. "I'm going to really miss Lark. He's helped us a lot on this journey. It was smart of you to take him from Gunner."

"Gunner owed me," Asher said, making a sour face. He stood and held a hand out. "Come on, get up."

"Huh?" Jen asked in confusion, but took his hand and allowed him to pull her up.

"It's time for some fun." His eyes squinted as he pointed at a white building in the distance. "See that building over there? That's where we're going."

"What is it?"

"You'll see." He smiled, pulling her away from their blanket. Jen couldn't believe Asher and his surprises, but she had to admit she was very excited to see what lay inside.

Ten minutes later, they stood in front of the building, hand in hand. Asher pulled her up the steps like an excited little boy. He opened one of the large double doors and motioned for Jen to go inside.

Jen smiled and walked past Asher into the building, freezing at the sight. It was as if she was staring at a large indoor Olympic swimming pool. She stood at the edge of the large body of water and watched two dolphins doing back flips as a blonde female instructor stood on the edge, giving them hand signals. Once the dolphins flipped, they swam up to the woman, who threw fish into their mouths and petted them affectionately.

"Good girls," the blonde said with a bright smile and Australian accent. Jen decided instantly that she liked her. "Now let's impress our guests and wave to them." The blonde made a hand gesture and the dolphins quickly dived underwater. Jen wondered what they were doing, until they emerged in the middle of the pool, looking at the instructor. She lifted her hands and waved, and the dolphins mimicked her movements.

"Oh my gosh," Jen exclaimed, covering her mouth with one hand. "They waved!" She heard Asher chuckle behind her.

"Let's go get up close and personal with them." Asher tugged on Jen's hand, but she stayed planted in her spot. Asher turned back around with a frown.

"What do you mean get up close and personal with them?"

"Ever wanted to ride a dolphin?"

"Asher!" Jen wanted to scream with excitement. "Really? We can get in the water with them?"

"Of course." Asher said and pulled Jen toward the instructor. The blonde woman stood and smiled as they approached. She looked to be in her late twenties and wore a huge diamond on her wedding ring. She held out a hand first to Jen and then to Asher.

"I'm Natalie, a marine mammal trainer here in Blue City. I have so many exciting things planned for the two of you today. First, you both need to change into swim suits and life jackets, and then you'll be escorted back to the dolphin pool where you'll get acquainted with my little friends here. So come follow me."

Jen followed Natalie to the locker rooms, changed into the swimwear provided, and met Asher back by the pool. Natalie briefed them on the dolphins, and Jen learned she was going to make them do different tricks. She'd even be able to get her picture taken with them. Sure, this was something she could do back home, but it wouldn't be with Asher. This was special.

Jen and Asher spent the next hour interacting with the dolphins by making them wave, do different types of dives, and even speak. When it came time for Jen to get a picture taken, she was able to kiss the dolphin, which she thought was the cutest part. Asher didn't want to kiss the dolphins, even when Jen begged, but he did hug a dolphin for his picture, which made Jen happy.

Eventually, they returned to the beach, where their food sat perfectly untouched, and decided to go swimming. Much to Jen's protest, Asher swept her up in his arms, ran toward the ocean, and dived in the water. He lifted Jen out of the water long enough for her to get some air, and then dived back in, taking her with him.

It was a beautiful day—different and relaxed as they played in the ocean. Jen was so used to drama that she kept expecting something to go wrong on their date, but it didn't. It was like a dream date, one she wished would last forever, but she knew reality would soon be knocking on their door. She tried to forget what lay ahead of them, but it was an impending cloud, looming near her head, threatening to bring a terrible storm.

After swimming, Asher and Jen made a campfire and cuddled. They talked about everything, from her world to his, with all of its differences and similarities. Jen noticed that Asher stayed away from any topics that had to do with his father.

"What are you thinking about?" Asher asked as Jen sat next to him, resting her head on his shoulder while looking out at the fire.

"Your father," she admitted. "Thinking about how badly he treated you and yet how good of a man you are. I bet you're nothing like him."

"My father isn't all bad. He just chose harsh methods of punishment, but in the end it made me the person I am today."

"You're strong," Jen began. "And headstrong. But you're also very thoughtful of other's needs, and you're always a step ahead of everyone else. I wonder what type of guy you'd be if you lived in 2016."

"Maybe you'll get the chance to know, if I go back with you."

"Well, one thing I know for sure, if you did come back, you'd be worse off than me."

"How so?"

"It's like if I were to go back to medieval times. I wouldn't know how to adapt to no electricity or cars or cell phones. And you? You could say goodbye to flying cars and robots. Oh, and you'd manually have to cook everything yourself, go shopping for yourself, and pretty much do everything for yourself. I would never hear the end of your complaints."

"Did you forget I'm in the military? I've lived on practically nothing at times. I had to live for six months in the desert, and all I had was a gun and a canister filled a quarter of the way with water that I had to make last a whole day. I know how it feels not to have electricity and to survive off basic instincts. I wouldn't only be able to live in 2016, but I'd be successful."

"You're right," Jen said, admiring his survival instinct. "You'd survive anything."

"And so would you," Asher told her.

"You're just being nice."

"I'm serious. You've held your own on this mission. You've adapted pretty quickly to a new environment, which shows me that you'd be able to handle extreme changes and survive. You're tougher than you think."

Jen smiled, loving his praise. Maybe he was right. Maybe she was strong in her own way. She fell silent as she continued thinking about how much she'd grown as a person.

She knew their moment in paradise would end soon. Tomorrow they had another mission, one that might lead directly to her father. She had heard the saying, "Be careful what you ask for," and was hoping the answers she was searching for wouldn't cause her to regret ever asking.

CHAPTER NINETEEN

Hoggs

This is it," Asher said, as he pulled the hover to a stop near a decrepit white house. Its windows were boarded up, and the uncut grass stood as tall as the front porch. Jen looked over to Asher, confused why they had stopped there. She wasn't expecting Frank Hoggs to be in a place like this.

"This is an abandoned house. Why would he be here?"

"On the outside, it looks abandoned but it's actually a secret facility for the military. No one would ever expect it to be here, which makes it a perfect hideout. Around this time of year, most officials are overseas, so a couple of guys will take turns running their shift, which consists of sitting around and watching TV because there's nothing else to do. My guess is that Frank Hoggs is the only one on-site, meaning we shouldn't have too much of a defense problem. You guys know the plan. We stick together this time. I'll do all of the questioning. Jen, did you bring the book cover?"

Jen felt for the cover neatly tucked away in her backpack and nodded. After they'd left the campfire, Asher drove back to the condo and told Jen to get some rest for their early mission. But Jen lay awake most of the night, tossing and turning, overly excited about their date.

Jen noticed Asher's soft, reassuring smile and smiled back. She wanted more than to just smile—she wanted to pull him in for a reassuring kiss that would make them each determined to survive their mission. She looked behind her and saw Rogue staring her down. Jen quickly turned back in her seat.

"All right, let's go," Asher said, and jumped out of the hover, pulling a black mask over his face. He kept a few steps ahead, giving Lark the perfect time to whisper to Jen.

"What if Frank Hoggs isn't here?" Lark kept his voice low so that Asher wouldn't hear.

"Let's not think that way," Jen whispered. "We didn't come this far for nothing." Rogue snickered behind her, but Jen ignored her. If she had her way, Rogue wouldn't have tagged along to begin with. She couldn't wait for the day to get rid of her. Why was she still tagging along, when it was clear Asher no longer wanted her? Jen thought. Maybe she's going to fight until the very end. Well, so am I.

Asher reached the front door and lifted his hand on a barely visible sensor screen that Jen wouldn't have noticed on her own. The light flashed green, and the door opened. It still shocked Jen how much access Asher had to all things military related. It was impressive. Out of all the people Jen could have run into after going through the portal, she'd met Asher, and she was truly grateful for that.

"Be quiet," Asher commanded before stepping inside the house.

Jen followed behind and let out a soft gasp as she stared at her surroundings. Asher hadn't lied. She hadn't stepped into an abandoned house, but some sort of open compound, with large TVs plastered across the metallic walls in a circular command room similar to that of a spaceship. There was one blond man sitting with his back to them as he worked on a computer. He was dressed in a metallic military uniform, similar to Asher's, with thick, black combat boots. From Jen's focal point, he looked to be unarmed, but she also didn't know what lay hidden under his uniform.

Asher signaled for them to stay put and pulled out his shooter while walking toward the man. He managed to get directly behind him without making a single noise, and pointed the gun at the back of the man's head.

"Turn around," Asher demanded with a low growl. The man froze, lifting up both hands as a sign of surrender. He slowly began to turn around, revealing a frightened and yet irritated expression as he stared up at Asher's hidden face. It was a good thing that Asher had covered his face for fear of the military finding out about his involvement in the portal scandal.

"Who are you?" the man asked, his voice laced with anger, as

Asher took the time to study his profile. He appeared to be in his early thirties, with a long, thin nose, small lips, pasty skin, and green eyes. The nametag directly above his heart read "Major Frank Hoggs." Bingo! "How do you know about this compound? This is a private facility!"

"I didn't come here for you to question me, Major," Asher said, leaning down so that his face was inches from Frank, who had started to sweat. Frank's eyes cut to where Jen, Lark, and Rogue stood feet away.

"Who are they?" Frank asked, ignoring Asher's statement. His eyes landed on Jen and briefly studied her before gazing at Rogue. Frank narrowed his eyes at Rogue and opened his mouth to speak, but Asher lifted a fist and slammed it into the side of Frank's jaw.

"What did I say about questioning me?" Asher walked a couple feet, picked up a chair, and slid it over to where Frank sat. Asher took a seat in front of Frank and got comfortable. Jen thought Asher looked like he'd interrogated someone before, and maybe he had. He hadn't told her yet about all of his military adventures, including the war stories. "Do you know why we came?"

"I could take a guess." Frank replied.

"I'm not a fan of the guessing game," Asher said with no trace of amusement in his voice. "My friends and I are on a very important mission, one in which you can help. We can do this the easy way or the hard way. You can tell us everything we need to know and then we'll get out of here, or I can beat the information out of you. Your choice."

"What do you want?" Frank asked through gritted teeth. His hands clawed at his wooden armrest as if he was fighting the urge to attack Asher.

"Where is George Kallis?" Asher asked simply. Frank scowled in response.

"Who is that?" Frank asked. His eyes cut to Rogue again as he sweated nervously.

"Oh, so now you don't know?" Asher scooted his chair even closer. "George Kallis came through the portal ten years ago and was taken in by the military. Your name came up in our search.

Seems as if you know a lot about this man's whereabouts. Don't play stupid—talk."

"I don't know who you're talking about," Frank said again with a wicked smile. Asher wasted no time connecting his fist with Frank's jaw, causing him to spit out blood.

"Next time," Asher began, "I'll strike you with this shooter, and if you still don't cooperate, I'll shoot you right here." He pointed the gun at Frank's crotch. "Where is George Kallis?"

"Maybe you should ask one of your friends," Frank said with his scrunched up in agony. Asher turned around to look at Jen, Lark, and Rogue, then turned back to Frank.

"How would they know? Stop playing games!" Asher yelled, hitting Frank with the shooter. Frank groaned and leaned forward in his seat as the pain coursed through his head. "Where is he?"

"Okay!" Frank said, gasping for air. Jen had to look away when she saw blood trickling down his forehead. She settled her eyes on Rogue, who looked more nervous than she'd ever seen her.

"Are you okay?" Jen asked. Rogue jumped at the sound of her voice.

"What? Yeah, I'm fine...just..." Rogue's eyes drifted to Jen's backpack then back to her eyes. "I think I need some air. Can you step outside with me for a minute?"

Jen thought about it, looking back to where Asher interrogated Frank. It was obvious Frank was about to reveal her father's whereabouts, a moment she'd been waiting for since she was seven years old.

"Jen?" Rogue asked. Jen nodded in response, even though she didn't even like Rogue. Jen looked over at Lark, who stood a few feet ahead of her, completely consumed by Asher's efforts. She decided not to ask him to tag along. Jen turned to ward Rogue, but paused as Frank's voice filled the room.

"George Kallis," Frank began. "Yes, I know him. At the time, I was young and wanted to do anything to impress my sergeant. He gave me a secret mission to keep watch over a terrorist until further orders were given."

"Why? Why did they keep George Kallis locked up? Is it because he came through the portal?" Asher asked. "Was he considered a terrorist on that basis? Was he a threat to the government...or was it the other way around?"

Frank laughed. "What do you think? Everyone knows the government is corrupt. George Kallis hadn't even entered Blue City willingly. They hunted him down and brought him back."

"Why?"

"Because they wanted the blueprint to the portal."

"Why did George Kallis have the blueprint?" Asher asked, earning him another laugh from Frank.

"You never asked yourself who invented the portal?" Frank acted amused by Asher's question. "Obviously it's the man who went through great lengths to keep the blueprint hidden. George Kallis invented it."

Jen gasped, holding a hand to her chest in shock. Her father had invented the portal? How was that even possible?

"Your friend back there looks shocked. I bet she'll be even more shocked when she hears everything else. I hate the military, anyway. They promised me a lot of money for keeping George Kallis confined, and guess where I am now? Stuck in a secret compound by myself all day long. Where's my money? They don't care! So why should I? Go ahead, ask me anything, but I should warn you. Things aren't always what they seem. You won't like the truth. Not one bit!"

"Can you please come with me?" Rogue whispered into Jen's ear. Jen nodded, completely in shock of the news she'd heard and absentmindedly led the way out of the building.

"Why does the government want the portal?" Asher asked impatiently.

"Now that, I don't know," Frank said. "They didn't feel the need to fill the pawn in on the master plan. But I can tell you who gave these orders, and I can also tell you exactly where George Kallis is. But first, your friend—"

"Who gave these orders?" Asher yelled, cutting Frank off.

"None other than the first commander in charge, the mastermind behind the whole plan," Frank said, causing Asher to jump out of his seat. His heart beat wildly with this news. It couldn't be, he thought. This can't be happening. Asher felt wild inside as he grabbed Frank's collar and shook him.

"My...my father is behind this?" Asher asked, not realizing he'd revealed his identity.

"You're the commander's son?" Frank asked in bewilderment. "Wow. Now that's interesting. But what's even more interesting to me is how Rogue disappeared with your little friend back there."

Asher frowned and turned around, just to see Lark standing by himself. Then Lark looked behind him for Rogue and Jen, but they were gone. Asher turned back to Frank.

"What did you do with them?" Asher asked, shaking Frank even harder. "Wait. How did you know her name was Rogue?"

Frank smiled and watched as Asher slowly let go of his shirt and pull his black mask off his face. Worry lines stretched across his forehead as he took a seat.

"This is where it gets really interesting," Frank said.

Once outside, Rogue walked a few feet away from the building and laughed. She then looked up at the sky and breathed deeply. The sky above was darkening by the moment, meaning a storm was on its way. Jen shivered. She hadn't seen such a dark, cloudy sky since she'd arrived in Blue City.

"This is my kind of day," Rogue said, with her back still turned away, but even so Jen noticed the eeriness in her voice.

"What do you mean?" Jen asked, as Rogue slowly started to turn toward her.

"Today is a day of revelation," Rogue said with a light, almost happy tone, but her eyes were dark and low. "Jen, let me see the blueprint."

Jen instinctively reached for the backpack hanging from her back but then stopped. There was something off about Rogue, and Jen didn't trust it. She'd noticed the way Frank watched Rogue with knowing eyes, as if he wanted to say something. She'd noticed how weird Rogue had started acting. She was not passing the portal over to her.

"No," Jen said. "Definitely not."

Rogue laughed and took a step toward Jen. "Why not?"

"Because I don't trust you."

"Well, you should've thought about that a long time ago," Rogue spat, moving even closer until she faced Jen with an intimidating scowl. "Give me the blueprint."

Jen lifted her chin, showing no signs of weakness. "I said no."

Rogue bit her lip in anger, balled her fist, and threw a punch at Jen, hitting her directly on the nose. Jen collapsed on the ground, grabbing her bleeding nose. She couldn't believe Rogue had just hit her.

"You have no idea how long I've wanted to do that. Probably since the day I opened the portal and watched you come stumbling through," Rogue admitted, laughing at the horrified look on Jen's face.

"It...it was you?" Jen asked, her voice barely above a whisper.

"Yes, it was me," Rogue said impatiently. "I've been tracking you this whole time. It wasn't supposed to happen this way, honestly. My job was to open the portal and go back to your bedroom and find the blueprint. But I didn't expect you to be in your room! Not only that, I'd heard footsteps in the alley and had to hide. I definitely didn't expect to see my ex and the third commander come walking into the alley, and I definitely didn't expect him to help you.

"I trailed you two. I saw the high speed chase with the two cops. I'm the one who reported it to the commander in charge and then he called off the whole chase, wanting you two to get away. But you see, he's always had you right where he wanted you. In fact, Commander Moore has been watching you and Asher this whole time...through me." Rogue studied Jen's shocked expression with twisted joy. "But you don't even fully understand what I mean, do you? Asher's father has been searching for the blueprint for over ten years and he knew your father had escaped with it. He's the one who devised the plan to get it back.

"Your father isn't who you think he is, Jen. He's not even from your time period. He's from Blue City. Twenty years ago, your father worked on a special project for the government to create deadly weapons for war. Your father was the smartest man around. A genius. Even smarter than that irritating ginger. Your father was also best friends with Commander Moore and didn't mind creating the portal for a friend.

"After that, he managed to create twenty replicas, all government-owned property. Then he and the commander tested the portal out, and time traveled to the future. Afterward, Commander Moore decided that he wanted the portals for his own malicious intent. There are men who want to watch the world burn, Jen. See, I like those kind of men. I wish Asher was more like his father. Asher is a lover, even though his father tried to toughen his heart. It's so sad to know he'll never live up to his father's expectations. I never really liked Asher, anyway."

"How is that possible? You've been a jealous lunatic since the moment you stepped foot into his house. You fell in love with him at boot camp."

"Commander Moore never liked his son and definitely didn't trust him, so he always had someone keeping an eye out on Asher. He never told me why, though, but I'm guessing he had a good reason. So I pretended to be this sweet girl. I dyed my hair blonde, wore extensions, and made sure to get him on my good side. I heard Asher Moore needed me for a more important mission. I left boot camp and pretended to go AWOL so that everything appeared legit.

"The commander then gave me the mission of finding the portal. I would've had enough time to get the blueprint if Asher hadn't been there. I was furious. I only had one chance to get it right and failed, but I knew that if I trailed you, I'd find my answer. I was then instructed to get close to Asher again and keep him from falling in love with you while I worked to recover the portal. His father was extremely set on making sure you two didn't fall in love. But we all know how all of the love stories go. I wasn't able to keep him from loving you, but none of that really matters now. I lied to the commander and told him that you two weren't falling in love. I have one mission and one mission only. Lucky for me, you guys found another portal and managed to do my work for me. Now I'm collecting what I came for. I want the blueprint."

Jen couldn't believe everything Rogue had revealed. This whole time, Rogue had been the enemy. This whole time, Rogue had wanted the blueprint. It made sense, given that she'd kept asking to see it. She probably wanted to steal it the moment Jen found it, but had bided her time. Not only that, but Rogue had never really loved Asher. The reason she tried to interfere was because of duty, not jealousy.

Worse than that, Asher's father was behind everything and knew exactly how his son was involved. This whole time, they'd been playing someone else's game, running around for answers that they wouldn't be able to handle once they learned the truth. This went beyond Jen's need to find her father; now Asher's fate was tied to his. It was his father who had kidnapped her father. It was his father who was evil. Rogue was right. Commander Moore had them exactly where he wanted them. Jen felt sick to her stomach. She needed to think, and quickly.

"I'll give you the blueprint if you take me to my father," Jen said, jumping to her feet. Rogue laughed and spat on the ground. She was back to the same girl Jen had met in the alley. There was no trace of femininity anywhere. Jen had known something was off and she couldn't trust Rogue. She wished she'd realized why a lot sooner.

"Or...I take the portal and let you live," Rogue offered, levering both hands as if weighing Jen's options. Jen shook her head, backing up.

"Asher's going to realize I'm gone, and he'll be out here in no time."

"Oh, really?" Rogue pointed to the door. A metal pole was pushed through the door handles, preventing anyone from getting out. Jen blinked in surprise. "You really should pay more attention to what people are doing around you. So naïve."

"You're crazy," Jen told Rogue. "What's in it for you? How does helping Asher's father benefit you?"

"Don't worry about that." Rogue took slow, calculated steps toward her. "You have your life to worry about."

Rogue charged toward Jen with full force. Jen tried to turn around and run, but Rogue was too quick. She tackled Jen onto the ground, climbed on top of her, and punched her in the face.

Jen's vision went black as she struggled against Rogue, who rolled Jen onto her stomach and tried to rip the backpack off of her back. Somehow, Jen managed to crawl out of Rogue's grip.

Rogue cursed and grabbed Jen's leg as she tried to crawl away on her hands and knees. Rogue yanked on her leg, causing Jen to fall onto her stomach again. As Rogue pulled on her leg, Jen managed to kick her right foot out, connecting it with the side of Rogue's face. Rogue instantly let go of Jen's leg and fell backward. Jen jumped to her feet and ran toward the door. Even though her head was pounding, she didn't slow. She had the blueprint to protect. Her father had hid it with her all her life, and she wasn't going to let Rogue steal it.

Jen didn't get far. She was tackled from behind and landed hard on the concrete ground. She quickly rolled onto her back, making it harder for Rogue to get the blueprint from under her. Jen swung her arms at Rogue, punching her in the face a few times, before Rogue managed to grab her hands and subdue her.

"You're only going to make this harder on yourself," Rogue said, struggling to keep Jen still.

"Asher!" Jen shouted, hoping he'd hear her. "Somebody! Help me!"

"No one can hear you," Rogue screamed, and lifted a fist in the air. Jen tried to block her face but was too late. Rogue's fist came slamming down, momentarily dazing her.

Rogue used the distraction to roll Jen onto her stomach and unzip the backpack. When she found the blueprint, she made a victorious sound. Rogue stood with the blueprint in hand and pointed the shooter at Jen. With a ringing head, Jen managed to roll onto her back and meet Rogue's hateful gaze. Jen's eyes then traveled down to the shooter in Rogue's hand.

"I could kill you right now and end everything," Rogue told her. Her hand moved to the trigger and began to press down. This was it. Asher had been right to say he and Jen may never live long enough to be together. Jen had failed her father, her mother, and now Asher, just because she wasn't strong enough to protect herself. She closed her eyes, preparing to meet her death.

BANG!

After a few seconds, Jen opened her eyes. She felt no type of pain anywhere on her body. Wouldn't a gunshot wound cause a lot of pain?

BANG! BANG!

It was then Jen realized that the noise hadn't been coming from Rogue's shooter, but from the door.

"I guess your friends finally figured out you went missing. Frank must've told them that he knew me." Rogue sighed and tucked her shooter back into her pants. "I'm sure we'll meet again. I'll kill you then."

Rogue took off running, leaving Jen lying in the alley. The pounding in her head started to subside as she focused on the sound of hands beating on the door. She sat up and looked around for Rogue, but she was long gone. Jen managed to get to her feet and made her way over to the double doors. She removed the heavy metal pole and set it down. Seconds later, Asher burst through the door and found her, leaning against the building, dry heaving.

"Jen," Asher said, grabbing her and wrapping her into his arms. "I was so scared." He pulled back and cupped her face with his hands, examining her. "You're hurt. What happened? Where's Rogue? Jen, she's not who she said she was. She's been working for my father this whole time."

"I know," Jen said, fighting back tears. She wanted to cry, but knew she had to be strong. "She told me everything. Asher, your father..."

"I'll handle him," he said, looking determined. "When the time comes. I'll repay him for everything he did to hurt you and your family. "

"Where's the blueprint?" Lark asked Jen. She'd finally noticed him holding onto Frank, who was in handcuffs. Jen gave her attention back to Asher as dread filled every inch of her.

"Rogue took it. She fought me for it. She won. She pulled a shooter on me. She was going to kill me."

Asher's face turned red as he let go of Jen and took a few steps away from her. He bent over in frustration and screamed. Jen finally allowed her tears to flow. Her eyes watched a blurry image of Lark as he stepped away from Frank Hoggs and walked toward her.

"We'll get it back," he reassured her.

"How do you know that?" Jen asked.

"Because," Lark said, with a knowing smile. "They don't call me boy genius for nothing."

CHAPTER TWENTY

The Unexpected

W here to?" Asher asked Frank, looking at him through the rearview mirror.

"192 Buck Street. It's an old military compound, much like the one we were just at, except this compound is used for illegal purposes. It's heavily guarded. The only way in is to be dragged in."

"Figures," Asher said, gripping the stick in frustration. "My dad probably already knows we're on the way. He'll be expecting us." And with that, Asher took off into the sky.

He spent the rest of the ride thinking about what Frank's revelation had meant: that Asher's father was a bad guy, a monster. That the man who had raised him to be a tough man was truly a coward himself. He hid behind lies and deceit, he killed and imprisoned people because of his own greed, and he did it all in secret, like a coward. He was corrupt, and he had to die.

Asher didn't want to kill his father, but he knew he was the only one capable of doing so. He didn't understand why his father wanted the blueprint, but he knew that if that type of power got into his hands, the world in grave danger.

Of all the things Asher had a right to be worried about, his own safety came last. If anyone could stop his father, it would be him. It was a surprise turn from how afraid he had once been of his father, but those days were long behind him. What Asher was actually worried about was Jen. She sat in her seat, so fragile and on the verge of cracking, and he wanted to hold her, to tell her everything was going to be okay, but he didn't know if he really believed it himself.

He understood Jen's pain. She'd just learned that her father wasn't who she thought he was. The life he'd created was a cover-up, a way to escape Blue City and be free from the commander. Did her dad ever really love Jen and her mother?

He couldn't fathom what she must be thinking.

He was right. Jen tortured herself with the idea that her father never really loved her or her mother. She found herself asking the same questions over and over: Does my father really love me? Does he even want to come back home? Will my family ever mend from this? Would the truth mean this whole trip to save him was in vain? Jen didn't know, but she was close to finding answers. She was anxious for the truth.

Twenty-five minutes later, they stood in front of a beautiful glass compound that mirrored its surroundings, creating an almost transparent illusion that was intriguing enough to pull Jen out of her stupor. If she hadn't known better, she would have thought the building contained a magnificent museum with wonders she couldn't begin to imagine. However, the multiple soldiers dressed in metallic uniforms, who were standing on either side of the glass door leading into the building, reminded her of the dangers that lay inside.

The guards noticed them approaching and raised their shooters in defense.

"Who are you?" one of the soldiers asked, taking a brave step toward them. Unlike the other soldiers, his face was covered by a mask, making his speech sound muffled.

"Third in command, Asher Moore, son of Commander Moore," Asher responded, reaching for the shooter in the back of his pants. "And this is Major Frank Hoggs."

"The other two, sir?" the soldier asked.

Asher clenched his jaw. "Two friends of mine whose identity is not needed. Please let us in."

"I don't have orders to let you—" the soldier said, but then stopped mid-sentence, lifting a hand and touching the earpiece in his ear as he listened to orders. He nodded his head once and met Asher's eyes. "I have just been given orders to let you in."

The soldier opened the door and moved to the side, allowing them to pass. Asher grunted, grabbed Frank's arm, and began moving forward, but the soldier quickly stopped him before he could get through the door.

"I have specific orders for your friend here," the guard said, pulling Frank from Asher's grip.

"No," Frank shouted, his eyes ablaze with fear. "They're going to kill me." Frank reached for Asher, but Asher turned his head away and continued walking. Asher knew that Frank was going to die—it was possible they were all going to die soon, but his loyalties weren't with Frank. "I helped you! You can't just let them kill me!"

Sure, Frank had helped, but he'd also helped keep Jen's father locked up for years. That made Frank no friend of his. And although Asher had a heart, he wasn't going to cave and cause a scene to help an enemy when he had another task at hand. He needed to focus, and so he reached behind him, grabbed Jen's arm, and continued to walk. He heard Frank's screams quiet down as the thick glass door closed behind them.

Jen trembled hearing Frank's muffled screams as the door closed. She turned around to see Lark walking behind them with both of his ears plugged, as if he didn't want to hear Frank's pleas. She wanted to reach out and comfort him, but found the only thing she could do was put one foot in front of the other and continue following Asher.

Another soldier up ahead was waiting for them as they approached. He didn't say a word, but simply turned around and began walking, expecting the group to keep up. Asher squeezed Jen's hand and forced a smile.

"We can do this," Asher whispered to her, causing her heart rate to increase. His soothing words did something to stop the ache that was growing inside her. She nodded and grinned again to satisfy Asher.

The soldier stopped at a large silver door, knocked once, and stepped aside. Seconds later, the door opened, revealing a large room with five soldiers surrounding a tired looking man tied up in a chair. Jen instantly recognized his frail face, sad eyes, and graying hair.

It was her father.

All of the anger and confusion Jen had been feeling toward him vanished within seconds. She wanted to run to him, but knew it wasn't a good time. Instead, she stood there, staring at him with her heart beating out of her chest. Soon she'd be in his arms...soon.

Next to her father stood a tall, brooding man, who looked like an older version of Asher. He was handsome, but the icy, cold glare in his eyes made him look haunting and sent chills down her spine. You must be the commander, Jen thought, as she glared at him in an attempt to hide her fear. Jen shifted her eyes to Rogue, who stood next to the commander, looking proud with the blueprint ensconced in her hand. Jen's fear vanished as her eyes narrowed on Rogue, and the memory of the attack in the alley resurfaced. She wanted to kill Rogue, but it would have to wait.

Jen's eyes cut back to the sight of her father and the knowing look in his eyes as he stared back at her. Was it a look of longing that she'd caught? Was he just as happy to see her as she was him? Jen was filled with so many emotions and questions, and wanted only to run into his arms again.

A moment ago, Jen had felt nothing but fear tinged with anger, but seeing her father alive had given her hope. She'd spent three weeks searching for him in Blue City. She'd almost been killed multiple times, had fallen in love Asher, and had made a true friend out of Lark. And now, the very reason she stepped through the portal was within her reach.

"Father," Asher spoke, pushing Jen slightly behind him to keep her protected. He saw the way the soldiers held weapons, ready to fire at his father's command. He saw the worried look on George Kallis' face, as if he knew something they didn't. He also saw the smirk in Rogue's eyes, as if she knew the same. Rogue. The girl he'd fallen deeply in love with was a traitor and pawn in his father's schemes. Jen had explained Rogue's involvement during the hover ride, and Asher wanted to be the one to destroy her.

"You've finally pieced it all together," Commander Moore said, clapping his hands together as if overjoyed. "You've done well, son. Because of you, I now have the very thing I've spent so many years searching for. The blueprint..." The commander's smile faded as his eyes drifted to where Jen stood slightly behind Asher, holding his hand in her own. "...although, I would never have taken you for the romantic type, boy."

"Why did you do all of this?" Asher asked, ignoring his father's last words.

Commander Moore's eyebrows shot up as if surprised by his son's question. He stood regal in his metallic military uniform, with columns of buttons, medals, and pins lining the right side of his chest. His eyebrows were thick like Asher's but darker, and his thin lips smiled brightly, warming the icy glare in his eyes. If Jen hadn't known what he was capable of or if she hadn't seen his death stare, she would have fallen for the friendly smile plastered on his face.

"I thought you heard me when I said it moments ago, Asher," Commander Moore said, his voice a slow purr. "I wanted the blueprint. And now I have it."

"But why?" Asher snapped, losing his cool, and yet his temper barely fazed his father. "You run the military! How can you be a criminal and still work closely with the president?"

"This," Commander Moore said, lifting both arms as if to present the room they stood in, as if it held all of his answers. "This is for our country. What I'm doing is beneficial to the state of this country! And if you try to stop me, you'll be considered a terrorist."

"What do you plan to do with the blueprint?" Jen asked, causing Commander Moore to lower his eyes as he stared at her.

"Little girls don't speak without permission."

"She's not a little girl," Asher said through gritted teeth, taking a step toward his father.

"Oh?" The commander laughed and went to stand directly behind where Mr. Kallis sat with his mouth tied by a piece of white cloth. "I'm sure George here would disagree." He removed the cloth covering his mouth, and George let out a gasp that pierced Jen's heart.

"Jen," he said, staring at her. "My baby girl. I've missed you so much. I'm so sorry for leaving you and your mother. Please know it wasn't intentional."

"Did you ever really love us?" Jen asked. She knew it was the wrong time for the conversation, but she needed to know. "Or were we just an escape and cover up for this monster?"

"Of course I loved you. I still love you and your mother very much. I'm so sorry. I..." her dad choked on his words. "I lied about everything. Please forgive me." He lowered his head as a single tear slipped from his eyes.

"So much for a sweet family reunion, huh?" The commander laughed.

"Please, just let him go," Jen begged. "You have what you want: the blueprint. Just untie him and let us return home."

"I can't do that," Commander Moore said. "If I send you two back, how do I know you'll stay put? George here may build another portal to stop my plans."

"What plans?" Asher asked. "You still haven't told us why you've gone through the trouble to hold him captive for ten years just to get this blueprint."

"There are plans far greater than you could ever imagine," Commander Moore said. "Plans to help Blue City prosper."

"I don't believe you," Asher said, and as his father silently watched him, he took the time to evaluate their situation. Commander Moore had five of his best sergeants lined up and ready to shoot if Asher, Jen, or Lark even moved suspiciously. But Asher's father had trained him well enough to survive even when the odds were against him. "You did all of this for your own personal greed. It has nothing to do with the state of our country!"

"Believe what you will, Asher, but you will not get in my way." Commander Moore focused on Jen. "I can't give you what you came for, but as a way of saying thank you, I'll let your friends keep their lives." Commander Moore turned to one of the soldiers standing behind Jen. "Escort these two out. Keep Asher here."

The soldier moved to grab Jen, but she quickly wrapped her arms around Asher, pulling him into a tight hug. "No!"

"Let her go," Asher said, pushing the soldier away. He could almost feel the energy as every shooter pointed at him. He pulled Jen away from the soldier and took a few steps back, turning toward his father. "I don't trust you. You'll kill them. I know you, Father. They stay with me."

"Fine. Have it your way." Commander Moore waved dismissively. "You're just hurting their chances of survival."

"They have a better chance sticking next to me."

Commander Moore signaled to one of the guards who lowered his shooter and moved forward. He walked over to a long table, grabbed a wooden box, and handed it to the commander. As the commander slowly opened the box, he smiled at what lay inside. He then turned it around so that everyone else in the room could see.

"Well, I guess it won't hurt to tell you my plans if you're going to die anyway. I'm sure you know what this is," Commander Moore said. "It's the very last portal ever made. But not for long. Soon I'll travel three hundred years into the future and begin mass production of the portals. Then I'll have enough portals to go throughout time and change the course of history so that Blue City may prevail in all its glory."

"Don't believe him," George Kallis yelled. "Asher, you'll kill him with your own hands. I've seen it. He's seen it. He's done all of this to prevent that from happening! He's—"

"What?" Asher asked, confused. Before Mr. Kallis could respond, Commander Moore covered his mouth with the cloth and laughed.

"That's exactly why I can't let him loose," he said, with irritation evident in his hard voice as he handed the wooden case to the soldier next to him. "He knows too much." Commander Moore turned toward one of his guards. "Be ready to kill him when I tell you to."

"No!" Jen screamed. She tried to break away from Asher's grip to run to her father, but Asher kept her at his side.

"Don't," Asher warned her. "Jen, this is bigger than your father. Think about the whole picture."

But how could she think about anything other than the man she'd been searching for more than ten years? How could she return home to tell her mother that he'd died? That she was unsuccessful in saving him? Asher had promised to help her get him back. Was he breaking that promise? Jen only thought with her emotions; she didn't care what logic Asher saw. She only saw her father.

The commander went back to the soldier holding the case and removed the last portal. He began to maneuver it, twisting and turning it at odd angles, until it grew into a large frame. Commander Moore sat the portal down on the ground and moved away. With a loud crack, the portal, as glorious as ever, roared to life. Commander Moore turned around, walked over to Rogue, and grabbed the blueprint.

"You've done well," the commander said to Rogue, softly caressing her check. "But I have no use for you anymore." He then turned toward the soldier. "Kill them all once I'm gone, including Rogue," and he quickly stepped through the portal.

"What?" Rogue cried, backing away from the portal and turning toward the soldiers in the room.

Asher knew they only had three minutes to kill every enemy in the room and follow his father through the portal before it closed up. "Take Lark and find cover, quickly!" he ordered Jen.

He didn't wait to see if Jen obeyed before pulling out his shooter. In less than three seconds, he'd shot two soldiers, and turned just as the soldiers behind him sprang to life. Asher jumped and twisted in the air, as two blasts of energy zoomed past him. He landed low to the ground and pointed his shooter with precision, quickly taking out the two soldiers near the door. Asher got back on his feet and ran toward the soldiers surrounding Jen's dad and shot one, watching as he fell to the ground.

He heard another shot go off and spun around to see Lark shooting a soldier who had been approaching Asher from behind. He'd come out of nowhere and it was a close call. Lark then turned and shot another soldier in the leg. Two guards stood with pointed weapons, not to mention Rogue, who had managed to avoid the fight.

Rogue.

He was glad his father had turned against her. It meant that she now knew what it was like to feel betrayed. But he still wanted to be the one to kill her, hating her for playing with his heart. Momentarily blinded by his rage, Asher moved toward Rogue, but a soldier appeared to his right, hitting him on the side of his head with a shooter. Asher fell to the ground, completely dazed. He heard Jen scream in the background, and he tried to stand but collapsed onto the ground, drawing a blank in his mind and shaking his head to rid himself of the pain.

Jen had hidden behind an overturned table, but quickly stood up after witnessing Asher's attack. Lark managed to shoot down the last two soldiers and covered Jen as she ran toward Asher. She stopped, feet away from where Asher lay, as she watched Rogue walk toward her with an evil smile.

"Remember when I told you I'd kill you later? Well, it's later now."

"Why would you still try to kill me? It's obvious the commander no longer wants you." Jen clenched her fists.

"I can win back the commander's affection, just like I won back Asher's. Once he hears that I'm the one who killed your father, he'll send for me."

"I didn't come this far to watch you kill my father. And you're not getting away this time."

Rogue laughed. "I thought I already proved who'd win this battle. Are you really stupid enough to try to fight me again? Hey, this time, I'll even go easy on you."

Jen was the first to run toward Rogue and swiftly tackled her to the ground. Jen used all of her strength to get on top of Rogue, pinning her underneath her weight, and punched her as hard as she could manage.

"That's for earlier," Jen shouted as she tried to hit Rogue again, but Rogue's hand shot out and blocked her punch. Rogue pushed Jen away and tried to stand, but Jen pounced back on her, grabbing her black hair and banging her head into the ground. Rogue let out a cry and tried to fight Jen off, but Jen was a wild woman. "This one's for Asher!" Jen balled her fist and connected with Rogue's nose, watching blood squirt everywhere.

Rogue had no chance at all as Jen hit her again and again until she no longer struggled against her. Jen reached into Rogue's pants, pulled out her shooter, and stood, pointing it at her head. After many battles lost, she was finally going to win the war with Rogue. She put her hand on the trigger.

"This one's for me."

"Jen, don't!"

Jen heard her father call to her, and she became distracted as she lifted her eyes to where he stood, staring at her. She forgot about Rogue and dropped the shooter, running to her father's side. She didn't care what else was going on around her—whether Lark was okay, or what happened to the soldier who had attacked Asher, or that the portal was closing. The only thing that mattered was her father.

She pulled him into a hug and began crying. "I found you," she said, removing the cloth from his mouth. "I knew you hadn't left us, Dad. I missed you so much."

"Jen, as much as I'd love a sweet reunion, it's not going to happen. You have to listen," her father said, the seriousness in his voice frightening her. "After I created the portal, Commander Moore accompanied me on the first journey. We didn't know where we'd end up; we only knew it would work. Well, it didn't take long to figure out that the portal knew exactly where a person wanted to go most, even when they didn't know it themselves. It takes you to the very place you desire. And what the commander wanted was to see his own death.

"We ended up in White City, over five hundred years into the future. It was there that we saw you and Asher just as Asher killed his father. At the time, we had no idea who you two were. Maybe if the commander had known from the beginning that it was his own son he might not have gone crazy. But after watching himself die, something inside of him snapped. It didn't take long for him to begin asking me to build more portals so that he could stop the events leading up to his death.

"That's how it started. But Commander Moore became obsessed, and it no longer became about preventing his own death. The power of the portals meant he could control all of time, not just his death. He wants world domination.

"Jen, he plans to create an army of men and transport them all back to Blue City, where he'll take over and rule the world. And this time period is just the start. He wants to rule every major city in every major time period, simultaneously. He wants to play an omnipotent God.

"Once I understood his plan, I'd decided to take the blueprint and escape Blue City. I traveled to different time periods, never settling long before going to the next era for fear that the commander was searching for me. I eventually settled in the 80s, where I met your mother and fell in love. Our love was real, Jen. I've never been happier than being with the two of you. I decided to stay there and raise my family in hopes of never getting caught.

"I knew the day would arrive when the commander would come for the blueprint. As you got older, I began to understand that you were the girl present at the commander's execution. That's why I implanted hints in your head about the blueprint being in the fairy tale book, hoping you'd uncover the truth and one day would help kill the commander. In my own way, I was preparing you for right now. Listen to me, baby. You don't have much time. The portal is starting to close. You have to go stop him!"

"But Dad, I want to take you home where you belong, with Mom," Jen cried. She cupped his sad face in her hands. "Mom did so badly after you left. It broke her spirit. You have to come home."

"Baby, I love you. Don't worry about me. You have the world to save."

"No, don't say that!"

"I love you, Jen. The commander isn't the only one who knows how he's going to die. So do I. And it's right here, with your love surrounding me."

"Dad..." Jen's heart sank as she sat down on his lap. "Stop talking crazy! I'm going to get you out of he—"

"Jen!" She heard Lark's voice sound behind her, but it sounded very far away. In fact, everything around her slowed down as her father looked at her with peaceful eyes. His lips curled upward into a smile.

BOOM!

Jen felt something beginning to soak through her shirt, but she didn't dare look away from her father long enough to see what it was. She knew. And the world around her was still a slow blur of events, waiting for her to catch up. But she didn't want to catch up. She wanted to stay in the moment before the pain hit; she wanted to live in the quiet before the storm.

The sound of her father choking on blood shook Jen out of her stupor. She felt her father go limp before she could even meet his eyes again. "No..." she whispered, clinging to her father's shirt. She looked down at the open wound in the side of his stomach that was gushing blood. It was too late. She met her father's eyes again and saw the life drained out of them.

Her father was dead.

A scream started in the bottom of her chest, but it never reached her mouth. She turned toward where Rogue stood, pointing the shooter directly at her head.

The shooter. Jen had dropped the shooter and Rogue must have gotten to it and shot her father. It's all my fault, Jen thought, as she welcomed her own death. I killed my own father.

Everything was silent, save for the wind from the portal, which was beginning to close. Lark calculated that they only had a minute to come up with a plan. From the looks of it though, Jen would use that minute to mourn her father. Lark shook his head and ran to the portal, watching as it closed even further.

"Dad," Jen wept, breaking out of Asher's grip. She stood and stared at her dead father as he leaned forward in the chair. She couldn't pull her eyes away from him, even though he was covered in blood and was missing half of his side. "This isn't real! No! Dad. Oh god. No!"

"Jen." Asher wrapped his arms around her, but she fought against him. "Jen, I'm so sorry. I really am. But we have to go."

"My dad!"

"Jen, you'll have to mourn later. You have to pull yourself together. If we don't go now, we'll never stop my father. This is the last portal. We have to go! We need to get the blueprint back."

"I can't leave him like this!" Jen cried, hysterically. "I don't even care anymore. Let me go! How could you ask me to continue on with this mission, Asher?"

"Because I love you," he said, turning Jen around and cupping her face. She looked into his eyes and saw the desperation as he confessed his heart. She momentarily forgot the horror of her own heart as his words sank in. "I've loved you from the moment you stumbled into Blue City, and I love you enough to pull you away from your worse moment and keep you pressing forward. Jen, trust me. Please. Our future is being decided in this very moment. Don't let your pain blind you from the truth. I didn't realize when I signed up for this that I'd get in so deep. But I am. We are. So is Lark." Asher stopped and looked to where Lark stood watching the portal. He turned around to Asher with a worried look.

"W-we literally have thirty seconds," Lark said. "N-now or never." Asher turned back around to Jen and searched her eyes.

"Avenge his death," Asher said. "If you stay, he died in vain. He spent ten years away from you trying to protect the portal. We can still stop my father, Jen. But we have to go now."

Jen knew Asher was right, and even though her pain was unbearable, she needed to avenge her father's death. She needed to keep going, because if she stopped, she not only failed herself, but everyone she loved. Jen nodded and allowed Asher to take her hand.

"Let's go," he said, and led her toward the portal.

"Ten seconds," Lark warned.

"You go through first," Asher told Jen, and she turned back around to take in the devastation one last time. There were bullet holes in the walls and debris that had spilled out covered the ground with white dust. Dead bodies lay sporadically on the ground, looking like a war scene from a movie. Jen was glad that they were able to kill their enemies, but she wasn't happy that one of those bodies belonged to her father. She felt the urge to go to him one last time, but knew she couldn't.

"I love you, Daddy," she told him one last time. "Always."

She turned back around and met Asher's eyes. He quickly stepped through the portal and pulled her with him, keeping her in a tight embrace. She shut her eyes as she felt the familiar warmth of the portal engulf her. Jen didn't know if she had it in her to honor her father's death and get the blueprint back, but she knew she had Asher, Lark, and God. With them, she'd be able to do anything.

Jen heard Asher gasp in shock and tighten his arms around her. A second later Lark cried out as he stepped through the portal. Jen opened her eyes and saw they were standing in her own pink-and-white bedroom.

"How...how..." Jen turned back to the portal, but it was already sealed.

They hadn't followed Asher's father 300 years into the future. They were stuck in the past, with no way of getting back to Blue City or to where the commander now hid. They were stuck in the place Jen had secretly hoped she'd go back to after watching her own father die: back home.

"Now what?" Lark asked, and Jen felt their eyes burning into her face.

He's right, she thought. Now what?

ABOUT THE AUTHOR

Charlay Marie always knew she wanted to be an author, having already gained internet rave over her fan-fiction stories as a teenager. In 2012, she began writing her debut Christian fiction novel, *Under the Peach Tree* and followed up with her second novel *When Willows Weep* just a year later. Charlay took a small break to focus on producing her hit stage play, *The Holy Shop*, which won a spot in the 3rd Annual Columbus Black Theater festival! At the age of 27, she is now months from releasing her new YA series, *The Portal Series*, in which she has high hopes for. She aspires to inspire woman and youth with her stories that speaks to the heart, heals the soul, and intrigues the mind. Charlay Marie writes and directs in Columbus, Ohio with plans of beginning her own film production company.